HEART OF A WITCH

REBECCA L. GARCIA

ISBN: 978-1-912405-94-7

Editing by Angie Wade
Proofreading by Janna Bethel
Cover design and interior formatting by Dark Wish Designs
Map by Daniel Garcia
Character art by Art by Steffani

"If he wanted to believe all witches were evil, then I was going to prove him right."

– Victoria Amberwood, Heart of a Witch

Salvius
Blackburn
Dawnridge
Redforest

Deadwood

Navarin

Istinia

Raven Grove

HEART OF A WITCH

Prologue

Elijah

I wrinkled my nose at the stench of smoking flesh tainting the brisk autumn air. Leaves whipped at my sides as I ran behind my father through the cornfield. The moon, full and red, hung low in the sky, casting everything in a condemning red.

We fell out into a barren field. Shadows reached toward us, rippling out from flickering orange. As I climbed my gaze to the scene, my stomach lurched. A woman cried into a cloth tied around her mouth. Her hands were bound to a stake standing among a pile of chopped wood. Smoke pillared upward in an illusory dance. My hand shot to my mouth when I saw the fire at her feet, licking her ankles.

Her dark hair fell like ink around her shoulders, matching the deep brown of her eyes. She wrestled against the ropes binding her to the stake. Bile bit up my throat when her pleas turned to screams.

I glanced up, waiting for my father to do something, but he didn't move. Instead, he watched with a sparkle in his blue eyes. No one there was going to do anything, and the woman was dying.

I ran at the small crowd of five priests surrounding the woman, but a hand gripped my shoulder, stumbling me backward. Steadying myself, I turned. "She's burning to death."

My father's eyes narrowed. "Don't let its human cries fool you. It's a demon masquerading as a human, and you running to its aid is exactly what it wants. Those screams, son, are the sweet sounds of victory."

I ran cold. The witch's bloodshot eyes found mine through the orange hue. The smoke continued upward, the flames growing when she turned her attention on me. "Please! Boy." I could just make out her muffled begging through the cloth. "I'm innocent."

My breath hitched. "But what if she's not a demon, and we're mistaken—"

His nails dug into my wrist.

I flicked my eyes up to look at him.

A trail of saliva glinted against his lip. "That's what it wants you to think." I trailed my gaze along the large scar covering his right eye and the pentagram burned into his forehead. They were battle scars from his war against witches. He'd earned them when he'd run into particularly nasty witches who hadn't gone down without a fight. I'd caught only glimpses of the ones on his body a few times, but they were just as grizzly. "You must see it for what it truly is. You too, one day, will be a protector of mankind."

I averted my eyes from the burning woman. A murder of crows took flight from the branches in the forest beyond the field when she howled into the night. "Watch her." His fingers grappled at my cheeks, forcing me to look at the fire enveloping her body. Her screams withered as the flames grew and wood turned to ash. I didn't speak. I couldn't. Mostly in fear I'd vomit.

"You're fifteen now. It's about time you saw an execution in person. So you can see what we're up against."

I couldn't help the tears that fell from my eyes. I wiped them before he could notice. "What did she do?" I asked, recalling the laws in our kingdom. When a witch was discovered in Salvius, they were sent to the witch territory, Istinia, to live among their own kind. If they committed one of the high crimes, however, then they'd go to trial, and most ended at the gallows.

"What does it matter what it did? They're evil, and burning them makes sure they can't come back. That or ripping out their heart, but this was far more satisfying."

I swallowed hard. He wanted me to agree, to share in his hatred. I could see it in the crinkles by his eyes and in his waiting stare. I couldn't bear to hear him call me weak again, not like he called my younger brother every day. "I understand. You're only protecting us."

He paused, then slapped my back. "Good. I was your age when I killed my first."

I ran cold. "I still have my studies and—"

"Times have changed. I wouldn't expect you to start now. My own father pushed too hard for me to join the family business too soon. He didn't understand my calling to join the priests or become a hunter, and I will not do the same to you. You will join in your own time when you're ready. Until then, you will focus on your studies."

I feigned a small smile, although I was certain the color had drained from my face.

He continued, looking up at the sky with wonder in his star-flecked eyes. "It is our legacy to protect the world from the plague of these creatures. Zerheus and his angels have blessed us with great wealth so we can carry out the purpose."

Goose bumps crept over my skin. I was certain the god, Zerheus, and goddess, Celeste, did not spend their time worrying about me or my purpose. If I became a hunter, it would have nothing to do with the divine. It was only our legacy now because Father believed it so.

I didn't want to tell him, but I couldn't think of anything I wanted less than becoming a hunter—not if it meant burning people and carving out hearts, witch or not. At least he didn't want me to become a priest too. Being a witch hunter was an addition to his priesthood, and though it paid well, I was sure he'd do it for free.

The temperature dropped a couple of degrees. I breathed in ash, then coughed to cover a gag when I realized I was tasting the essence of a witch. I angled my head to get a better look at the dark mass unmoving against the embers.

My father joined the other priests, brushing ash from his blue robes as he walked. I couldn't help but wonder if any of the witches captured here in Redforest had received a proper trial. I'd never heard of one sent to Istinia. All were killed. I supposed it was why most stopped coming to our town, except for the occasional straggler. Dawnridge, the main city in the kingdom, was infested with them, or so I was told.

I turned my back toward the scene and stared out over the cornfield and up at the indigo sky. In the distance, the white walls of our mansion stood out against the rest of the houses. Red and orange hues flickered in one of our windows. Corbin was still awake. I was glad my brother hadn't been forced to see this too. He'd already seen enough darkness to last himself a lifetime.

***

Dappled light trickled through the gaps in the drapes of my brother's room. I tightened the knot of my tie and looked at his untouched uniform lying on the bed.

"I'm not going." Corbin crossed his arms over his chest. "I hate it there."

I glanced at the bedroom door, which was slightly ajar. I wrinkled my nose. I could still somehow smell the ash from the dead witch on my skin. Shaking it off, I cleared my throat. "Please don't do this, brother. You'll only give him more reason to hurt you again."

His brown eyes glossed with tears. He looked so much like our mother, Zerheus rest her soul. I was the spitting image of my father, having inherited his ash-blond hair, blue eyes, and pale skin.

"No." He kicked against his bed frame. "You can't make me go."

I knew this was going to happen, when he'd left Saint Baltazar's School for Boys and started the prestigious King's Crest Academy. "You need to give it time. It's only your second day."

"The others think I'm weird."

"You can always put them in their place."

He recoiled. "I don't like to do that. I'm not like you… or your friends."

I sighed. "Fine. The next time someone calls you weird, come and find me, and we'll set them straight."

His frown faltered. "I'd rather not go."

"You must." I ran my hand through my blond strands, tidying my hair to the side. "Just try to act more… normal around the other kids."

"All I did was bring Edward out in our etiquette lesson. He wasn't harming anyone." He pulled an earthworm from his bag.

I closed my eyes, praying for patience.

"My teacher threatened the cane."

"Of course she did." The brown worm curled up in his palm. "Leave him home today."

"If Damian finds him, he'll kill him."

I scowled. "Don't call him Damian! He's our father, and if you can't address him properly, then at least call him sir."

"Why do you defend him? He does it to you too."

"Not as much." My mind flashed with a memory of the sting of leather against my back. Squeezing my eyes shut, I let out a tense breath. "Don't give him reason any more than he already has to punish you. He only wants us to behave." I tried to reason with my brother, but the words felt wrong in my mouth. "We should go before we're late." I straightened my suspenders, then attempted to flatten a wrinkle in my shirt. "Remember, Corbin," I said. "You're a Shaw. You're town royalty. Don't let anyone talk down to you. You're better than them."

We bade good-bye to our housekeeper before stepping into our carriage. I rested against the plush green and inhaled the smell of horse dung. "They need to clean that up." I made a face. "It's like we pay them to stand around and do nothing."

Corbin wrung his hands. "You sound just like Father sometimes, you know."

I rolled my eyes. "I do not. I'm just saying, there was a pile of it before we got inside."

"Who cares?" He shrugged. "Anyway, where did you go last night?"

A shiver snaked up my spine. I masked it with a stretch. "Nowhere important."

"You're lying."

I kicked my legs up onto the empty seat space next to him. "It doesn't matter where I went. Just be glad you didn't have to go."

"But—"

"Enough talk now. I have a headache," I lied, then rolled my shoulders back and closed my eyes. The wheels bumped along the cobblestones, jolting us as the stallion dragged us up the high street. I'd tried everything to get rid of the smell of the witch clinging in my nose, to no avail. Whenever I closed my eyes, she was all I could see.

Sleep had been brief last night, between dreams of my mother screaming her last breath out and the witch who'd caused her death. Seeing one burn last night brought back memories I wished would stay buried. Even though the memory of my mother faded, I still felt her absence every day. So did Corbin.

I looked at my brother and sighed. He was living proof that witches were demonic creatures, and last night, I'd almost felt sorry for one. The realization of it made my skin crawl. Witches posed as humans—a dark trickery, appearing to cry, love, laugh, and feel like we did. They did it to entangle us, so they could hurt us. Like they had my mother. My dream served as a reminder of why I hated them in the first place.

I licked my lips, casting the memory of the execution from my mind. If I was to one day become a hunter, I had to get used to it. Nights like last night were going to become my new normal, whether I wanted it or not.

The carriage pulled up to the wrought iron gates of the academy. Protective charms against witches hung from the fences surrounding the obsidian building. I stepped out before Corbin, forcing a stoic expression.

I spotted my friend, Charles, and nodded in his direction. He pushed one of the girls walking by into a mud puddle. He looked at me, and I did what I had to: I laughed.

Because I was Elijah Shaw. I wanted anyone who thought about bullying my brother to think again.

One

Six Years Later
Victoria

Staining the silk handkerchief with my bloody hands, I let out a tense breath and climbed my gaze to the branches above. Dappled light cast shadows to the ground as the sky lightened with the first pinks of morning. Spiders climbed the low-hanging twigs, spinning their webs toward the leaf-carpeted ground.

One landed on my hair. Careful not to crush it, I pulled it from my black strands and let it crawl over my fingers and onto a branch next to me. I returned my gaze to the mess of feathers and crimson-stained leaves at my feet, surrounded by a circle of symbols—symbols that would earn me a one-way trip to the gallows if they were ever found.

Normally, I wouldn't dabble in dark magic, the kind pulled from the depths of the underworld and the demons that inhabited it, but I was desperate. I kicked the symbols made from sticks, scattering them. I kneeled at the site I'd labored over for the past four hours. Under the cover of darkness, innocence quickly suffocated, and nothing seemed as bad, but when day dawned, the cruelness in performing these types of rituals was laid bare. A breath of wind caught my dark curls, sweeping them over my shoulder.

The bird's talons were curled up beside the silver blade between them. I pulled the dagger from the crow's stomach, releasing its body from the ground. There was so much blood for such a small creature.

I sighed at the makeshift grave I'd dug in haste. The creature had already been close to death when I'd found it, but it didn't make me feel better.

Grabbing the grimoire pages and the five pieces of jewelry I had hoped to succeed in spelling, I sighed. I threw them into my satchel alongside the black and purple half-melted candles.

"Victoria." My mother's sharp voice found me. I hadn't heard her coming. "Get inside before someone sees you."

Closing my eyes for a moment, I reined in the pain that threatened to crack my voice, composing my emotions before turning on my heel to face her. Her honey-blonde hair fell flat around her shoulders, lacking the life it once had, matching her face.

"No one comes out this way," I replied. I hated being on my own with her, ever since the incident.

"Please, honey." Her voice lowered to a whisper, and desperation tugged at her words. "We need to be cautious. That *hunter* is in town. I can't risk anything happening to any of you. Think of your sisters and brother."

My fingers flexed, then curled. That was precisely what I was doing. The hunter was the whole reason I was out there in the first place, trying to shield our family from his wrath. Damian Shaw, Salvius's most esteemed witch hunter and priest. I wished I could spell the skin to peel from his bones, but I couldn't without the rest of my family paying the price for it. My actions had already cost my mother too much.

"I'm coming," I promised. "I won't do anything to put our family in danger."

The skin under her eyes had sagged, appearing as if it had lost contact with the bone beneath. Her snake-green eyes matched my sister's, Ember, and in them, I found her, softening me. "I'll be in before the shop opens."

"Hurry, sweetheart." She brushed a fallen wisp of moss from her shoulder, snagging her apron on a twig as she found her way out of the tree line. I supposed we were fortunate to have an entry to the forest in our backyard. The trees were the perfect place to hide the remains of our rituals and spells.

I stepped backward, crunching a bone under my boot. Finding dead birds was easy in this part of the forest. Many who landed among these branches seldom lasted long. The lingering effects of magic seemed to drag the life from the area. It wasn't the worst thing; their bones made for good grounding items when casting more forbidden spells. The temptation over the years to practice the darker arts on occasion had become too much. I'd performed four successful rituals in my life, using magic from the underworld. Each time, it left me feeling unwell for a short period, which was why I was careful about how often I did them. Using that kind of magic frequently could cause a person to lose their mind.

I turned back, emerging from the trees into the first rays of purples and gold. Beyond the grassy bank sat our manor house.

Yet another day had passed since my cousin's murder, although the people of Salvius would disagree with the term. They believed he had been rightfully executed, as he'd broken the law and killed another, but I know for certain he hadn't done anything wrong. Damian had found him, and everyone knew that once he set his eyes on a witch or warlock, it wasn't long until they were dead. He was the cruelest bastard in the entire kingdom, fabricating evidence against good witches and stringing them up. It didn't matter that we were supposed to get a fair trial if found hiding among the humans here. The hunter was after blood, and the humans didn't care. They turned a blind eye as long as it suited them. Why would they fight it?

Ambling over the grassy yard, passing the leaf-covered swing that hung from a low, thick branch of a maple tree, I gazed upward at the alcoves over the windows, then at the glass panes and the ivy smothering the stone. It would have been easier for us to live in Istinia, where witches lived separately from the humans here in Salvius, but my mother hadn't been able to leave my human father. Our manor bordered the cemetery where he was buried too, and she visited him often.

Living in the human kingdom wasn't the worst thing. We weren't forced into covens when we were children, like they were in Istinia, and made to leave our families behind so the young could serve their communities.

Although, we did have to hide what we were because if anyone found out, especially someone like that hunter, we were as good as dead. The treaty between our lands didn't mean a thing to most humans, as was proven by what had happened to my cousin. I supposed they didn't care that we were made from gods—even older than the ones in Istinia—from a race spanning back a millennium, and we had their magic in our blood. When they'd had children with humans, the first witches had been born.

Running my fingers along the stone banister of steps leading down from the garden to the front lawn, I smiled. Ember waved at me from the downstairs window. She ran out the front door, clutching a book, then dragged her disapproving gaze down to my bag of candles and spells. "You were out again all night, weren't you?"

"I'm trying to protect us—protect you." My dark eyes met hers, and she softened.

"Did it work?"

My stomach dipped. I hated admitting I'd failed, again. "I was closer this time."

She leaned forward, then grabbed my free hand, squeezing it softly. "You do too much for us. You're killing yourself."

"I don't do enough," I said as heaviness drowned my heart. "You know Mother can't do much anymore."

"Stop blaming yourself. I can't bear it." She scorned me as if she could read my mind and every dark, hate-filled thought in it. "Every single time you see her, you're tortured." She shot me a watery smile. "You didn't know any better. You were a child."

"I shouldn't have opened my mouth about us," I snapped, then inhaled deeply, calming my inner demons. As much as my mother and sister wanted to relieve me of the burden I'd caused, they couldn't.

She squeezed my fingers again. "Forgive yourself."

"I've never been one for forgiveness. Even for myself," I said. I couldn't even think it, because I was the one responsible for our mother's deteriorating health. She'd used the worst kind of magic to cloak us, to make my friend lose her mind, so that what we were wouldn't be revealed. I had been seven, and my friend eight. I'd trusted her and told her I was a witch. It was the single biggest mistake of my life. She'd threatened to tell her overtly religious parents, and if my mother hadn't stepped in, I was certain we'd have all found ourselves attached to the gallows.

My sister's eyes widened, reflecting my worried expression in her green irises. "If it takes your mind off things, the winter season is upon us. Noelle is in three months, and you know how much mother likes to prepare."

A small smile tugged my lips upward at the corners. She wasn't the only one who liked to prepare. Noelle meant more customers at our family shop, and as it was our only income, we needed them, but this year would be a little different. "Speaking of Noelle, there will be no spelling of the luck charms this year. Just leave them as a human would make them. We can't risk anything with the hunter here. We have no idea how long he plans to stay. If he makes a connection between our cousin and us, we're done for." I sighed with relief that we could hide under our father's name: Amberwood. It was a respected—and more importantly human—name that went back generations.

She swallowed thickly, then shuffled from one foot to the other. Her white lace-up shoes reached her ankles, complementing the peach dress that stopped at her knees. She'd always worn light colors, quite the contrast to me. "Right, yes. I'll be careful. On that note"—she looked down at her feet—"there's something I want to talk to you about."

"What?"

She scratched the back of her neck, tugging on one of the curls that had escaped her knotted bun. "You know how I've been wanting to open my own line of perfumes."

I frowned. "We've gone over this several times. As I've said before, we can do it in the future at the shop. We just need to plan for it. Learn to be patient, Ember."

She pressed her lips together. "We will never be able to afford to do it."

I bit the inside of my lip. I would have to crunch the numbers, and it could take a couple of years, but if we cut back on—

"I've taken a job at The Black Card," she announced, interrupting my thoughts.

My eyes widened, my stomach lurching as I took in her words. "Have you lost your mind?" I pressed my fingers against my forehead. "That's a black magic club." I lowered my voice to a whisper, though it was unlikely anyone would hear us. Rarely did anyone come up to the house from the shop, situated a stone's throw away from the house, but it had happened a few times over the years. "That is the *first* place Damian will look, and any other witch hunter for that matter."

"Humans go there too." She placed a hand on her bony hip, her expression swirling with attitude. I missed the days when I was fourteen and she was twelve and she'd follow me around everywhere, always taking my advice. Now, she was nineteen and her own woman, which meant making her own mistakes. For the most part, I let her, but not when they were life or death.

"I'll find a way to get you out of working there. I'll explain to the owners."

"No!" She was seething. "Cas was right. He said you'd react this way, but I said you'd be supportive."

"I'm only looking out for you. I understand at your age—"

"Oh, stop." She rolled her eyes. "You're only two years older than me."

"Yes, and you can tell."

The muscle in her jaw feathered. "What's that supposed to mean?"

"I wouldn't be stupid enough to make myself a target while a hunter is around. We are meant to hide what we are. Even the humans know something isn't right with that club."

"I'm not an idiot. I know how to protect myself." She shook her head. "I'm finally doing something with my life. I'm branching out. I thought you'd understand, so thanks a lot."

"I can't support it when it's your life in danger, Ember."

"But it is *my* life, Tori."

"Not for you to throw away."

"The truth behind the club has remained hidden for years," she said. "No hunter is going to find out it's run by witches now. The Blackwoods are good at covering up after themselves. The humans think it's just a bar, and they even drink there. Besides, they pay really well, and we need the money. I can help our family and get the materials I need to make my perfumes."

"I don't need you to find a job." I shook my head. "I'm making things work."

She rolled her eyes again. "I know, I know, you have a plan, but you always say that, and nothing happens."

"That's because plans that work take time, organization, and a slow but steady rise. Our shop has grown in profit by six times since four years ago."

"I can't wait years to start my life, Tori. I want to open my own shop one day. There's a place next to the apothecary shop, the old spinner's place. The owner is selling, and if I had been saving, Cas and I could have bought it."

"Ember, think for a moment—"

"I'm not you. I can't waste years of my life waiting for something to happen." She turned on her heel toward the front door. "I'm starting tonight, and you can't stop me."

Ouch. I waited until she walked away to let out the tense breath I'd been holding. She was going to get herself killed. I wasn't surprised my brother had sided with her. He had a "be free and damn the consequences" way of living.

I stepped inside and hung my fur coat on the coat rack. I brushed a couple of leaves off my black lace sleeves, then tugged at the waistband of my navy-blue skirt, pulling out an escapee twig. I dumped my bag next to the umbrella holder and rolled my shoulders back, moving my head around until my neck cracked, releasing the tension. I needed a hot bath and a nap, but the shop was opening soon so they'd havc to wait. I still needed to buy some mice in town to feed Ebony and Buttercup.

I couldn't help but smile at the thought of her name, even after our fight. Only Ember could have named one of the most venomous snakes in Salvius after a flower.

I walked into the living room. Above the unlit fireplace, stone ran upward, into a point. Surrounding it, shelves of dusty books took up the entire far wall. Above it was a balcony to the next floor. My brother leaned over the polished ledge, looking down into the living room. "Morning, sunshine."

"Good, you're awake," I said by way of greeting. He ran his hand through his dark waves, grinning. He really did think far too much of himself. He, like Ember, loved the humans in our town. Maybe a little too much. "Although, stranger things have happened. Didn't you get enough alcohol in you last night to keep you in bed until noon?"

He pretended to shiver. "So cold, sister. Let me guess, you were out all night too. For different reasons," he drawled. "Obviously."

"You know I was. The only difference is my night was productive."

He forced a clenched smile. "I'm glad to see the cold air didn't dim your sunny disposition."

I rolled my eyes. "How was the human girl?"

"She's already gone. They never stay long."

"No." I pursed my lips. "You make sure of that." I paused, thinking about what Ember said. I was sure Cas picked a girl up from that club. "It seems our dear sister is following in your footsteps."

His nose crinkled. "Ember, out fucking strangers? That's a little hard to believe."

I winced. "No. I mean going to the same bar where you pick these girls up from. I can't believe you're on her side with this.

Actually, I can. You're too reckless, and now you're dragging her down with you."

He rubbed his temples, sighing loudly. "It is way too early for this. I knew getting her that job would earn this shit from you." He dropped his head back, staring up at the ceiling. "Can we skip the lecture for once?"

My jaw clenched. "You're going to get her killed!"

"Don't be dramatic, sister. She'll be fine."

I balled my fist at my side. "The witch hunter is in town."

He waved his hand dismissively, as if the man who killed our cousin was nothing but a harmless fly. "He'll leave in a few days."

"We don't know that! He executed Jackson, unless you've forgotten."

"Our cousin was careless."

I shook my head. "Not unlike you. Not unlike Ember."

"I'll tell her to hold off starting work until he's gone."

I swore under my breath. "You better, Cas, else I'll—"

An amused smirk curved his lips. "You'll what?"

"Just sort this."

He huffed and pushed himself away from the balcony, rolling up the sleeves of his blue shirt as he walked back to his room. I waited for his footsteps to creak to nothing and draped myself over the couch.

A headache pounded through my head—probably from the lack of sleep, water, or both. I'd been overdoing it, but no one else was taking the threat seriously, except my mother, who couldn't do anything to help. Ember and Cas didn't know Jackson well enough to really care that he'd been killed, but it did shake them a little, even if Cas didn't show it. I, on the other hand, did know our cousin. I'd played with him when we were children, and he'd always been the first to spur on adventures. He was a free spirit, which was probably what had got him killed. He was too trusting of humans.

I closed my eyes, letting my thoughts drift. I'd need to open the shop soon. Today marked the beginning of autumn; the frosty air circling the house through cracks in the walls and windows confirmed it. It was the perfect time to make more coin, with the townspeople more willing to spend their dramair on things they didn't need.

My youngest sister, Alex, bottled crystals and made some into jewelry. Ember made different charms—for luck, love, marriage, and health—packaged sage, and made different types of candles with intoxicating scents. My mother knitted scarves, blankets, hats, and gloves and stayed behind the till, taking payments and talking to customers.

Cas begrudgingly wove dreamcatchers between his shifts at the apothecary, which was what my father did before he passed.

I oversaw the finances, the bills, supplies, ordering, and everything else that helped our shop run. Together, we made up Amberwood Boutique.

Before I could muster motivation to get up, Cas walked down the stairs and stopped next to me. "These will help with energy and the headaches." He placed two green capsules on the side table next to the sofa.

"How did you know?"

"It's not a far leap. Besides, I figure if you can give me a headache within only a few minutes, then hearing yourself all the time must be a constant migraine."

I shot him a look but swallowed the capsules.

Damn, if he wasn't talented. They worked almost too quickly. He waited, tapping his foot against the ornate rug. "Admit it."

I rolled my eyes at his stretched smile. "They worked."

"Always so giving with the praise," he sassed and pulled on his blue coat. "I'll be back this evening. I need to work a double shift. People are worried another plague is coming."

Ah. That was why he was up so early. He was doing the morning shift instead of his usual evening one. "Idiots." I clicked my tongue. "Herbs are not going to help against it. You'd think they would have learned from the last time."

"Those so-called idiots are keeping the shop open." He pointed at me when he reached the door. "Try to rest and take it easy today. You look like death."

"Have a terrible day," I called after him, half joking. "I know I will."

Two

My fear of Ember working at the club followed me throughout the day as I tempered finances and checked inventory. She finally joined me in the back after the final bell tinkled over the door.

"We didn't make much today: four gold and twenty-two silver dramair."

"Put it in the safe. I'll join you back at the house once I've finished counting inventory."

She arched an eyebrow. "I'm going straight to The Black Card. My shift is in an hour."

My fingers flexed. "I'll assume Cas hasn't had a chance to talk to you yet, but even he agrees you should hold off until the hunter leaves."

"Oh, Cas." She rolled her eyes and smiled. "He came to see me at lunch and didn't say a word. Wished me luck for tonight actually. He probably just said that to get you off his back."

I gritted my teeth. "Aren't you too tired to go? It's been a long day."

"Nope." She grinned. "Only excited."

"Is there anything I can say to stop you from going?"

She shook her head. "Nope, but you can wish me luck."

I gave her a look. "Ember."

"Tori," she snapped back, angling her head. Amusement flicked on her features. "Lighten up a bit, please. I'll be fine. You worry too much. If you're so concerned, maybe you should come down to the club, have a drink. You know, actually talk to other people. Maybe you'll even meet someone."

"I have no interest in fraternizing with humans."

She cleared her throat. "They're not all bad."

"You're right. For every hundred, there probably is a decent one, but I don't want to waste my time looking for them."

"Really? For every *hundred*?"

"They're ignorant, Ember. They don't care about us. If they found out what you really are, you'd be killed, and the people you think like you would watch with a smile."

"Yikes, Tori." She looked down at her feet, shaking her head gently before climbing her gaze back to meet mine. "I pray every night that you'll learn to trust. You're so cynical. The world isn't all bad, you know."

"You can pray to all the gods and angels you want, but it won't change what the humans are capable of."

"I just want you to find happiness. There has to be a sliver of it somewhere for you too."

"I am happy. I have you, Alex, even Cas sometimes."

"I mean outside of the family. You need to start a life of your own."

I could see she meant it, yet the sentiment made me angrier. "Try not to get yourself killed tonight," I said, ignoring her statement, and moved on to counting a box of dreamcatchers.

"Love you too," she whispered as she made her way to the door.

The indigo sky rolled with rain clouds, sprinkling droplets onto my black dress. I reached the front door, then stepped inside, greeted by smoke-tinted, musty air. Mother was embroidering flower patterns by the crackling fire, which cast an orange hue around her.

Cas appeared from the kitchen. "How dreadfully boring." He ran his hand through his brown waves and shot her his widest smile.

She chuckled softly. "I find it calming. You should try it."

"I'm good."

"I closed up," I said, announcing myself, though I was sure they heard me coming in. "I'm taking a bath, then feeding my babies."

Cas made a face. "Stop calling them babies. They're vile little things."

"Why so cruel?" My eyes brightened, a smirk dancing on my lips. "Afraid of them?"

"I'm going out." He turned to face Mother, ignoring my question. "Ember's meeting me at the club."

My eyebrows pulled together. "Oh, I am well aware. You lied about getting her to wait."

"You wouldn't have stopped nagging me if I didn't, so yes, I did."

"Take care of her, Cas, or I swear, you'll find those 'vile little things' in your bed in the morning."

He angled his head. His amused smile faded instantly. "Don't you dare."

I placed a hand on my hips. "Then make sure she gets home in one piece—both of you, if that's possible."

"Enough!" Mother snapped, pausing her embroidery. "What's going on?"

Cas clicked his tongue. "Nothing. Tori's just being controlling again."

I heard footsteps behind me. "Arguing again?"

I whipped my head around. Alex stepped forward, her young face looking much like mine, with barely a hint of our mother or Ember in there. She was all Father, just like me, just like Cas. She had angular features, sharp, dark eyes, thick lips, and warm, golden-brown skin. "You should be in bed. It's ten."

She pouted. "Cas is going out."

"He's an adult… and an idiot," I said.

She laughed. "I know."

"Hey." Cas walked by us both, messing her hair up when he passed. She slapped his hand away and peered around me toward the fireplace. "Mama, do you want a tea? I'm making one."

She nodded. "I'll have a chamomile, baby."

She was the only one Mother called that anymore. I supposed she was the baby of the family, still attending school. She'd finish school the year she turned seventeen, like we had. Only one more year to go.

"Good night," I said before climbing the ancient staircase to my room.

Once inside, I kneeled in front of the glass tank, moving the lid. I placed my fingers inside, and Ebony was the first to slither over them, knotting and slinking around my hand. I pulled her out, stroking a finger lightly over her rough, black scales.

"Did you miss me?" I smiled, stroking her as she curled around my wrist like a bracelet. Buttercup's inky tongue darted from her mouth from inside the tank. I dipped my free hand inside and let her slither onto my hand.

I placed them both on my bed. They slithered along the sheets, creasing the satin as they moved to their favorite place: my bedpost, which knotted up to the ceiling of my four-poster bed. I lay among my pillows and blankets and sighed, feeling one of the snakes move across my thigh and back onto the bed. I remembered when I'd found them, barely hatched. Ember and Alex were the only ones who were supportive of my keeping them.

Cas and Mother were dead against it, mostly because they were black Salvian vianas, Salvius's most venomous snakes, but they'd never bitten me. I connected with them, like I did with spiders and other creatures—at least the ones people didn't like much. I was like them in that way. People didn't like me much, but it was okay. I didn't like them either.

I had so much to do, but tiredness loomed over me like a storm cloud. I'd need to wear my raincoat out in this rain. The sound of it against my window lulled me deeper into thought. Tonight the ritual *had* to work. I needed to cloak our powers from detection until the hunter left, and I still had to feed the snakes. I felt one slither against my black curls scattered out around my head, and I closed my eyes.

I peeled back my eyelids, sitting upright, panic clutching at my chest. I grabbed the standing clock on my dresser, my eyes bulging. It was four in the morning. I rubbed my eyes, then my temples. I must've fallen asleep.

I hadn't had a chance to go out and work on the ritual. The protection spell I'd found in the grimoire could only be done at night. I'd failed at it for a week, but each time I came closer.

My breath hitched and I stood. Ember and Cas had to be back from The Black Card by now. I darted out of my room and ran down the hallway until I reached Ember's room. The lights were off. What if she hadn't come back? If the hunter had found them? Throwing open her door, I jolted her from her covers.

"Oh, good gods!" She clicked the lamp on her side table, then peered at me. "Tori?"

"Sorry." I steadied my breathing. "You usually have a light on when you sleep."

She placed a hand over her chest. "I got back late and passed out."

"Good. I was just checking you got home okay."

She croaked groggily. "Of course I did."

I stepped inside. "How late was it when you got back?"

"I don't know." She checked the time. "An hour ago maybe."

"Is Cas here?"

She shrugged. "He left before we closed."

I didn't like the "we." I slid my disapproving gaze to the outfit flung over the back of a chair. A green, slender dress glittered atop the red velvet upholstery. "They've already given you a uniform."

She rolled her eyes. "Actually, I chose to wear this. It's... pretty."

"Green has never really been your color."

"Don't be bitter, Tori." She rested back against the pillows. "Please."

I sighed softly, then sat on the edge of her bed. "How did it go?"

Her face lit up. "I met someone."

I tried not to frown. "Who?"

"His name is Chester. He works there too."

My stomach knotted. "As what?"

She shook her head. "I knew you'd judge."

"I'm not judging."

"You used to like that place."

"Before it was taken over by heathens, Ember."

She scoffed. "They're not. Chester's the son of the owners, and he's well-mannered and perfectly lovely."

"Perfectly lovely?" My voice rose an octave. "The son of those *vampires*."

"Vampires don't exist," she shot back with a scowl, "and yes, they use dark magic on occasion, but that doesn't mean they're heathens. You've used it too."

I stared at her incredulously. "Huge difference there. They *kill* people."

She waved a hand. "Rumors. They use animals."

"You're okay with that now, are you?"

"No." She crossed her arms over her chest. "But they're not killing people, and Chester doesn't get involved with those rituals at all. He uses magic like I do."

"They do kill people," I replied. "You know they do."

"Before tonight, I believed it was a possibility, but after meeting Chester and everything he told me, I know those rumors are wrong. I think they're good people, and many witches think they're bad because they're... different." She looked me up and down. "I thought you'd understand, of all people."

I glanced down at my silver-and-black rings, my navy nails, and my black lace dress. "I'm not a murderer."

"They're not either—well, Chester's not. He has a good soul."

Her eyes glazed over. I'd seen that look before in people. She *liked* him liked him. Underworld help me. "We'll talk about this tomorrow."

"There's nothing to discuss," she said simply, then gestured me out of her room.

I paused by the door, then glanced at the dress again. I hated being in an argument with her. It felt so heavy, but I couldn't be okay with her putting herself in danger. I also didn't want her to feel bad. "You can borrow my red dress tomorrow."

"Really?"

She'd begged me to let her wear it countless times. "I'll leave it out for you. If you're going to insist on working at that horrible place, you should at least look good doing it."

Silence hung between us before she finally said, "I love you too, Tori."

I left, then stopped by Cas's room to check he was back and moved on quickly when I heard faint moans from a woman inside.

I went back to my snakes, who'd coiled up on my pillows. "At least you both listen to me," I said, shaking my head, and lifted them both to return them to their tank. I could swear Ebony gave me a smile, in her own snakelike way, before settling between leaves. Buttercup, however, hissed in defiance when I placed her down. She always had been the bitch of the two.

I threw myself back on my bed. I'd try the ritual again tonight. At least I wouldn't be as sleep-deprived. The morning was barely here; I could go back to sleep for a few hours. My thoughts drifted to what Ember had said about me going to the club. To meet someone. It had been a long time since I'd shared my bed with anyone. I'd only ever dated warlocks, and there were so few in our town. I remembered the way it felt to be touched, to feel their mouths against my breasts, and the heat of their bodies becoming one with mine. I missed it, but with no warlocks I didn't already know in this town, I had no choice to do without. There was no way in the underworld that I'd ever kiss, let alone share my bed with a human.

Three

The earthy smell lingered after the rain finished that evening. I fell out into a clearing among maple trees. Red leaves carpeted the ground, sludging under my boots, as I made my way with my bag and oil lamp. I pulled my black and purple spell candles from a pouch, along with the torn grimoire pages detailing the ritual instructions because there was no way I was carrying that ancient, massive book with me into the forest.

I placed the lamp on the ground at a clearing. I grabbed handfuls of twigs and stones, creating symbols in the dirt. Around them, I placed the candles and jewelry, then closed my eyes. It was only eight o'clock, but the sun was setting earlier each day, as it always did this time of year. I smiled, looking up at the darkening sky. I welcomed the darkness.

Once I whispered the incantation of a shield, a bubble appeared over my head, sheltering me and the candles from any delayed rain drops. I pursed my lips. Dark magic required a price. Unlike the magic we could play with naturally, it fulfilled desires with no boundaries, pushing against the fabric of timelines that shouldn't be messed with, and normally I'd steer clear of it. I'd seen firsthand the damage it had done to my mother all those years ago, but with the hunter prowling, there was no other magic that could prevent us from detection. Magic lived in our blood, and if a hunter used a detection object near us, it would reveal who we really were.

I glared down at the grimoire page copies. "You require more than a near-dying bird, don't you?"

I'd suspected so for a couple of days but wanted to believe otherwise. Every animal I'd found so far to use for the ritual had already been close to death.

At first I'd used bugs, but it wasn't enough, so I moved on, but—

In the distance I spotted the silhouette of a doe, grazing on tall grass. They seldom came to this area of the forest, especially at night, but she was perfect, as if the gods had sent her to me to complete the spell.

With a heavy heart, I stepped forward, unsheathing the dagger that had been inside various creatures this past week.

I whispered a spell to quieten my movements. I needed only to incapacitate it for a moment. As I neared the doe, the dark magic running through my veins throbbed, pushing me onward. I pushed away all empathy, all kindness, letting my inner villain take over; I needed her to do this.

The creature wasn't quick enough for my magic or blade. The light left her eyes quickly, a swift end. At least it had been painless. I dragged the carcass to my circle of symbols, coating the ground and the ring, bracelet, and necklaces in its blood.

Less than an hour passed, and the ritual was complete. I pressed my lips together, then buried the animal and my deed along with it.

All dark magic came at a price. By the time I finished washing the blood from my hands and jewelry, trying to push away the image of what I'd done in the forest, the voices returned. Every time I succeeded with a ritual, it brought me closer to madness, where things reached out in the dark beyond this world, and spirits loomed closer, waiting for me to move to the dark side, like other witches who played with dark things did.

I held onto the bow and violin as if they were a rope keeping me from the black hole where I might lose control. We'd heard the stories growing up, among us witch families hiding among humans for various reasons. When a witch cast too many hexes and performed rituals that fell outside of the normal magical boundaries... When they were sourced from a place of spirits and wild, evil things, eventually, they lost their minds.

I shuddered at the thought and placed the violin under my chin. I didn't do the magic frequently enough to truly hurt myself long term. My mind would heal, but the first day after a dark ritual was the worst.

I played. The music was my voice, and with it, I could say anything. Music tore the emotions I kept so far down, flooding them outward in melodies for all to hear. I closed my eyes, perfecting each stroke, every movement calculated to deliver the perfect sound.

By the time I finished my song, I was crying. I had no idea why. Wiping my tears on the back of my sleeve, I placed the instrument on my bed. I jumped when a shuffle sounded behind me, accompanied by a footstep so light, it could have been mistaken for something else if I hadn't already been so on edge.

"You always did play so beautifully."

"Mother." I swallowed thickly, wiping my cheeks again. "I wish you knocked."

She smiled. "You were so engulfed in your music; I didn't want to disturb you."

I cleared my throat. "Is there something you want?"

"No. Just to listen."

We stood merely feet apart, but it may as well have been miles. Cold circled my room, only adding to the feeling between us.

"Don't worry." She softened her tone. "I won't tell anyone." Her gaze climbed to my red cheeks, evidence of my tears. "I'm always here for you, Victoria. You will always be my little girl no matter what—"

"Thanks." I cut her off. I stared at her sagging skin and dull eyes, and my stomach knotted. I wouldn't take anything more from her. My stupidity had already cost her her health.

"I don't blame you," she said, as if she could read my thoughts. "I know you're thinking it. I've always known." Tears filled her eyes. I hated it. "It's why you push me away. You didn't know any better, honey. You were so young. I chose to do that ritual. Everything that's happening to me is a result of my choices. That girl lost her mind because I made it so."

She reached out to touch my hand, but I flinched my arm back. Goose bumps spread along my arms, and a lump formed in my throat. "I was foolish."

She let out a small but sharp exhale. "Victoria…"

"Please," I said sharply. "I'm busy. I have to find Cas, Ember, and Alex. I need to give them these." I pointed at the purple velvet bag. "I completed the ritual."

She brought her hands to her mouth, shaking her head. "I told you not to use black magic."

"It's done," I said simply, then pulled out a delicate silver bracelet. Turning to her, I held out my hand for her to give me hers.

"I can't."

"You will." I gritted my teeth. "It is the only way to protect us from detection. The hunter is in town, and I am taking no risks."

After several long seconds, she held out her arm, looking at the ceiling with tears in her eyes. I clasped the bracelet around her thin wrist, then stepped back. "I washed them," I explained as she examined it. "But there still might be traces of blood."

She paled. "Oh, Victoria."

"I'll go find Cas." I looked at the window. Dappled moonlight slid through cracks in the black drapes. "If he's not out."

"Caspian is downstairs, eating dinner."

"Good. Ember should be down there too."

"Oh, honey, Emberly left an hour ago. She went to meet some boy."

I clenched my jaw. "Chester?"

She smiled. "Yes, that's what she said."

My eye twitched. "He's the son of the couple who runs The Black Card. He's trouble."

Her thin brows pulled downward, warning in her eyes. "Emberly is a smart girl. She wouldn't get involved with someone dangerous."

"Well, he is."

She gave me a look. "Have you met him?"

"I don't need to."

She sighed heavily. "Don't think about it." Warning laced her words. "I mean it."

"Think about what?"

"Getting involved. I know you're protective when it comes to our Emberly, but she's old enough now to do what she wants. If we try controlling her, then we're no better than the rest of this society."

My fingers flexed at my side. "Well, someone has to. I'm going to go find her."

"Victoria!" she called, but I was already out the bedroom door. She didn't see it yet, but that was okay because, in the long run, she'd understand. I knew in my gut that Chester was bad news, and his family was worse. They could all think me the bad one, but they'd thank me for it later.

"Heading out," I called to the kitchen, placing a necklace and ring on the side table. The ring was for Cas because he wouldn't be caught dead in anything else.

"Where ya going?" Cas shouted back. He appeared in the doorway to the kitchen, adjoining the hallway, and leaned against the frame. "Don't tell me you've finally made friends."

I ignored his smirk. "I'm going to the club."

He frowned. "I assume not to relax, like a normal person."

"I'm looking for Emberly."

His shoulders slumped. "Of course you are."

Ignoring his quip, I pointed at the ring. "It's spelled. It'll hide your magic from anyone using detection objects." I frowned at the thought of them possessing dark objects that should belong to Istinia, but the humans had kept some. One was powerful enough to detect our powers. All the hunter had to do was touch our skin with it, like he had Jackson. As soon as it glowed, the gathered humans roared in excitement, anticipation for his death.

He grabbed the ring, examining it with a smile. "It's not terribly ugly."

"Good." I pulled on my short black jacket before heading out into the chilled autumn day.

I walked down winding streets until I reached the town center. Obsidian buildings lined the road, with alcoves and statues half out the walls. I rushed past tall, terraced houses and through an open wrought iron gate into a narrow alleyway. Branches reached overhead, like grappling fingers. Wind creaked the gate and rustled leaves down the cobbled stone. A spiderweb glistened between a flickering oil lamp over a back door, and a lonesome spider climbed the silvery weave. I turned left where the alley veered off, into a smaller alley, and walked until I reached the familiar, glossy black door with a single playing card as its door knocker.

I tapped it three times, and within seconds, a slot opened in the door and a pair of brown eyes found mine. "Victoria Amberwood," I drawled.

Their eyes regarded me, then the slot shut and the door opened. "Come in."

I handed the woman three silver dramair. I'd seen her before, one of the nights I'd come to bring Cas home after he'd blacked out drunk. "I'm looking for Emberly Amberwood."

She moved back to the doored arch leading into the club, where music slithered through the cracks around the entrance. "She's in the back." She peered around me. "Will your brother be joining you this evening?"

"No." I rolled my eyes. Chester Blackwood and his entire family were already bringing unwanted attention to our town. "Thanks. I won't be long."

I pushed open the double doors, walking between a polished bar and cocktail tables. Humans and witches mingled, and the doors were spelled shut behind me by the woman. I ambled toward the back as pipe-smoking men stared at me. I hated feeling their gaze trickle over my figure, underdressing me with their eyes. Turning my back toward a group of them, I walked to the guarded door. The man, in his thirties, who had more muscles than was necessary on any person, looked at me. "Do you have an appointment?"

"No, but my sister is in there."

He angled his head. "I can't let you in if you don't have an appointment."

His hands were clasped over his stomach, his shirt buttoned to the top, and his cufflinks had been shined to an inch of their life. Most importantly, he didn't have one of the rings yet. Most of the staff who'd been working there for over a year were gifted a green club ring, which gave them immediate entry to the club at any time.

His eyes darted to my breasts, but he looked away when he noticed my frown. I took a step closer, tentatively placing my fingers on his wrist. Tiptoeing, I leaned upward, letting my whisper dance around his ear. "I know the Blackwoods well. You must be new here. They won't mind me going back there, and I would be so grateful if we didn't cause a scene. Those men back there won't stop gawking at me." I stepped back, watching his tight expression loosen. "Please."

He swallowed thickly. "I really should go check."

"I'm sure they wouldn't want to be interrupted for something as small as this." I knew Emberly would turn me away the second she heard my name. There was no way they'd let me back there.

He wrung his hands, a bead of sweat visible above his brow. "I don't kn—"

"I'd really appreciate it. Maybe I'll thank you with a drink after your shift. Only if you want." I forced a smile, then traced a finger along my collarbone.

He cleared his throat, peering behind me, then moved his attention back to me. A smile unfurled on his lips. "What's your name?"

"Victoria, but you can call me Tori."

The corner of his lip tugged further upward. He opened the door behind him a crack. "I'll make sure they don't bother you." He gestured toward the men staring from the table at the side of the room.

I placed my hand on his bicep. "Thank you."

I swept inside and hurried down the long corridor when I heard the door lock behind me. I shook my head. I hoped he wouldn't get in trouble, but I had no choice.

I peeked inside each room, but they were empty. Finally, I reached a closed door. Chanting whispered outward, and the dark magic in my veins sang back.

That couldn't be a good sign.

I creaked it open, and my jaw slacked. A woman lay bare on a large mahogany table. Her paper-white skin was sliced into various black-magic symbols, blood spilling through the cuts like small rivers. She didn't move when they knocked into her arm, hurrying to push me out and close the door.

Pockets of smoke hit my nose. An herbal, burning stench filled the room. The owner of the club, Katherine Blackwood, glared me down, her thin lips tightening into a hard line. She wrung her bony fingers together, her crimson robe swinging around her legs as she walked. Behind her was her husband. Richard watched me, his eyes narrowing.

The door shut in my face, and security appeared behind me.

I felt the blood drain from my face when I was forced out into the open air. The woman was dead; I was sure of it. Nothing alive was that still.

It confirmed my worries. They really were murderers, and my sister had gotten mixed up with them. I rubbed my forehead, pressing my lips together. Ember couldn't have known what they were doing. She'd never have been okay with it. They were leaving her in the dark, but their son had to know. Chester was, at the very least, lying to her. Before letting my imagination get carried away, I turned and looked at the matte-black sky. I steadied myself, then pressed my lips together. I had to get back, to tell my family what I'd seen.

I ambled through alleyways until I couldn't smell the ash-tinted air from the main street. A figure appeared at the end of a narrow road, striding with his fingers wrapped around the handle of a lamp.

A blue robe floated around him when he walked. On the front was the mark of a priest. I had seen both priests of our town, but I didn't recognize him. Before he could get a good look at me, I slowed my pace and ducked down a side alley. I pushed my back against a rickety fence, disturbing a nest of spiders. A scramble of ivy and vines on the fence hid me from sight.

I heard footsteps near, then fade, crunching stones underfoot. Once I was sure he'd passed, I stepped out from the side alley and focused my eyes on the back of his robe. The magic in my veins tingled at his presence. He moved his robe to the side and pulled out a dagger, followed by a pair of shackles. I knew those shackles. Each town had a pair, gifted from the witches in Istinia as a show of peace. They disabled a witch's powers. If he had them, it meant only one thing: he was the hunter.

I swallowed thickly, watching him fade out of sight. He was heading right for The Black Card.

Four

I walked back to the house, my heart racing as a carousel of scenarios flitted through my mind. The hunter was staking out the club. He wouldn't go in there alone. The dagger and the shackles were a precaution; I was sure of it. I'd heard the stories. He was as dangerous as he was clever.

I was grateful Ember hadn't been there after all. Wherever that Chester boy had taken her, I hoped it was miles from here.

I curved around a corner to where the ancient church stood. Stretches of grass surrounded the crumbling building, shadowed by maple trees carpeting the entrance with red leaves. Their low branches stretched out, contorted over pale tombs housing the dead. Among those graves stood a small group of ten holding oil lamps. They all wore blue robes, signifying they were priests in training.

The men's eyes landed on me as if they could sense what I was. I reminded myself there was no way they could. I had my necklace on, one that had come at the cost of a life of an innocent; animal or human, it didn't matter to me. A life was a life, a soul still a soul.

It took every ounce of restraint I had not to stare at them back, to show them I wasn't afraid of them, but I knew better. I lowered my head so they couldn't see my face. I didn't want to make an impression. Being forgettable was the first lesson of being a witch in hiding.

By the time I reached the house, the temperature had dropped a couple of degrees. I fingered the pendant on my necklace as I hurried up the driveaway, then into the house.

"Ember!" I shouted, letting her name reverberate around the walls of the living room, praying she had come home in the time I was gone. "Ember!"

"She's not here." An irritated Cas appeared from the kitchen, running his hand through his brown waves. "No luck finding her?"

"No," I snapped.

He turned the ring around his finger. "Are you going to tell me how you managed to pull that ritual off?" He arched an eyebrow, knowing glittering in his eyes.

"Not right now. Look, something terrible has happened," I explained. "I went into the back of the club." I looked around for Mother, but she wasn't there. "The Blackwoods sacrificed a woman. She was dead, Cas, on an altar, with symbols cut into her body."

The light faded from his eyes. "Are you certain?"

"I didn't fucking hallucinate it, brother."

His jaw tightened. "I know you don't like them, but they're good people. They wouldn't just—"

"You too? What is it with my family and liking those awful people?" I grabbed his arm, my eyes wild as they clamped onto his dissociating stare. "Cas? What is happening?"

The bulb of his throat moved when he swallowed hard. "What did the woman look like?"

"I don't know... She was naked and dead. I was mostly focused on the blood."

"Her hair? Was it black? Did she have a scar over her lips?"

I searched my scattered memories. "I think so. Why does it matter? They killed her, Cas. That's what's important. We have to find Ember and get her away from Chester." I snapped my fingers in front of his face. "Hello? Brother? Have you finally used those last few brain cells?"

The color drained from his face. His glazed gaze finally moved back to me, and his lips parted, a tense breath passing through them. "I can't believe she'd do this."

"Who?"

"Katherine—I mean, Lady Blackwood."

My eyebrows pinched together. "*Katherine*," I stated. The soft tone caressing her name on his lips made me nervous. "Oh gods, Cas. What did you do?"

"Well, she was lonely and—"

I put a hand up to stop him. "Don't. I'll vomit." I shuddered away the awful image. Having a strong imagination was both a blessing and a curse. "So you and Ember are both sleeping with the murder family now?"

Goose bumps spread along his arms, standing his hairs erect. "The woman they killed, she might have been the same one I brought here the other night."

I rolled my eyes, swearing under my breath. "Tell me Lady Blackwood didn't choose that woman because she was jealous?"

To his credit, he looked as if he were going to throw up. At least he hadn't gone entirely over to the dark side. "I hope not, but she was just a one-time partner. You know how it is."

"Not really." The muscle in my jaw feathered. "Did Lady Blackwood see you with this woman?"

"Yes, she knows her. She's a local at the club."

"Human?"

"Of course."

"Fuck." I balled my fist. "Don't you realize the hunter is here? That he has a team of priests in training with him, and they're looking for witches? If you were seen with that dead woman last and now she shows up dead, fingers will point to you, especially if she shows up covered in black-magic symbols." I inhaled sharply. "We can only hope they dispose of her well, so she's not found."

He closed his eyes, tightening his lips as a grimace pulled the corners down. "What have I done?"

"Perhaps be careful who you bed in future," I snapped.

"You can't be a little nicer? I just found out my lover is dead." He shook his head. "Never mind, I forgot who I was talking to."

"A one-night partner, you said." I was seething. "Don't act like the victim here. If you want babying, go find our mother, or better yet, wait for Ember to return, and you can both share in the depression together at your awful romantic choices. Do you know where she is, by any chance?"

"Yes, I do."

"You didn't think to tell me earlier?"

"She came back while you were out. I told her to leave before your neurotic ass got home."

"Now who's not being nice?" I placed my hand on my hip. "Are you going to tell me where she is?"

"So you can judge us both even more? No fucking way."

"Cas," I said in warning. "I saw the hunter. He was heading for The Black Card. No doubt checking it out. If you know where she is, you need to tell me."

He hesitated, then rolled his eyes. "You don't need to worry about the hunter. The Black Card has the best security and magic defenses."

"I couldn't care less about that club or the people in it, as long as Ember isn't there."

He rolled back his shoulders. "Fine. They went to the kissing tree."

Great. They were in the forest at the ridiculous spot with the tree carved with hundreds of initials of teenage couples who'd no doubt broken up shortly after carving them. She must really be smitten to go there with him. We both used to laugh at people who went there to avoid a scandal. It was improper for a girl to be alone with a boy. Normally I hated society, but at that moment, I wished Ember would adhere to their rules.

"Leave her be."

I snapped out of my thoughts. "She's with Chester, the son of those heathens."

"She's away from the club and the hunter. That's what's important." He angled his head. "Besides, he's a kid, like Ember. He isn't involved in whatever his parents are doing. He barely even goes into the back with them. Trust me, she's safe."

"Don't blame me for not taking your word for it."

He grabbed my arm when I took a step toward the front door. "She'll hate you for it. Stop, sister. Let her make mistakes and live a little."

"It's too dangerous."

"He's just a boy."

"He's a Blackwood."

He squared his stance. "You've always been protective of her. I get it. We all do, but there's a time when it turns into just being controlling. Don't be that person. It's not a good look on you."

I swallowed his poisoned words, my mouth twisting. "I'm only doing what's best for her."

"You're not the judge of what's best for her or any of us."

I pulled my wrist from his grip, biting the inside of my lip as I took a step back. She'd told me as much last night. "When she gets back from the forest, you tell her about the club and the hunter. I don't want either of you going back there."

"One." He put a finger in the air. "You're not my boss, but... right now it *might* be best if she doesn't go there," he admitted. "I'll make sure she knows. You should get some sleep. You look tired as shit."

"Thanks," I said, then moved past him. "Give her the necklace too. It'll conceal her magic. Don't forget, Cas. I'll still put those snakes in your bed."

I heard him murmur "I don't doubt it" as he walked away, and I headed up the stairs. I was exhausted. The ritual had drained me, and with the string of sleepless nights and broken sleep, I could almost hear my bed calling to me.

I dropped a couple of dead mice into Ebony and Buttercup's cage before heading to bed.

My dreams were like an ocean of layers. They got darker the farther I fell. Blue robes, daggers, and dead people haunted my nightmares, and in the last one before waking, shouting erupted, words pounding against my soul as I felt hands grab my arms.

My eyes fluttered open, and I jumped to my feet. I punched Cas in the arm, pushing him away from me. "What in the underworld are you doing?" I asked breathlessly.

Tears glossed his dark brown eyes. "I had to wake you! You were right."

I ran cold. I'd never heard those words leave his mouth. "Cas?" I asked tentatively.

"It's Ember. I waited up for her, but she didn't come back, and it was almost three in the morning, so I went down to the club and..." His hand shot to his mouth, and a tear escaped into the gaps between his fingers. "The hunter attacked with his team. The whole place is torn apart, and they found dead bodies, sacrificed." He paused for a short moment. "It's enough to condemn everyone inside. I ran, but I couldn't find Ember. I went to the kissing tree, but she wasn't there. Y-you, don't think she would have gone back to the club?"

My heart somehow felt heavier in my chest. "Where did he take them for trial?"

"He's already begun the..." He tugged at his collar. "Punishments."

Bile bit up my throat. "Where?"

"Town square. I was going there next."

I pushed him out of the way and grabbed my boots, sharing a glance with my brother before running out the door. I prayed to deities I didn't believe in that Ember was far away from all this. Anyone who'd heard of Damian Shaw knew that no witches passed a trial with him. If he caught us, we were already dead.

My stomach knotted as I ran toward the town square. Stars twinkled against the matte-black night, but the first hues of blue had already faded the speckled silver in the distance. It had to be four, maybe five o'clock, based on the sky. I'd heard he held trials at night because it was when he believed a witch's powers were weakest. His logic was stupid, but then he was human and a priest to boot.

Please, Ember, don't be there. Please.

If she was, then I'd have to expose us, because there was no way I was letting her die. I'd fight them. I should have brought weapons. I mentally kicked myself for not thinking of it back at the house. I heard footsteps behind me in the distance, but I didn't turn to see who it was.

The town square was alight with torches and oil lamps, illuminating the freshly erected gallows and jeering crowd. My gaze climbed the wooden platform, and I found my worst nightmare come true.

Five

Ember's bloodshot eyes found me when I stumbled into the town square, falling out through hordes of people. Her lips parted, and a raspy breath passed through them.

Flames flickered on torches carried by humans, licking the sides of their faces with hues of orange and yellow. A shiver shuddered my bones, slinking down my back and spreading goose bumps along my arms. The usual softness of her expression was warped with fear, her bottom lip trembling like it had when we were kids and she was afraid.

I hadn't seen that look in a long time.

"No." The word had barely left my lips when the floor of the gallows fell away from under her feet. I fought my way through the swelling crowd and focused on the rope cutting into her throat as she hung from the noose. I still had time. If I could get to her, I could cut it down, then boil the townspeople's blood. It was enough to get her away, even if they killed me for it.

I watched in slow motion as the hunter stomped across the gallows, pulling something shiny from his pocket when he reached her. Fury forced adrenaline through me, speeding me to the edge of the gallows, when something hot flicked my cheek.

Blood spattered as he carved out her heart. He was too fast, too skillful for me to reach her in time.

My jaw dropped, a breath barely escaping as everything fell into slow motion. I gaped at the hole where her heart was. Her legs had stopped kicking, her fingers twitching, then stilling. My brain faltered. I stared, slack-jawed, my mind numb to the scene playing out in front of me. Someone nudged me when the crowd lurched forward, cheering for her death.

Death.

That was what she was: dead.

Choking on her name, I dropped to my knees, my heartbeat stopping for a soul-shattering moment. *Ember.* The word was faint in my mind, swallowed by another: *sister.*

It had to be a nightmare. It couldn't be real. I was still asleep. I had to be asleep. It couldn't be real.

Hands gripped my shoulders and pulled me, but I couldn't move, couldn't think. "Not here," my brother's broken voice whispered and tugged me again. A sob rippled through my body, and all I could think about was killing every single person in this crowd. They were rejoicing. My sister was dead. Gone.

Forever.

I didn't want to be right. Not like this.

"Please," he begged.

Chills spread along my arms, my legs, and my neck, fading the numbness that had forced me to my knees. My body filled with pain instead, a type of pain that couldn't be helped with herbs or bandages.

He was right. Not *here.* Not *now.*

I stood. My shocked silence had bought me anonymity. No one was paying attention to me; they were far too engulfed in cheering at her fall.

I recognized several people in the vicinity, ones I'd seen around town. Bringing my fingers to the droplets on my cheek, I swallowed thickly. Climbing my gaze to my sister's lifeless, blood-drenched body and angled head, hot anger enveloped my remaining emotions.

The hunter squeezed her bleeding heart between his fingers, rejoicing in holding the heart of a witch. I vowed that one day I would do the same to his.

I turned, taking in my brother's expression, pleading for us to leave. He never turned to face our sister. I opened my mouth to speak, but he gave me a knowing look, pulling my hand.

It took every ounce of strength I had to turn away from the gallows, to pretend I was another face in a crowd. It took all the control I possessed to not launch myself at Damian Shaw.

I let his name swirl in my thoughts, burning into my mind until it was all I could think about. It kept me walking, out of the square. I glanced back, noticing the Blackwoods being brought up to the gallows next. It was only Katherine and Chester, I noticed. Richard had probably been killed first.

Once we were out of earshot, Cas spun on his heel, covering his mouth with his hand as tears glossed his fingers. "This is all my fault."

I brought my trembling hands up, examining my crimson-stained fingerprints. I sorted through the searing rage in my mind, through the sheet of shock that desensitized everything else threatening to break me.

Alex. Cas. Mother.

They were in danger. It was all I had left to hold on to. Their names splashed through my grief and pain, forcing adrenaline through my veins. Clearing my throat, I shook my head, as if to scatter the image of Ember's last look at me, as if she was expecting me to help her, save her.

The pain would swallow me whole if I wasn't careful.

"We need to get home." I croaked the words out, my voice barely a whisper. "Before they come to the house. They'll know our family name. They'll assume she has a family, and we'll all end up—" I couldn't finish the sentence. Cas cried harder. At least he'd waited until we were alone, bordering the edge of the forest, before he broke.

"Mother, Alex," he said slowly, as if their names also woke him up. He dropped his arms to his sides, then looked me dead in the eye. "What do we do?"

I inhaled sharply, deeply, holding my breath as ten thoughts formed. I needed time to work out the best course of action, but we didn't even have hours. Each second brought us closer to capture. They could be on their way to the house already. That hunter would come too. A part of me wanted him to, so I could slide a knife across his throat and listen to his gurgled screams like a melody until the miserable bastard took his last breath, then use the same knife to carve out his black heart.

"Tori." The bulb in his throat moved as he watched me carefully. "The plan?"

Plan. I steadied my breathing, closing my eyes. "We need to get out of here, then decide what to do later." I glanced at the red trees, the leaves reminding me of our childhood, of Ember. "They'll expect us to run. He'll hunt us. Us gone will be all the proof he needs that we're witches too, but if we don't, it won't take long for evidence to show up, even if it's not real. This necklace won't protect me from him finding a way to kill us anyway." I soured. That was what he'd done to her. She'd never gotten involved in the sacrifices at that club. Her biggest crime was more likely pouring the wrong drinks. "We go to the house first, get Mother and Alex, then go to the club."

His eyes widened. "The Black Card? What? No. They'll kill us there."

"It's the last place the hunter will expect us or any witch to be. You said every witch in that place has been taken to the gallows. They'll have money there. We need dramair if we're going to get away."

He didn't have time to argue as I rushed past him, every step feeling heavier as the realization of Ember being gone swept through me in waves. I didn't let it in. I couldn't. Not now.

Not yet.

The house came into view. Ivy had spread along the walls, entwining in and out of the cracks formed over centuries of the building being in our family. A lifetime of memories would soon be gone, because of one man.

I reached the front door and pushed it open in front of my mother. She angled her neck, peering around me, and when only Cas appeared with me, her face paled. "Did you not find Emberly?"

"I told her before I left," Cas explained as a sob bubbled up his throat.

I licked my dry lips, forcing back a cry that was screaming to be let out. I couldn't say the word, not without choking on it.

Cas took over. "She's gone, Mother. The hunter found her."

Mother dropped to the floor, inconsolable in her grief, as her howl of pain ripped through the house.

"Alex," I said, turning toward my younger sister, who'd been dragged from her bed by our mother's cries. "We need to leave. Pack only your essentials, only the things you cannot bear to be without. We need to be fast."

Tears glittered her pink cheeks. "Ember… Is she?"

"Now," I snapped, unable to answer her. "We leave in ten minutes."

She turned and ran, and Cas leaned over our mother.

"Cas." I grabbed his shoulder. "Bag the essentials and any dramair we have lying around. We need all the money we can get. Get your traveling cloak and Mother's. Leave everything else behind."

He nodded, glanced at our mother who'd curled into a ball by the door, and swept up the stairs. There was no point trying to get her to pack anything. She could barely breathe as it was.

I cleared my throat. "We're leaving. You have ten minutes to cry before you need to get it together." I glanced at Alex when she appeared at the top of the stairs, a satchel in her hand and wearing her cloak. "For Alex and Cas."

I didn't wait to see if my words affected her. I ran up the stairs and grabbed my snakes, my coin purse, and a change of clothes, then ran back down to the front door.

I grabbed the keys from the hook by the door and ran to the shop at the end of the drive. I forced them into the lock, then practically fell into our store. My gaze found the charms Ember had made. I grabbed a charm and shoved it into my pocket—a piece of her—then ran to the safe.

I pulled out all our savings. Years of our family's work were reduced to being escape money. Bitterness curled my frown. I bagged the dramair and hurried outside. There was no point in locking the door. They'd break it down once they saw we were gone.

I glanced back one last time before gesturing to my brother to come to meet me. Alex walked behind him, and my mother a step behind her, her blotchy red face a picture of despair. Grief crippled me with every step. I felt as if I were living in a dream, going through the motions, barely able to keep a hold of each moment before it passed into another. All I knew was we had to keep going.

Barely twenty minutes had passed when we reached the club. The door hung from the hinges, and in the distance, the townspeople cheered as more witches were hung from the gallows, one by one, to make an example of us. All of them were murderers, supposedly, when only a few I knew of were.

As we creeped inside, my boots crunched atop a broken bottle of liquor. Alex pulled her black curls into a high ponytail to get it out of her face. Sweat slicked her forehead. She pulled up the hood of her cloak. "Where are we going after this?"

I eyed Cas and Mother, who were sifting through the bags and slips to find more dramair. We couldn't go to our aunt's, two towns over. The entire family would be under threat. I'd have to send them a letter, if it ever reached them in time. We had to get out of town, but then we'd need a carriage. It was late. "We're going to a hotel."

She gave me a look. "Here?"

"No. Dawnridge," I said. "It's far enough not to be searched straight away, big enough to disappear in, if temporarily, and unexpected. The witch hunter will think we'll flee to a small village."

"Why would he think that?"

"Because that's what we *should* do."

Her eyebrows knitted together, but I stepped away before I could be bombarded with more questions. We had no room for compromise. Each decision could cost us our lives. I had to think like the hunter. I had to do the opposite of what he expected us to do, because once he was done with the witches from the club, we'd be next.

Six

Elijah

Kicking an empty bottle across the marble floor, I sighed. "Ignore the mess." I scowled in the direction of the housekeeper. "The help has been slacking since my father left town."

She glared back, then inhaled sharply. "I will get this cleared up immediately, Mr. Shaw."

Charles grimaced. "Corbin back on the bottle again?"

I shook my head, eyeing the empty scotch bottle, discarded for anyone to find. He was lucky we owned the police in Redforest; otherwise, he'd be arrested for it. Alcohol has been illegal for as long as I could remember, and our father absolutely despised it, calling it demon water. "I'll deal with my brother later."

Charles smirked. He ran his finger around his ear and then briefly along his slick, dark hair. "We're on our tenth housekeeper." I glanced at his shoes, which had been shined to death, enough to reflect the chandelier above our heads. "They keep stealing from us."

His family was the second most prestigious in our corner of the kingdom, next to mine. He picked up the black invitation discarded on the side table in the lobby and grinned. “Only a week until you turn twenty-one.” He turned it over, reading the gold calligraphy. “A party in the honor of Mr. Elijah Shaw.” He enunciated in a voice that sounded too posh to suit even him.

I hit his shoulder, then pulled the card from his hand. “My father demands the best. He wanted the ball.”

“Naturally. I suppose we won’t just be honoring your birthday but also your new title. Won’t be you be Sir Elijah Shaw next week?”

I couldn’t help but smile. “What can I say, the king acknowledges excellence when he sees it.”

“Excellence?” He laughed. “What did you do again, to deserve this title? Then again, I suppose you don’t really have to do anything to get one, lucky sod.”

I paused. I hadn’t technically done anything. They said I was getting it for being a community leader, whatever that meant. “I need to get going soon. Need to go to the club,” I said, changing the topic.

“Aren’t you going to give that place up soon?” he asked. “Once you become a hunter? I mean, you’re of age.”

“I don’t know if I’ll go on to be a hunter yet,” I replied. “The club is doing well. He’ll see that and lay off the pressure. I just need to get the numbers to him.”

He chuckled. “Why not? Afraid of getting your freshly pressed suit dirty?”

“I’m not afraid of anything. I just don’t want to spend my time chasing demons when I could be making real money.”

“We both know you don’t need it.”

"We mustn't become complacent, Charles. I want to make my own name, build my own wealth, not run around tearing out witches' hearts."

The door creaked open, and a bleary-eyed Corbin trudged through. "Don't let Damian hear you talking like that, or you know what will happen."

I shot him a warning glare. "Shouldn't you be at the academy?"

He shrugged. "You going to make me?"

Charles whistled, then clicked his tongue. "If you were my brother, I'd have kicked you to the curb already."

I placed a hand on my friend's shoulder. "Settle down. Corbin's just going through something."

"He's an embarrassment to your family's name."

Corbin rolled his dark eyes. "I'm right here."

Charles gritted his teeth. "I need to go anyway. I'm meeting Elizabeth downtown. I'm taking her to the theater."

"Have fun." Corbin hissed, then opened the door for him to leave.

Charles shot him a look before walking out the door, then called back to me. "Good luck."

Once I was certain he was gone, I grabbed Corbin's wrist and pulled him into the parlor, clicking the door shut behind us. "Has the liquor gone to your fucking head, brother? Do you know what would happen if that got out? You're lucky Charles didn't catch on when you said 'or you know what will happen.'"

He slumped into a forest-green armchair. "We'll be disgraced," he said with a smirk. "So? The people in this town should know what Damian's really like."

"So?" I paced in front of the antique fireplace, catching my worried expression in the mirror. "We have a reputation to uphold."

"No." He put a finger in the air. "You have a reputation to uphold. I have liquor to drink and books to read."

I inhaled deeply. "Don't tell me you're still reading that poetry?"

He moved his dark strands from over his face. "It's called fiction, and I like it. The stories feel so real. They connect me to something deeper than I have in real life."

I pressed my fingers against my forehead, briefly closing my eyes. "Fine, just don't go telling anyone. It's bad enough everyone already thinks you're strange."

"Do you, brother?" He arched an eyebrow. "Are *you* ashamed of me?"

I thought for a moment. "No."

A hint of a smile crossed his lips. "Good. You haven't completely turned into the asshole you pretend to be—well, the one you actually are sometimes."

"Are you done?" I walked to the drinks cabinet, which masqueraded as an old globe. I poured a whiskey, relishing in the sharp spicy aftertaste. "On another note, you need to be careful about leaving bottles lying around for anyone to find."

"We're in our own home."

"You know as well as I how many people come through here."

He clicked his tongue. "When Damian is here, yes. Not right now though."

I'd given up a long time ago trying to get Corbin to call him father. As long as he addressed him in person as such, it was all that mattered. "The maids still talk, and you know how they are for gossip."

"Oh yes, and I'm sure the many women you bring home give them *nothing* to gossip about."

"I need to go to the club," I said, ignoring his snark.

He laughed, draping one arm over the arm of his chair. "You know, for someone who berates me for leaving evidence of my drinking, you're quite the hypocrite when you own such an establishment."

"That establishment is our future, Corbin. It's time to get out of the witch-hunting trade." I poured him a scotch, only because he'd drink one when I left anyway. "We will make our own names as men."

"That, brother..." He lifted his glass in my direction. "I couldn't agree more with. I only wish you told him."

I finished my whiskey, then blew out a fiery breath while checking my pocket watch. "I must go if I'm not to be late."

"Zerheus forbid Elijah Shaw is late."

I hated when he called me by my full name. "Try to do something with yourself today, if you're not going to attend school. Maybe bathe."

He called after me, "I can't make any promises."

I walked downtown, my gaze inadvertently landing on the old gallows as I passed. Since Father had gone hunting witches in a club of black magic, Redforest had been quiet. No hours-long sermons at the church. With most of the priests traveling with him, we'd been left to guard the town from witches ourselves, not that any would ever be stupid enough to come here with our reputation. Most of the time, the people put on trial weren't witches at all, but ones who'd gotten tangled up in trying to perform a spell with no magic—or something along those lines. During the trial, they were tested for magic but sometimes freed with moderate punishment.

When he found a real one, they were brought to these gallows to be killed in front of the town. He'd hang them first, to weaken them, after placing shackles on them to take away their magic. Then for good measure, he'd either rip out their heart or burn them. Those were the only ways to destroy the demons inside. Fortunately, witches didn't come here often.

I unbuttoned the top button of my shirt, then tugged at the collar. I dipped down a dark alley, the only shortcut to the club. Shoving my hands in my pockets, I walked the gas-lamp-lined cobbled streets, past the dressmakers, cigar shop, and bakery as it wafted the smell of fresh bread into the autumn air. I could have taken the carriage, but I enjoyed long walks. They helped me clear my head.

The dark double doors to my club was a welcome sight as I turned left down the narrow street. A lamp flickered overhead, and Tim and Greg stepped apart when they saw me, making an entrance.

"Mr. Shaw," Tim said, adjusting his jacket, which was far too small for his muscular arms. I didn't mind. The customers would be warier of making a scene once they saw him. It was why I had hired him as my security.

"Any troubles tonight?"

Greg shook his head. "Nothing of note."

I nodded curtly, then stepped inside, inhaling the smell of liquor, smoke, and polished wood. Denise was the first to greet me, pushing her chest out and sucking in air as if she could look any thinner in her corset. I pretended not to notice. "Hey, sweetheart." I leaned down and kissed her cheek.

"Is your father back yet?" she asked, her eyes glittering in curiosity.

"No, he's still away on business."

She nodded. "He's only doing Zerheus's work. Someone must protect us from the demons. We miss him at church is all." She leaned over a stool and whispered into my ear, while her fingers traced up the inside of my leg. "As long as you're all alone in that big mansion..."

I offered her a clenched smile. "Not alone, love, but as always, I'm charmed by your forwardness."

She smiled, then leaned back. "If you get lonely tonight, you know where to find me."

I exhaled slowly. "I'm a lucky man."

She grinned, and I moved to the other side of the club. I was sick of hearing about the god's work, about demons and witches. For one night, I wished I could not have to hear about my father or any of it.

I ordered a whiskey, then rubbed the back of my neck, undoing a knot. Moving my fingers downward, enjoying the release of the ache in my back, I hit the top of one of the many large scars hidden under my shirt.

A lump formed in my throat, and I downed the whiskey to keep dark thoughts from invading. Maybe it was why Corbin drank so much too, to keep the pain at bay. After all, he had far more than I.

Seven

Victoria

We were rich for the first time in our lives, but it meant nothing without Ember with us.

The host greeted us at the front desk of the Diamond Hotel, the most expensive establishment in Dawnridge. It was a risk coming to the main city of Salvius, but it was also the smartest move. Going to a small hotel on a rundown street was anticipated, and I didn't put it past Shaw to search our town and every neighboring village through the night before coming here.

"Felicity Moreton," I said, with the plummy accent of high society. "We require a room for the night."

Cas stood next to me. Mother and Alex waited outside. The host's brown eyes slid toward my brother. Agitation shuddered through me. She waited for him to speak, and under different circumstances, I'd slap her for ignoring me. "Sir?"

He cleared his throat. "Yes, uh, one room for me and my…" He looked from me to the host. "My wife."

My nostrils flared, but I forced a smile when she looked at me. Discreetly, I pulled one of my rings from my other hand and put it on my ring finger. He wasn't wearing one on his, but I prayed she wouldn't look.

"That will be three gold dramair."

His eyes widened at the price, but I placed a hand on his shoulder gently, a show of affection for the host, but a reminder to him of the position we were in. With a slight squeeze of his shoulder, he tensed, then handed over the coins.

She handed him a key and gestured toward a man wearing a fancy uniform to take us to our room. I glanced at the front door but walked in step with my brother as the man led us to a gold-furnished room. Once he was gone and the door was shut, I grabbed Cas's wrist. "Wife? We agreed we'd say I'm your business partner."

He raised his eyebrows. "Come on, Tori, this was more believable."

I gritted my teeth. "You're not even wearing your ring on the right finger."

He looked down at his hand. "Oh, I'm sure they didn't notice."

"I'm not fucking around, Cas. Move your ring to the right finger." I grabbed his bag and dropped it on the bed. Anger steeled my heart when I saw his hair cream. "You did not bring your fucking hair cream as an essential."

His sheepish stare found me across the room. He ducked when I threw the cream on the bed. My eye twitched. He'd expected me to hurl it at him. "I'm not Ember," I said thickly, recalling their banter and affinity to throw things at each other when they were mad.

Silence befell the room. He ran a hand through his waves. "It was stupid of me to grab it. I wasn't thinking. I just grabbed things and... It was all a blur. I'm still in shock."

I shook my head. "Forget about it."

He peeked through the crack in the drapes. "Mother and Alex are still outside."

"I am well aware of where they're stationed, brother, considering that's where we left them."

"Stationed?" He let out a long exhale. "You sound like a prison guard."

"Stop." Tears glimmered in my eyes. It was a rare show of emotion, but I was barely holding it together, and I needed him to see it, to see how close to the edge I was. I wouldn't play games.

He sat on the bed, slumping his shoulders and drooping his head in his hands. I wanted to do the same. To drop and do nothing but sit in silence, but I couldn't stop moving.

I walked downstairs, running a hand through my long dark hair and pushing it back over my shoulder, giving half smiles to passersby as I made my way through the lobby. I did everything I could to look as normal as possible, for someone who'd watched her sister die a few hours earlier.

Once I'd snuck Mother and Alex into our hotel room, I let myself pause, until the pain threatened to break through again. I looked at them in turn, jutting my chin in an attempt to look half together, for them. It was mostly for my mother, who appeared fragile thin, as if she might break at a moment's notice into another crying fit, but it was also for Alex, whose brown eyes shimmered with tears. She wrung her small hands together as she shifted from foot to foot. Cas could handle it himself, I decided, but even he needed me. "*What do we do?*" he'd asked after—

Alex pulled Ebony and Buttercup out of her pocket. "I kept them safe."

"Thank you." I took them, letting my snakes entwine and coil around my fingers. They stayed there as if they could feel my pain, as if they knew.

"Settle down for the night. We're as safe here as we can be. In the morning, we will leave, but we need sleep."

"Mama and I were talking outside, and we think we should go to Aunt Terra's."

I shook my head, stealing a look at Mother. Her eyes were far too like Ember's for me to hold. "Absolutely not. That's where the hunter will go next."

Mother looked up at me for the first time since we left the house. "We need to tell her."

"We can't risk it."

Tears trickled again down her cheeks. I was surprised she had any left. "I can't let my sister die."

I pursed my lips, placing the snakes in my deep pocket. I understood. Truly. I'd lost mine to the same man, but we couldn't, and it broke my heart to say it. "It's her or us." The words came out colder than I'd wanted, but they were true and harsh yet necessary. We couldn't risk it. I could send a letter, but it would be too late, and we all knew it. If we tried going there, to warn them, we'd be walking into a trap, or be captured shortly after.

After tonight, when he'd find no sign of us, he'd follow the Amberwood name to our mother's maiden name, Vineroot, which would lead him to our aunt and cousins. I tried not to picture what would be waiting for us if we returned. "I'm going for a bath," I said. "Try to sleep. Cas and I will take the sofas in the living area, and you two can take the bed. I'll tell you the plan in the morning."

I didn't wait for their replies. I slinked quickly into the bathing room and locked the door behind me before anyone could say anything.

Once inside, I breathed.

One. Two. Three. Steady, careful not to let anything out. I couldn't afford to feel things, to stop and allow them to surface.

I stole a glance at my reflection in the mirror. My bloodshot eyes looked back. My painted crimson lips had faded to pink, my cheeks red from constantly wiping them, as if some semblance of blood may still be there.

I took a deep breath, then turned on the taps, watching it slowly pool with clear water, steam billowing up in an illusory dance to nothing.

I slid Ebony and Buttercup out of my pocket and plugged the drain before placing them in the sink. "Stay in here," I whispered.

I undressed, careful not to let out the sob quaking softly behind my closed lips. If I started crying, I was afraid I wouldn't stop. I stepped into the hot water, letting it comfort me as it relaxed my muscles. I thumbed out an ache from my shoulder, then the top of my arm, working my way over to the back of my neck. Ember was always the one who'd give me massages. My shoulders were always tight and tense, or so she'd say. My throat closed over when I thought about her. I felt myself slipping away, into memories and emptiness, where I'd stay forever.

No. I had to hold onto something. A tether. Anything. I couldn't focus on her being… no. Then I would be dead, because I couldn't live with that kind of grief.

I closed my eyes. I pushed Ember from my mind, filling it instead with the witch hunter. The townspeople. The club owners, but they were already dead. A quick fate, really. For centuries, witches had been demonized, but like humans, there was good and bad in all of us, and Ember was good. She trusted humans. She gave to charity and tried to do and say the right thing. She danced around people's feelings, careful not to hurt them. She and I couldn't have been more different, but I loved her for it. She was the light I didn't have, but they'd killed her. They had squashed her light as if it were nothing, and they had been left only with darkness. Me.

I gripped the edges of the sunken bathtub. Fury clouded my vision, and my nostrils flared as every injustice suddenly felt like a mountain collapsing on top of me. I'd let too much slide over the years, and it had cost us everything. I let what happened to our cousin go. I hadn't fought back. I'd never fought against the hunters or anyone who demonized us.

If humans wanted to believe us evil, then I would become precisely that. If they wanted darkness, I'd shroud them in it until they choked. If the hunter wanted another reason to hate witches, I would be that, for him, because in his vengeance against us, he'd turned me into his own personal poison.

I sat in the bathtub, plotting, planning until the water turned cold and pale-blue light filtered through the window.

I wouldn't kill him straight away like he had her. Instead, I'd destroy him from the inside out. Death was going to come for him eventually, but I wanted to ensure he'd be begging for it when it did.

***

None of us slept well. Morning stole the night from us too soon. I wasn't prepared for the world to continue moving, as if the worst thing hadn't happened. My stomach ached, a growl rippling through my torso, reminding me I still required food.

Mother was awake already, though she pretended otherwise. Her bloodshot eyes flickered open every couple of minutes before they closed again. I wondered what was going on inside her head. Out of all of us, only Alex was still snoring.

Cas didn't even try to appear as if he were sleeping. He stood at the window, staring out of it blankly. I dropped my arms at my sides and cleared my throat. Mother's eyes opened, and Alex stirred. Cas didn't turn around.

"Family meeting in ten." I gestured toward the adjoining living area from the bedroom in our suite. "We'll need to leave soon."

Cas checked his pocket watch, his voice raspy when he spoke. "We should decide on where to go next."

"That's what this meeting is for." I leaned over the bed, then nudged Alex's arm. "Wake up, sister."

Once everyone was sitting on the sofas, I explained my plan. "We can't run forever."

Alex nodded in agreement. "Should we go to Istinia?"

I winced. "You can go if you'd like, with Mother. You'd need to cross the mountains. It's dangerous."

"What about you?"

Cas leaned forward, propping his elbows on his knees. "Yes, what about you?"

"I'm staying. I'm moving to Redforest."

His eyebrows shot upward on his forehead. "Where the hunter lives? Have you lost your mind?"

Alex's tone softened. "We will understand if you have."

"My mind is perfectly clear." I shot Cas a look. "I'm going to Redforest precisely because it's where the hunter lives. I'm going to make him pay for everything he's done to us. To Ember. To our cousin. He won't stop hunting us until he's dead, and I plan on making sure he ends up that way, but first, I'll make him suffer."

I saw Ember in Mother's eyes, then averted my gaze to my brother. She stood, moving to my side. She placed her hand on my arm, a soft, gentle touch, but I shrugged her away.

"Victoria," she said slowly, her voice cracked from the crying. "Darling, we cannot go into the heart of the snake's pit."

Alex placed her fingers to her lips. "Actually, I'm with Tori."

My eyes widened as I took her in. Anger glittered in her stare.

"He deserves it. They all do. Look what he did to Ember. He tore out her heart, Mama."

My mother clapped her hands against her ears, letting out a whimper. "Please, don't. I can't bear it. My baby girl."

I pulled her hands away, giving Alex a look to stop. "I know it's hard to hear, Mother, but if we don't put a stop to him, we'll forever be hiding. Aren't you angry?"

"Of course I am." She looked at me incredulously, then wiped her nose on the back of her black sleeve. "But I care more about you three and your safety than vengeance."

Cas drummed his fingers against a side table. "I do too."

"I don't want you all involved," I said. "I'm happy to go alone. You can all travel to Istinia."

"I'm not leaving," Alex said. "I want to kill the hunter too."

"I'm not going to kill him straight away," I admitted. "I'm going to take my time, make him suffer for all he's done." I angled my head at my mother. "And probably what he's on his way to do to your sister. I'm going to make him wish he *was* dead before I end him."

She buried her head in her hands, and Cas was right at her side, consoling and comforting, taking the role of our dead sister.

Cas looked up. "You're only doing this so you don't have to grieve."

My heart palpated. "It's not. It's because he deserves it. I'm doing this for Ember. Someone has to, Mother."

Alex nodded along.

"He'll kill you," Mother said.

My eyes glossed. I knew it was a possibility if he found out who I was. The truth was I didn't care if I died. I knew she could see that too, but I saved her hearing those words aloud. "I'm going to be careful. He won't know who I am. I'm changing my identity."

Cas thumbed the back of his neck. "Then I'm taking Mother away. She's not going to Redforest."

"That's for the best," I stated. "Because once I'm done with the hunter, I am going to hurt every single human who allowed this to happen."

Mother shook her head. Her voice was hoarse. "You can't take down an entire kingdom. It's been this way for as long as witches have been alive."

"I have to at least try." I glanced at Cas. Guilt was etched into every worry line, every crease around his eyes as he looked from me to Alex. "She's just a kid."

She scowled. "Hey, I'm more mature than you."

If I wasn't drowning a pool of anger, I'd have smiled. "Alex can come with me; I'll take care of her. We have the necklaces to conceal our magic, and the hunter didn't see our faces." I paused, only relenting because she was far too much like me. There was no way she'd allow herself to be left behind. "You're only coming if you don't get involved with my plans with the hunter. Promise to stay out of it?"

She huffed but nodded. "I promise. I won't get involved. I just want to watch."

Cas growled, then clicked his tongue. "I guess at least it will be unexpected. He won't see us coming."

I arched an eyebrow. "Us?"

"Yes," he said. "I'm in."

Mother cried. "No."

"We won't get caught," he said with promise, looking her dead in the eyes and holding her shoulders. "I'm taking you to Blackburn. Uncle Richard will take care of you until we return."

Alex pressed her lips into a hard line. "Dad's stepbrother?"

"It's a good idea," I said. "He's a sympathizer, and he doesn't have Dad's last name. It's far away from the hunter. No one will look for her there. Take her, then come back."

"Please," Mother begged. "Don't go."

I licked my dry lips, pressing my pointed nails into the arms of the sofa. "Please understand. He is going to look for us wherever we go. It's either we brave the mountains and try to get into Istinia, where we will be forced apart into covens anyway, or we spend the rest of our lives looking over our shoulders for the hunter. We're not safe anywhere, not in Blackburn, Dawnridge, or Redforest. At least this way I can protect us and make him pay too. Karma never happens to people like him. It's why people like me step in."

"Honey, it's never as simple as that."

"Then what?" I asked, tears swimming in my eyes. "Will you have me forgive him? Go about my life while he picks off our family one by one? No. I'm going, and if Alex and Cas want to come, they can."

It took an hour before Cas finally got Mother to agree to leave. I was sure the herbal tea he'd made, from ingredients he'd bought at the shop next to the hotel, had something to do with her sudden agreeability. I wasn't upset. She needed to be calm, else she wouldn't survive this.

I laid my snakes inside the pocket of my jacket and pulled the material outward, watching them curl around each other and go to sleep. Having them close helped, if only a little. I inhaled deeply, holding my breath for a few seconds. I'd never given much thought to revenge, but I thought it might be the death of me, and that was okay. As long as the hunter's death was just before mine.

Eight

Victoria

A rickety sign creaked when a breeze swept through the town center. It read, Redforest – May Zerheus Bless Our Town. Alex stepped out of the carriage behind me and flicked her midnight-black hair over her shoulder. “It’s… quaint.” She gave me a tight smile.

I hated the place as soon as I laid eyes on the weathered gallows, a stone’s throw from their church. Sun-bleached wood panels held up the structure, and boards were nailed over holes where the wood had rotted. Most towns didn’t have gallows up all the time. They were only erected on the rare occasion a witch was sentenced to death, but it was obvious executions were once a frequent form of entertainment in Redforest. I assumed Damian also kept them up as a warning.

“Stay close,” I said and grabbed Alex’s arm, rushing her past the church. The architecture dated back to the time when gods roamed the world. Tall arches welcomed the townsfolk inside.

The light bricks reflected the sun as if they were made of gold. The bell rang, signaling the beginning of their service.

I welcomed the smell of fresh bread as we passed a bakery, a stark difference to the lingering stench of horse dung that covered the main road, winding up between shops on either side. I eyed a rundown apothecary shop. Slanted shelves of jars and bottles filled the view in the grimy window. A faded sign hung from chains over the door, but the first part of the name was no longer visible. At least Cas would be happy once he returned from taking our mother to Blackburn. It was hardly competition.

Alex pursed her lips. "Are we going to buy this one?"

My nose scrunched. "No. We have a shop in a far better location."

"Do you really think we can afford it?"

"Yes. I've already told you everything. We discussed the plan on the way here," I whispered. "I will answer any more questions once we are alone." I forced a smile at a couple who were staring at us. A woman in a corseted purple dress looked me up and down, then moved her disapproving gaze to Alex. I tugged Alex's arm, moving us away.

Alex gritted her teeth. "That was rude."

"They're not used to how we dress." I looked around at their long dresses with boxy sleeves.

"You're telling me." She snorted. "This town feels like it's stuck fifty years in the past."

A man scratched at his knee-length breeches down to his stockings, then fastened his tailcoat. A couple of other men wore the more modern tailored suits I was accustomed to seeing back home.

A waft of leather hit my nostrils when we paused by a shoe shiner. I pulled out the map Cas had given us and ran my finger along the winding street. "It's left up here." I pointed at the dressmakers on the corner.

Alex grinned, pointing at a pink bow tied on one of the mannequins. "Will you be blending in with the fashion here too? That would look pretty on you."

"I'd rather strangle myself with it."

She chuckled. It was the first time I'd even felt close to laughing since… I held my breath. I turned my thoughts to Cas. He'd be here tomorrow. Sometimes it felt like we were looking after her when it should have been the other way around, but I didn't mind. Taking care of her was the only way I could make up for her health deteriorating in the first place.

"How long until we reach the house?" Alex asked, breaking me from my thoughts.

I checked the map again. "It's not far."

"I wonder how it'll look."

"It wasn't too expensive, so it'll be nothing like our house." A lump formed in my throat. I supposed our home was no longer ours. The king and queen would take it for themselves, declaring us fugitives or accomplices on the run and, worse, witches. Our beautiful family mansion and shop were forever gone. Hatred seared through my veins, bubbling a rage under the surface that only revenge could sedate.

Alex sighed. "I miss home. I miss Mama and…" She trailed off.

I didn't respond. What could I say? I missed our mother too? I didn't. It was the truth, and as much as I wish it weren't, I couldn't pretend. Her being gone took away the guilt I felt whenever I saw her.

A brisk gust of wind caught a dead, red leaf, swirling it toward us. Batting it out the way, I looked up at the low-hanging branches of the maple trees lining the street we'd veered down, leading away from the shops. "I guess the town is aptly named."

"It's kind of pretty in this part. Ember would have loved it here."

Her face floated into my mind, along with memories of us jumping in piles of leaves and running after each other among the trees in the forest with sticks, pretending they were swords. I felt the warmth drain from my face as the memory slipped away, forever gone. Just like her.

Alex's fingers squeezed my arm as I bent over. "Tori?"

I swallowed thickly, steadying myself. "I'm fine. Let's hurry before night comes."

She rubbed the back of her neck, then rolled her head around, rolling her shoulders back. I did the same, finding relief in the stretching of my tense muscles. It had been a six-hour carriage ride from Dawnridge. They had these things called automobiles in Istinia, but Salvius was always a step behind with technology. According to our late cousin, automobiles could take us from place to place five times faster than a carriage.

A small, red-bricked house came into view as we turned the corner. Its faded black door was slightly ajar, and the wind whistled through the tall grass in the front yard.

She frowned. "Is this it?"

I looked at the number forty-nine on the door. "It appears so."

"How did Cas get this?"

"Through one of the connections he trusts," I explained, realizing I had been wrong before. We hadn't included her in every detail of what we'd set up before leaving Dawnridge. "Let's get inside. It's getting cold."

She rubbed her bare arms, but neither of us moved, gazing at the house. A sickly dread crept over me as I took in the broken window on the side of the house, and its ivy-strangled black gate. It was our new home. I hadn't let it truly sink in, that I was leaving my old life behind for good.

***

I left the house after covering the hole in the window and unpacking our things into the old dressers and wardrobes. Alex took a nap on the sofa, and I hurried back into town before everything closed. We needed fresh linens for the beds and a few other things. Holding the makeshift list Alex had helped me write, I hugged my black jacket around myself. The fresh autumn chill tingled my fingertips and lips. Avoiding the disapproving looks from the locals as I walked, I realized with unsettling awareness that we may have to dress like them if we had any chance of fitting in.

Emberly would have done well here. She always did know how to blend in when needed, unlike me, or even Alex. Cas would have an easier time adopting his alias, Ambrose Weathermore from Dawnridge. I would remain Victoria, and Alex would want to take our mother's middle name, Evangeline, or Eva for short. We would be known as an orphaned family who'd inherited our family fortune and moved to start a new business. Cas, or Ambrose as he would be called, would be taking care of us, his younger sisters, until we married. Once he opened his apothecary, Alex and I would work there. I'd take care of the business side as I had back home, and Alex would help customers while Cas made the mixtures and treated patients.

I glanced back when I reached a road that stretched to a hill, then out to a forest. Expensive, grand houses lined the road. Had I taken a wrong turn? I reached for my map, then swore under my breath. I'd left it on the dresser. Fuck. I turned back, then paused.

My gaze climbed a four-story mansion. I recognized the name edged onto the sign: Shaw Family Residence. It was where the hunter lived. I held my breath, regaining my composure as I reminded myself that Damian Shaw was, in fact, not here and out still hunting—us.

I ducked behind a wall when I saw him. A man stepped out through the main gates and ran his hand through his ash-blond hair, then tugged the sleeves of his blazer. He looked like the hunter but younger, without the scars. I looked at his impeccable navy suit. He carried himself with an air of regality reserved for those at the palace in Dawnridge, but he wasn't royalty.

He was a Shaw.

I supposed in this town they might have been the same thing. He strutted down the road, hands in his pockets, so I did what any sane person would do in my situation. I followed him.

Shops were closing by the time I'd walked through town, but I didn't care. Dismissing my list for tomorrow, I shoved it into my pocket, focusing my eyes on the back of the man walking ahead of me. I couldn't get over how much he looked like Damian, so I assumed he must be his son, but I needed confirmation. I caught my breath when we turned a corner. I wondered why he hadn't taken a carriage.

The blond man slipped inside a black building in some seedy alleyway; above it, a sign swung. The Black Horse. I smoothed the black lace of my dress, took off my jacket, and ran my nails through my hair, taming the flyaway strands.

"Evening," I said when I reached the guarded door.

"Name?" the bigger of the security guards asked.

"Victoria."

"Common name, that one. What's your last name, miss?"

"Weathermore." I enunciated it clearly, playing the part of a woman in high society.

"Never heard of it."

I forced a smile. "You will."

"New to town?"

"Yes, and if you were in Dawnridge, you would know the name. My brother would be disappointed to learn of this disrespect *if* I tell him."

The two exchanged looks, then the bigger one cleared his throat. "New members are to use the guest pass." He handed me a card with silver writing on it. "Welcome to Redforest, Miss Weathermore."

I hurried inside, handing my jacket to a man waiting at the entrance. He gave me a number on a ticket and walked me to a small table. I gazed at the women who danced in skimpy dresses, much like they did at The Black Card back home. This club didn't seem too different. It operated in the shadows of Redforest, illegal like the Black Card, all because of one thing: liquor. Illegal and coveted.

A quartet played violins in the corner, while another musician played the piano in harmony. I'd heard better, but they weren't terrible. I took my seat, watching the blond man from the back of the room, my gaze following him to the other side of the bar.

"I'll take one of those." I pointed at a drink on the menu when a waiter appeared, who bowed his head and left quickly. At least they were efficient.

The man, whose features I noticed were sharper than what I remembered of Damian's, slapped his friends' backs by way of greeting, then smiled his pearly whites at anyone who looked his way. He brought a round of drinks for the men surrounding him, commanding the attention of the bartender within seconds, then moved his attention. He tapped his fingers against the shoulder of a woman who appeared to be in her early twenties.

She turned, her smile widening. Based on her slight smirk and the gentle nudge to his arm, she knew him. She ran the stirrer of her drink along her bottom lip and fluttered her eyelashes, gazing up at him, then she averted her gaze to her drink, where a lonely cherry bobbed next to ice.

My drink arrived. I thanked the waiter, handing him a gold piece. He didn't so much as bat an eye at the generous payment and tip, which confirmed my suspicions on the type of people who frequented the club.

It was a place for the wealthy and bored.

I examined the crystal glass, bigger than the size of my hand, and sniffed the smoking green drink. A hint of mint with lime floated to my nose. I took a sip and delighted in the fresh, albeit slightly sour, hit from the cocktail. Wafting away a cloud of smoke that had made its way from another table, I continued to watch the man I'd followed here and the woman at his side. She turned, her knees facing him the whole time. Minutes turned to an hour. His eyes glazed over her but didn't stay on her. Every so often, his gaze moved to other women in the room.

Two drinks later, I pushed my glass to the middle of the table, paying the waiter handsomely. The woman leaned in, ready to close the night, nudging closer.

"Elijah," the woman said, laughing. "Are you are trying to get me drunk?"

He laughed. "I have no need to get you drunk."

"Mr. Shaw," the bartender said. "Will you be wanting another scotch?"

The chatter from the surrounding tables drowned out their voices.

He almost seemed bored with his slight sigh and slumped shoulders. Standing with her, he walked to the other side, only a few tables from mine.

My waiter cleared my glasses, pulling my attention from Elijah. "How has your evening been here at The Black Horse?"

My lips stretched into a genuine smile. "It's been excellent. Thank you."

He bowed his head and left with his tray. I really did have a good night. I'd got everything I needed. A name. He was in fact a relation to the hunter, and I'd bet my dramair he was Damian's son. He was at his property, had his name, bore striking resemblance to Damian, and was at the right age. He had to be.

Elijah Shaw.

Son to my sister's murderer.

I let his name swim in my mind. He was everything I needed. He would be my way in, my revenge, my punishment. I watched him leave with the woman, a half smile on his face—curved lips but no crease to his cheeks. I knew the type. He wanted a challenge, and no one here was giving it to him.

If that was all it took, then I would be *exactly* whom he wanted.

Nine

Elijah

The same nightmare came for me again; I was glad it was Amber who was in my bed and not some other woman. I awoke in a panic of sweat and heavy breathing. She pretended not to notice, which I appreciated.

"Morning." The corners of her eyes softened.

"Morning, love," I said, then sat upright, noticing she was already pulling on her stockings. "You not staying for breakfast?"

She stretched her thin, rosy lips into a smile. "I should go before my husband notices, although I'm sure he won't after his night at his gentlemen's club. He will have drunk his weight in brandy—to our advantage." She whispered a kiss against my lips after pulling her shoes on. "You know, you should find yourself a wife sometime."

I wiped the beads of sweat that had collected above my brows. "Why ever would I do that?"

"For company, Elijah. I've known you since we were in school. You get lonely."

I smiled. I'd always liked Amber, and if she hadn't got married to that oaf, I supposed she would be the least objectionable option, but even she had tired of waiting for me to propose all those years ago. "I suppose you do make marriage sound so very charming."

She rolled her eyes. "You are a man, Elijah. You don't need to marry for security or reputation. You can choose someone you really like. Besides, my husband isn't that bad. He's just a little... boring."

"Is that why you're in my bed and not his?" I smirked. "I'm not complaining."

"You're so bad." She kissed my cheek. "I love it." She stood. "I best be going. Good day, Elijah. We shall see you at your ball." She squeezed my shoulder as she left.

I exhaled deeply. I wished she hadn't had to leave so soon, because once I was alone, images of the nightmare flooded back. Then came the sounds of Corbin screaming, but at least this time they weren't real.

I stood, forcing out a tense breath, then pulled off my shirt. Amber hadn't yet asked why I never took it off during the night. Perhaps she thought us so hot with lust that we couldn't fully undress before fucking.

A housekeeper knocked on the door. "Mr. Shaw, sorry to wake you," she said through the door.

I shook my head. She knew I was up. She'd have seen Amber leave. I pulled my pants up and opened the door. "What's wrong?"

"We've just received word Father Shaw is returning tonight."

"Where's Corbin?"

She cleared her throat, averting her gaze. "Master Corbin hasn't been seen since yesterday evening."

I closed my eyes for a moment, searching for the thread of patience I had to have somewhere. "Do you know where he went?"

"One of the maids spotted him when she left last night, down by the old apothecary shop on Canal Street, with some of his friends."

I gritted my teeth. That was kind of her to call those heathens his friends. They were more like users of his money to fund their habits. "I'll go to their hangout spot before my suit fitting. Please have the maids draw me a bath."

She nodded and turned to leave. I bit my bottom lip, feeling bad for what I'd said the other day. "Thank you."

She half smiled and hurried down the corridor. Once she'd gone, I rubbed my forehead, smoothing the wrinkles. I had to straighten Corbin up before Father returned. He was hard enough on my brother as it was, which was half the reason Corbin was down there to begin with.

Father had told him since he was young about how he was the product of witchcraft and the reason for our mother's death. It was bullshit, but my brother suffered for our mother's actions regardless. I wondered what was worse: believing he was the reason she'd died or being hated by the only parent he had left?

***

The town center was emptier today than normal. I straightened my shirt, glad for the walk to clear my head. Fractured dreams from the night before slowly faded the faster I went. I waved at the only remaining priest left behind, who was unsurprisingly about to enter a not-so-secret brothel, as he diverted himself past the white building. I wouldn't have said anything, but fuck if he knew that.

"We need to get your uniform first." A voice I didn't recognize pulled my attention to the other side of the narrow street. Straight, dark hair ran like silk down her chest and stopped at her waist. Her black dress hugged her curves, with lace barely covering her bronzed arms and neck. She argued with a younger version of herself, who I assumed was her sister.

Passersby glared at her when they walked past, looking her up and down. Their disapproving pinched frowns I knew too well. Whenever someone new came to town who was a little different, they were given the same welcome.

I shoved my hands in my pockets, crossing the road after a carriage pulled by. Her eyes found mine, widening as I approached. My heart skipped a beat when she smiled. I hadn't expected such a warm, approving smile, or kindness in her gaze.

I stopped in front of her, glancing at the young one, then back at the mystery woman. "Hello." I croaked but quickly cleared my throat. "Uh, I'm Elijah. You must be new to town."

Amusement glittered in her eyes. "I'm Victoria."

I extended my hand, and she shook it, taking a step closer. I breathed in her scent: jasmine and honeysuckle and perhaps something else, but I couldn't pinpoint what.

"This is... Eva." She hesitated, pointing toward the shorter version of herself, who smiled back at me broadly.

"It is a pleasure to meet you both."

Her eyes reminded me of honey and cinnamon, like the tea my mother would make me when I was a kid. "What brings you to town?"

"Business," she answered quickly. "My brother is opening an apothecary shop."

I turned my attention to the crumbling black building. "I had no idea they were selling."

"They're not. We will be opening another, farther uptown. This is a terrible location for one."

I leaned against the wall of the shop, my eyebrows flicking upward. "And why is that?"

"Because all the necessary shops are farther uptown, such as grocery shops and postal services. Medicine is a necessity." She glanced at the tailor's, then the dressmaker's. "This is the more luxurious part of town. The shops are sparser and for those with more… eloquent taste." She looked me up and down.

"Perhaps, but then one would think opening a business close to where the wealthy peruse would be most beneficial."

"The rich can afford to have doctors come to their homes. Why would they go to an establishment like this?"

The corner of my lip tugged upward. "It seems you have an answer for everything, Mrs?"

"It's Miss."

I smiled. "Miss?"

"Weathermore." She pouted her painted-red lips enough for me to notice them. Whether it was on purpose or not, it had the desired effect.

"Well, Miss Weathermore, welcome to Redforest. I hope you get a chance to visit my club sometime. It's not far from here."

"You mean The Black Horse?"

"You've visited?"

"Maybe." A smirk played on her lips. I honestly forgot someone else was there for a minute. I glanced at her sister and cleared my throat.

"Perhaps you'd like to come tonight? Of course, twenty-one and over only, I'm afraid," I said when I saw her sister's grin.

Victoria paused, placing her finger against her chin. "I'll have to see what I'm doing this evening."

"I hope you come," I said, knowing she would. I looked from her to Eva. "Good day, Miss Weathermore." I looked back at Victoria, my voice turning sultry. "You too, Victoria."

I felt her eyes gloss over me before she turned and left, her sister in tow. I stole a glance back at her and smiled to myself.

The sound of laughter from a passerby snapped me back to why I was there. Inhaling sharply, I slipped down the narrow alleyway between the apothecary and the draper's. I supposed Victoria was right. It was a terrible location for the shop. No wonder they were always behind with their rent.

I shimmied down the narrowest part of the alley, grimacing when a rat squeaked and ran between my legs. Falling out the other side, I pinched my nose. A pungent, herbal smell mixed with sewage water and smoke filled the air. I eyed the garbage thrown out the back of the shop, then turned toward the open concrete area that stopped at a tall, grey-bricked wall.

Stepping carefully over bits of broken bottles, broken ceramics, crumpled paper, and the occasional rat skull, I slipped down another narrow alleyway connecting the apothecary to a hidden alcove where two benches stood. "Corbin."

The two guys were still with him, both a couple of years older than him, whom he called friends.

"Br-brother?" His eyes rolled back.

"What did he take?" I stared at the one I recognized as Kapps. "Answer me!"

He passed me a brown bottle of opium. "Fuck's sake, Corbin." I rubbed my forehead. How was I going to get him out of there without being seen?

"He insisted," the other said.

"Leave, now," I barked. "If you whisper one word of this to anyone, I'll kill you."

They looked at Corbin and left.

I grabbed Corbin's shoulders, shaking him gently. His head flopped back as he incoherently mumbled something. It was going to take hours for him to be okay enough to walk.

"Stay here," I ordered, as if he could even move if he'd wanted to. I noticed his pockets were inside out. "They took your dramair, you fool." No wonder he was the only one hopped up on opium. They'd taken his money. Those bastards. I stormed out of the alley, then up the other.

I evaluated the area. If I had a carriage pull up directly outside the alley, no one would see if we were quick. I wanted to bet he'd seen a letter last night, alerting the household of my father's return. He was already trying to black out the thought of our father, but if Corbin was seen like this, I wasn't sure I could protect him from our father's wrath—not even if I fought like I had before, which had only made it worse.

The memory swirled unwantedly into my mind. Father had had Corbin shirtless, screaming, and buckled over a chair, with ten lashes. When blood surfaced and chunks of skin attached to the whip, I'd lost it.

I recalled the bruise on Father's temple, purpling toward his eye, and the spatter of blood covering my knuckles after I'd hit him. Corbin had sat gasping in the corner of the room as he held the whip in one hand.

That day had stopped future punishments, but it had also cost us the most.

Ten

Victoria

"He likes you." Alex grinned. "You played it well."

I scratched the back of my neck. "I was unprepared. I'd planned to meet him on my own terms, but no matter."

"Cas will be pleased you've already found a way in."

"He only invited me to a club. He's undoubtedly extended such an invitation to countless women."

"Will you be going?"

I laughed. "No. If I don't go, he'll spend the evening looking for me; therefore, I'll be on his mind. The more I remain an idea to him, the more he'll want me. That's how I get him."

"Are you sure you can do this? I mean, you don't have much experience in… seduction."

"Alex!" I scowled. "You're not supposed to even know that word."

She laughed, flicking back her black ponytail. "Fine. How do you plan to *win* him over?"

"I'm..." I paused, licking my lips. "Going to use my intuition."

"Oh, gods."

I arched an eyebrow at her. "Anyway, we still need to go get your uniform. Are you sure you're happy to finish your schooling here?"

She nodded, a little too eagerly. "Yes."

"I need to get used to calling you Eva. I hesitated in front of Elijah when introducing you. It can't happen again."

"You're too hard on yourself. Wait until Cas hears how you already met one of the Shaws."

"I'm just glad he's finally coming, after being delayed." I couldn't help but scowl. "As usual, he had a hard time saying good-bye to our mother."

She rolled her eyes. "You miss her too. Don't pretend."

I spotted the uniform shop for the academy. "I see it." I pointed, changing the topic. "I also spot our brother."

He laughed a little too loudly, deep in conversation with some woman holding a parasol against the sunlight.

We approached her, and Alex cleared her throat. "Brother."

He smiled broadly. "Ah, Eva, Victoria." There was something pointed in his eyes. "Maria, these are my sisters. Sisters, this is Maria. She's the wife of the priest Father Montague. I was telling Maria how devoted we are to the faith."

I forced a smile and looked at Alex, whom I hoped would go along with it. Out of the three of us, she was the most vocal about her hatred for Salvian's religion. "Yes, we certainly are."

"How wonderful." She practically sang. "I hope to see you at this week's sermon. We just heard our beloved priest, Father Shaw, will be attending. You should meet him. He's the most devoted and pious man you'll meet."

Cas lightly touched her arm, and she blushed. "We will be there, Maria." He took a step back. "My apologies. Mrs. Montague."

She laughed lightly with a coy smile. "Oh, it's absolutely fine. I mean, it was a pleasure to meet you, Ambrose."

He grinned, showing off his pearly whites. "The pleasure, I assure you, was all mine."

He bid her good-bye, then walked us down the road until we were alone. "That is my ticket into the church."

Alex grinned. "The pleasure," she mimicked, "was all mine."

He gently nudged her. "It's a full-time job, being this charming."

I rolled my eyes. "Let's discuss the main event, shall we?"

They both looked at me, their eyebrows raised.

Anger bubbled in the pit of my stomach. "She said Damian will be there, so he's back then—or will be." I clenched my jaw, wondering if he ever found our extended family and how many more hearts he'd held since we'd been gone.

Alex touched my hand, which had balled into a fist at some point mid-thought. I flexed my fingers and let out a long, shaky exhale. "I met Elijah, the eldest son," I said. "He invited me to his club."

He clasped his hands together. "Perfect, and naturally you won't be attending."

Good. Cas understood. "I'll wait for him to find me."

"It's the perfect plan. Now, you." He looked at our sister. "Let us get you your school uniform, then head home for some dinner. We all have a long night tonight."

"We do?"

"Yes. We must plot our next steps and clean up the house a bit. You've both done a terrible job at making it homely. I stopped in to unpack before I came here."

I crossed my arm, tapping my shoe against the pavement. "Then I suggest you take the role of decorator and housekeeper."

"It seems I have no choice."

Alex chimed in. "We can always hire someone."

"No," Cas and I said in unison. "We can't risk anyone finding anything..." He gave her a look. "Or seeing something."

She nodded slowly. "Right. Sorry, that was stupid."

He winked. "It's okay. You're still young."

I gave her a look. "It's nothing compared to the stupidity our brother would do, bringing a plethora of human women back to our house, so don't feel bad."

He tsked. "I'm so happy you're always there to bring me down a notch."

"Someone has to be." I looked over my shoulder. "Anyway, I think I might take a look at the shop we'll be buying again. I want to make sure it's all safe. Can you take her to get her uniform?"

"Okay, but I've already checked it out. It's perfect."

"We'll see." I left them and trudged back through town. The sun had come out in all its glory, as if it were saying good-bye to fall and welcoming winter with one last show. Soon it would be dark evenings and gray clouds. I neared the apothecary when I saw him again, but he was holding an unconscious boy. I angled my head as he heaved the boy into a waiting carriage. A couple of people were looking too but turned away before Elijah could notice them, but he did see me.

Panic flitted his gaze from me to the boy, and the color drained from his already-pale face. I took the few steps toward him as he waited mid-step into the carriage. If I turned back now, he'd be too embarrassed or worried to search me out again. I couldn't have this encounter ruin anything between us, especially as it was so new and nothing had truly begun yet. "Mr. Shaw," I said when I reached him. "Is everything okay?"

He sighed heavily. "Miss Weathermore."

I guessed Victoria was out the window. "Who is that?" I looked around to see inside. "Is he not well?" The stench of ammonia lingered in the carriage air. "Is that opium I smell?"

The boy muttered something unintelligible. Elijah glared at him, then looked back at me, tight-lipped. "It's my brother."

I blinked twice. "I can help."

"Really, there's no need."

"Please." I moved Elijah out the way, inviting myself in. If I was going to save us from this awkwardness, I would go along with it. I doubted he'd be at the club later, so my plan to not show up went out the window. On the upside, perhaps I'd see his home. More importantly, maybe I'd even see his father. "I'd hurry if I were you," I said as he stood at the open door. "People may see."

He relented, running his hand through his blond hair, tousling it. He closed the door and took the seat next to his brother. "You really didn't need to do this."

"I know a great remedy that can help him," I explained before he could stop me. "It's a mixture my brother taught me." I left out the part how I'd had to use it the few times Cas had taken too much. Opium was all the rage, but it was dangerous. I could feel it in my gut, no matter how many people tried to say it was safe. "What's his name?"

"It's Corbin."

"I'm going to help you, Corbin," I said with promise to the semi-conscious boy. He appeared to be around Alex's age. I saw something soften in Elijah's hard gaze, and I knew I'd done the right thing.

Elijah pulled Corbin into the house with the help of several servants, all of whom seemed immune to seeing Corbin this way.

I assumed it was a common occurrence. Every family had its black sheep, I supposed, though my family was full of them.

"Where's the kitchen?"

Elijah pointed down the hall, toward a corridor.

I nodded, heading there.

"We will be upstairs, in the second bedroom to the right," he called after me, and I couldn't help but notice the worry lacing his words. Caution swallowed his gaze as he watched me turn down the corridor.

I noticed the portraits and stopped in front of one of Damian, in his youth with far fewer scars. I glared into the eyes on the painting, my heart sinking into my stomach the more I stared. A single tear fell down my cheek, and I caught it on my wrist. "You," I whispered as I examined his face, recalling the way he had squeezed my sister's heart in his hand until her blood spilled through the cracks in his fingers. She was dead, buried in some unmarked grave like the other witches. No longer would she come to my room to play with Ebony and Buttercup or listen to me play the violin. Never again would we walk through the forest and find flowers to add to her pressed flower collection. She would never make another perfume again or get to live out her dreams. She was gone, and I couldn't pull her back from death. It was permanent, and I hated it. I could scream until my voice went dry and tear down every painting in this house. I'd burn it to the ground and dance in the ashes, then when Damian found me, I'd tear out his heart and force it down his throat.

"Excuse me, miss, are you lost?"

I turned slowly, curling my trembling lips behind my teeth. I had to rein my anger in.

I swallowed hard. "I'm looking for the kitchen. I'm a friend of Elijah's."

She gave me a look, as if she presumed as much, then led me down the corridor. I didn't look back at the painting in fear I'd burn it with my magic.

"I need, um, some herbs."

"I'll show you to the pantry."

I followed her closely, forcing the imagery of Damian from my mind. My hatred for him would swallow me whole if I wasn't careful. Even if it was alluring. Some days I wanted to give up, to let the darkness in and allow myself to shrivel into nothing until I didn't have to feel anything again. If it weren't for my rage, and Alex and Cas, I was certain that was exactly what I would have done.

Revenge was the driving force keeping me from tipping over the edge into nothingness.

I refocused. I had to gain Elijah's trust and help his brother. I found the herbs and gathered them in a wooden bowl. Cas was the one who had come up with the spell I'd place on the herbs. In fact, almost all the "remedies" in his apothecary shop at home were infused with magic. It was his favorite part of being a witch, being able to use magic to heal others. The magic in the remedies was in so small amounts it would only last in a human's body for a few hours, but it was enough to heal. Like Ember, Cas was inherently good, if not a pain in the ass with his vices, but then we all had those.

I crushed the feverfew, chamomile, catmint, dill, and sage, which would mask the magic from detection, and added them to clover oil. I took the mixture to an empty bathroom, locking the door behind me, and whispered the incantation over the bowl. "In our goddess Estia's name, take what is not of him and break it down, remove it from his body before he is bound. Loosen the coils of what ails him, and let him wake without feeling too grim."

I felt the energy pulsate through me and into the mixture and smiled. I quickly left the bathroom, finding my way to the second bedroom at the top of the staircase, where Elijah sat at Corbin's bedside. "Here." I gave him the bowl. "Pour it all in his mouth. It will help the opium leave his body quicker."

"He may choke." Fear danced in his eyes. I could see it as plain as day; his brother was his weakness. I understood that. Ember had been mine until she wasn't.

"He won't. Give it to him," I urged.

He hesitated before he opened Corbin's mouth, and he wrestled back, but Elijah was stronger. He poured the mixture down Corbin's throat, and as I promised, he didn't choke—only gagged. "How long will it take to work?"

"Not long. Maybe an hour."

He pulled his pocket watch from his jacket, then inhaled sharply. "Thank you for your help, but I must ask you to go."

My eyebrows knitted together. "Why…"

"I apologize, but now really is not the best time for you to be here. There will be a carriage downstairs waiting. My driver will take you wherever you need to go."

"I can wait to see if he'll—"

"No," he snapped, then lightened his tone. "Now is not a great time. Please leave."

I bit the inside of my cheek. Had I messed the whole thing up so soon?

I gave one last look at Corbin and sighed. "You're a good brother, Elijah. I know what it is to have the burden of loving your sibling so deeply. He's lucky to have you watching over him," I said and walked out the door before he could see the tears in my eyes. Something about the exchange reminded me of Ember. She'd never have taken opium, but I had tried protecting her like he was with his brother—especially the days before she died. He had the same look in his eyes I recognized in myself. He was terrified.

I shrugged it off, hoping his wanting me to leave so abruptly was simply out of worry for his brother. I wished I could have stayed to meet Damian in person, but this may have been for the best, if even his painting had made me so mad. I had to regain my composure.

I spotted an invitation on a table as I left: a ball, in Elijah's honor, for his birthday. I looked up. Perhaps Estia was rewarding me for saving the child's life. I shoved it under my jacket and left through the double doors. I was going to get us three an invitation to that ball, no matter what I had to do to obtain it.

Eleven

Elijah

"Father." I licked my dry lips, standing straight when he entered the room. He had a glint in his eye I recognized. "The witch hunt went well, I assume."

He slammed his leather-bound journal on his desk, wisping dust into the air. "Yes. Where is your brother?"

"Bathing. We didn't expect you for another hour."

His eyebrow lifted. "Has he been drinking?"

I didn't let a single breath falter. "No."

"You're too kind to him."

Someone had to be. I allowed the hardness in my stare to say everything I couldn't. "Are the other priests back too?"

"Some stayed behind." He waved his hand dismissively. "They had unfinished business."

I grimaced. "I'm sure they did."

He walked behind his mahogany desk, and his leather chair let out a groan when he took a seat. He moved some papers, then tapped a finger against the wood. "I know you think me cruel."

My eyebrows furrowed. "I don't—"

"Don't lie to me. I can always tell." He exhaled slowly. "Everything I do is for your benefit, whether you see it now or not. When you're older, you'll understand."

That lecture again.

"For Corbin too," he said. "I have to be hard on him. We know what darkness plagues him. The residual magic from his conception lives in his blood."

"He has never shown any powers, nor have you ever detected magic on him."

"It's dormant; I am certain. Regardless, if I were cruel, I would have sent Corbin away, but I didn't. He is my son, and while I am tough on him, it's for his benefit. I must keep him on the straight and narrow, to keep him on Zerheus's path in the light, so he doesn't follow another."

I swallowed the response I wanted to shoot back, only because it would fall on deaf ears. I wished he could see *he* was the one pushing Corbin down a dark path. He could have died yesterday. Our only saving grace had been the day delay in father's return due to flooding, else he'd have seen how bad his son really was. "How many witches did you find?"

"Seventeen." He smiled tightly.

I moved my gaze to the brown armchair in the corner. Above it was a gold-framed painting of my mother, him, and me when I was a baby. It was the only piece of the wall not made from shelves lined with leather spines of church books. "The club was indeed a black magic one then?"

"Yes. I found families of them hiding out." He sneered. "Some escaped, however."

"Oh, damn," I said, trying but failing to keep the sarcasm from my tone. I glanced at the chessboard on the small table in front of the unlit fireplace to my right. I'd never been invited for a game.

"I'll find them eventually," he said, taking no notice. "I have priests in every town on the lookout for the Amberwood and Vinewood witches."

"Amberwood? Sounds very human."

"It is. They took the name of some poor dead man." He shook his head. "They told the locals he was their father. Such lies they spill."

I heard a shuffle behind me, coming from the corridor. "I think I hear Corbin."

The muscle in Father's jaw ticked as the door to the study opened. My brother had at least had the brain to slick his hair back and powder his face, so it didn't appear so yellow. "Sir."

He allowed it. "What have you done in my absence? How are your studies?"

He hesitated, and I shot him a look. *Don't lie. He'll know.* He'd talk to the headmaster and know he'd been skipping school.

"I'm doing good."

Fuck.

"That is yet to be determined."

I chimed in before they could say anything else. "He's doing great, but I'll admit, I took him out of school for a few days while you were gone. I needed help at the club."

Corbin took a step forward, but I placed my hand out to stop him from saying anything.

"Is this true, boy?"

His expression darkened. I knew that far-off look, as if he'd desensitized everything. "Yes."

Father clicked his tongue. "You know better than to bring your brother to such a place of temptation. He is not like us. He can't withstand it."

I inhaled deeply. "I wasn't thinking."

"Don't let it happen again. Your brother must remain dedicated to his studies."

I nodded. "I won't."

"You're dismissed." He looked over his papers. "Both of you."

I touched Corbin's back and led him out of the study. Once we were outside, he breathed relief. "Why did you do that?"

"He'd have found out otherwise that you were skipping."

Something flashed in his eyes. "You don't need to protect me against him."

"I won't let him hurt you."

"Right." He laughed it off. "He still threatens to whip me, you know."

"He won't, not while I'm here. Besides, things will be different one day. You'll see."

"When the bastard's dead, yeah."

"Corbin."

"What? Don't tell me you haven't thought about it."

I had, but I wouldn't say it out loud. Nor would I wish on it. "He's the only parent we have left. He means well, but he doesn't go about it the right way. I'm confident he'll see the light one of these days. I've tried talking to him before—"

"Defending him, again. Like I should be surprised." He grabbed one of the ball invitations on his way to the staircase and tore it down the middle. "I should be grateful, in a way. In a few days, it'll be announced that you'll be training to be a hunter, which means I won't have to."

I gritted my teeth. "I plan on discussing that with him today."

"He will never allow you to refuse it. It's our legacy, remember?" He made a face. "Until you stand up to him, you'll never have the life you really want."

"He can be reasoned with. I've done it before. He allowed me to wait until my twenty-first birthday to decide."

"He won't, and when he says no, you should go. Take your money, leave the house, and do what you want to do."

"I won't do that."

He walked up the stairs, not looking back. We both knew why I'd never leave, not until Corbin was finished with the academy, until he could be his own man and leave too. I'd never leave him at the mercy of our father. Since I was there, he wouldn't hurt Corbin again. He hadn't for years now, but as Corbin had said, he still threatened it, and I didn't trust it not to happen without me around.

I ran my hand through my hair.

"Mr. Shaw." The housekeeper's voice rang behind me. "A Miss Weathermore is here to see you."

"Who?" I closed my eyes for a second. "Oh. Victoria." I hadn't sent her anything to say thank you for yesterday, but I also hadn't expected her to come back after seeing all of that.

***

Her smile caught me off guard. I straightened my jacket. "Miss Weathermore."

"Mr. Shaw. I see we're back to formalities."

I couldn't help but grin. "It's good to see you again, *Victoria*."

She knotted her fingers together. "How's your brother doing?"

"Better." I guided her down the winding path toward the gates. I didn't add how I planned to get revenge on his so-called friends who'd stolen from him and got him hopped up on opium. "Thanks to you."

She smiled again in response. "It's a nice day."

"It is." I looked at the pastel-blue sky. "A good day for a walk, don't you think?" I guided her away from the mansion.

She arched an eyebrow. "Is there something terrible about your house you don't want me seeing?"

I paused, and she laughed.

"I'm teasing. A walk sounds lovely, although I had hoped to rest my feet."

"I know a spot."

"Good." Her faded-red skirt flowed out at her ankles as she walked a step ahead. At her waist, a black band separated her skirt and a buttoned-up cream blouse with lace at the collar and long sleeves. Her lips were shaded in a softer pink too, softening the sharpness to her features. Her dark eyebrows raised slightly when she spotted me looking at her. "Something you like?"

I chuckled. "Nothing I don't."

She rolled her eyes. "You seem in quite good spirits, considering."

"There's little point wallowing in misery. Besides, those responsible for giving him the opium will get what's coming to them."

"So your brother is truly better then?"

I nodded. "Your… mixture worked wonders. He still has some lingering side effects, but he's better than he would have been. It appears I owe you a thank-you."

"I take payment in dramair or food."

I smirked. "I'm a terrible cook."

"Then dramair it is," she said teasingly. "I'm just glad he's okay. Really." She paused. "Does he take opioids often?"

I ran cold. "No."

She didn't look convinced. "If you need more of that ointment again, my brother will sell you some at his shop."

My eyebrows raised. "He's opening so soon?"

"Yes, in a week."

"Good to know. I'll make sure I'm there."

"Your presence will be appreciated. I'm certain with a Shaw attending opening day, we can attract quite the crowd."

"Ah, so you've already heard about my family."

She shrugged. "It's hard not to. Everyone we've spoken to loves your family."

"You mean loves my father."

Her expression flattened. "Yes. You're known as 'the asshole.'" She laughed. "Not my words."

"Now, that's only partly true." I curled my lips between my teeth. "Anyway, I will be there. It's the least I can do." We walked through the iron gates and then out onto the street, turning toward the orchard. "You say you are here with your brother and your sister, whom I've already met, but what about your parents?" I asked, noticing she couldn't be any older than me.

She looked at her feet. "They died. My brother inherited our family's wealth, and he's always wanted to live here and to open his own shop."

"I'm sorry for your loss."

She pressed her lips together. "It was cholera."

I'd heard of many dying from that. "If there's anything my family can do to make your transition here easier, please let me know."

"I will."

I grinned at her forwardness. "Where did you live before?"

"Dawnridge."

"Do you miss the city?"

"Not really. I prefer small-town life." She looked around at the maple trees lining the street. "What about you? Have you always lived here?"

"Born and raised."

"Where's your mother, if you don't mind me asking? I haven't heard anything about her."

"She passed away when I was a kid."

"Oh. Sorry."

I held my breath for a heartbeat. "It was a long time ago."

"That doesn't matter. Memories have a way of holding onto us, don't they?"

I nodded slowly, turning left at the corner and leading her down a narrower street. "We're almost there."

"Where are you taking me?"

"An orchard."

"Oh."

"My family owns it."

She let out a sharp exhale. "Of course they do."

We walked in silence, but it wasn't uncomfortable. A gentle breeze shifted leaves across the ground, sweeping between us. I should have had the staff pack us a picnic. It was a good thing I didn't have anything to do until the evening. The club wouldn't open for a few hours yet, and I wanted to check in. I'd hoped to talk to Father after his sermon about my career path, but it would have to wait.

I looked at Victoria, my eyes moving to her pockets, unusual things to have on a dress. My eyes bulged. They were moving "What is..." I stepped back when a snake's head popped out. "Victoria." I reached for the head of the viana, hoping to pull it out before it bit her. How it got into her dress I had no idea.

She turned, her skirt swirling back as she did. "Don't hurt her!" she shouted, pulling it from her pocket. It curled around her fingers and nestled into her palm.

"That's a fucking snake."

"Yes," she drawled and pulled a second from her other pocket. "Sorry if they frightened you."

"*They*?"

"There are two."

"You knew they were in there?"

"They're my pets."

"Good gods."

She stroked one's head. "This is Ebony. She's the sweet one."

My eyebrows furrowed. "Those are venomous. Kill-you venomous."

"They won't harm me," she stated. "This one is Buttercup. I'd be wary of her though. She won't bite me, but I wouldn't put it past her to go for another."

I was wary of both. I shuddered back. I didn't want to appear as a coward, but they were nicknamed man-killers. "How... did you acquire them?"

She placed them back in her pockets. "I found them when they were babies."

I scratched the back of my neck, hoping I didn't look too flushed. What could I say? She definitely made an impression. "We're here." I glanced at her pockets, my heart still pounding. If she had in fact had them as babies, then they must be safe. They were fully grown at twelve inches, so she must have had them for years.

I pushed open the creaking gate to the orchard. Apple trees ran in uniform lines down a stretch of green as far as the eye could see. I grabbed one of the rosy-red apples hanging from a low branch and handed it to her. "It's good. Trust me."

She crunched into it, her eyes closing. "Gods, what is this magic?"

I laughed. "Redforest apples are famous. You should try our cook's famous apple pie sometime."

She took another bite and walked under the tree. "I'd love to, if you ever invite me to your house again that is."

She sat in the shade, flicking her black strands over her shoulder. I crouched next to her, then sat back against the trunk. Her skin looked darker in the dappled sunlight, warming her brown eyes. "I'm having a ball this weekend."

"Is that an invitation?"

I smirked. "Do you want it to be?"

"Depends. Will there be any of this famous apple pie there?"

"I'll make sure of it."

"Then I may come."

"I'll have an invitation delivered. Just write down your address before you leave," I said. "I hope you'll save me a dance."

"If the pie's any good, I'll leave you a slot on my card."

I'd almost forgotten about everything, walking with her to the orchard. Corbin. Father. Becoming a hunter. But it always slipped back in. Even here. "I should be getting home soon. I will walk you home first."

She ran her finger along the core of her apple. "Do you not like taking a carriage? I saw several at your house."

"I prefer to walk."

She lay back, her eyes focusing overhead on the branches. "I live quite far from here, so if you wouldn't mind, I'd love to get a carriage back. I got one here, but it wasn't my own, so they wouldn't have waited."

"I'll have one take you back."

"Thank you. I'll need to use your restroom too." She stood, then grabbed another apple from a tree. "Thank you for showing me your orchard. It's beautiful."

"I should have sent something to you," I admitted, "after I knew my brother was okay."

She smiled. "There was no need. I simply came around today to see if he was feeling better."

Of course it was why she was here. Why else did I think she came back? "I appreciate it."

She reached her hand in her pocket, and I tried not to squirm, but she didn't pull it out. "I know it's a little unusual," she said when she saw my face, "to keep snakes as pets, but I found them when I was in a dark place, and they brought me comfort. They've never hurt me, although I wouldn't recommend anyone else holding them."

I saw a glimmer in her eyes, something dark and sad, but it was gone as quick as it had come. "I think it's sweet."

She cough-laughed. "Sweet? That's a first."

"You care about animals. Why wouldn't that be sweet?"

"Because they're not rabbits or kittens."

"Even snakes deserve love. Maybe more so."

The corners of her eyes creased. Her stare held an intensity I'd never seen in anyone else before. "Let's walk," she said after a moment. "You can tell me all about your club while we do."

Twelve

Victoria

I set a black candle on my altar, then ran my finger along the instructions on the open pages of my grimoire. I double-checked I had all the items: four coffin nails, a snakeskin, an ounce of black salt, three strands of Damian's hair, and a feather of a raven. Then one by one, I placed them into a brown woven bag.

"Won't this have repercussions?" Alex asked.

Cas shushed her. "Our sister knows what she's doing."

I cleared my throat. "I'll be okay, sister."

"After today, I believe in you." Cas nodded affirmatively. "You got your invitation."

"Actually, I got all three of us invitations. He didn't take much persuading once we walked back to the house."

Alex's nose crinkled. "It must have been so hard, pretending to like him. To be in the same house as that wretched hunter."

"It wasn't easy, but first impressions tell me he's not much like his father."

"Ew," Alex rebuked. "Don't tell me you like him."

"I don't, but saying he's not quite as bad as the man who ripped out our Ember's heart isn't high praise either, sister."

"Good," she snapped and looked at the bag of supplies. I'd swiped a comb from Damian's bathroom to get the hair.

"I need quiet while I work this," I explained and lit the candle, smiling when the flame flickered up. It danced smoke through the air, toward our wood-beamed ceiling. I lowered my gaze to the hex bag. "Sleep demons of the underworld, bring your fear to our world. Make Damian Shaw's sleep of horrible things; haunt his dreams until he weeps. Take his hair and my blood as a sacrifice for your magic." I pricked my finger with a needle and let blood drop into the flame, watching it fizzle instead of dull.

One had listened.

"For as long as this bag remains under his bed, his mind is yours to twist." The flame changed to blue, flickered, and disappeared into a thin line of smoke. "It is done." I picked up the hex bag, feeling the darkness of the energy I'd brought into this world settle uncomfortably into my shoulders and neck, like a tension that would never alleviate.

Alex angled her head. "How do you feel?"

"Right as rain," I lied. Nausea crept through me, threatening to reach my throat, but I kept it down. I had to. I couldn't have them worry any more than they already did. We all must sacrifice for our cause, and I would take the brunt of it for their sakes. It was no less than I deserved.

"Good." Cas stepped forward. "You distract Elijah and Damian at the ball, Tori. Alex and I will sneak upstairs and place it under his pillow."

I nodded, but anxiety tingled. "Just be careful. Don't get caught."

Cas scoffed. "Thanks for the reminder. We were planning on getting caught, right, Alex?"

Alex clicked her tongue. "Oh yes, but now you said that, we'll make sure we won't."

I was feeling too unwell to snap a quip back at them. "I'm heading to bed for a bit."

Alex paled. "Why? Are you feeling sick?"

"No. It's been a long day. I just need a short nap to rejuvenate."

Cas grabbed the hex bag. "Go sleep. I'll place an order for a new suit from the tailors. Shall I make one for dresses for you both too?"

Alex made a face. "I'll go with you. I don't trust your taste."

"You can make mine," I said and left them to head upstairs. Today had drained me. The walk with Elijah was longer than I'd expected, but at least I'd gotten into his house and grabbed the hair to make the hex bag. It was only step one in our plan, but at least I could see the light at the end of the tunnel.

Once I reached my bed, I collapsed onto the covers. I pulled the blankets over my body, shaking. Dark magic seeped through my body, which tried to fight it like a disease. I closed my eyes, and between waves of nausea, I found emptiness.

***

Sleep came for me in a shroud of blackness, pulling me deep into the cesspit of my mind, where dark things roamed. Shreds of magic remained there, pulled from the underworld by spells I'd used, and distorted my memories. For a moment, I understood madness. It was like looking through a filter of uncertainty, of rage with a spoonful of fantasy.

I roamed the farthest reaches of my thoughts. There, Ember waited for me. She was on the gallows as she had been that day, but her face was different. In place of my sister's wide eyes were deep, pitiless things: the eyes of a demon. When her heart was ripped from her body, I saw what they saw, a demon posing as a human, killed. I was angry at her for doing this to us. Rage filled me, and for a second, I saw her as the problem, as the destroyer of our happiness.

No. She was my sister. She'd loved me. We weren't the darkness plaguing the world. We had souls. I shook my head, trying to claw out of my own mind when hands shaking my shoulders awoke me with a jolt. My eyelids flung open, and beads of sweat trickled down the sides of my forehead and temples into my hair.

"Alex."

"You were screaming." Her wild eyes assessed me. "You've been out for hours."

"I have?"

Her cupid-bow lips tightened into a frown. "Were you having a nightmare? I've had them too… since Ember."

I shook away the mental image of my sister as the demon they all believed us to be, but I couldn't get rid of the rage prickling the edges of my mind. I looked into the eyes of my sister, unable to tell her the truth: that the magic we were using was slowly unhinging my mind. "It probably was a nightmare. I don't remember."

She took a step back, releasing me. "You don't have to pretend to care."

"I do care."

She arched an eyebrow. "Could've fooled me."

I gave her a look. "I care enough that I'm here. I cared enough to orchestrate all of this."

"Sorry. I've had a hard time at school. I haven't been in the best of moods."

I sat upright. "How so? You didn't say anything earlier."

She plopped herself on the end of my bed. "You were busy plotting and hexing." She paused. "I met Corbin. The Shaw junior."

My stomach churned. "I told you not to get involved."

"But it was so easy," she admitted, fingering her silver necklace with a slight curve to her lips. "The others tried bullying me."

I clicked my tongue. "I assume you retaliated."

"I haven't." She paused. "Yet," she mumbled quietly.

"Wait, is Corbin the one bullying you?"

She shook her head, averting her gaze from mine. "Actually, he's the one who's been sticking up for me. They think I'm weird."

"You are weird," I said, in an attempt to lighten the mood. "The best people are, sister. Would you prefer to be like the rest of them?"

"No."

I wiped the sweat from my forehead using a handkerchief from the nightstand. "So Corbin isn't a total ass then?"

"He's still a Shaw," she said with a ferocity lining her tone. "He's only protecting me because he wants to get inside my underwear. I can tell."

"We told you the terms of your coming here was you weren't going to get involved personally. You promised you'd watch from the sidelines."

She placed her hands on her curvy hips. "I think it's unfair you and Cas get to have all the fun."

"This isn't supposed to be fun."

"Fine." She turned, but I saw her roll her eyes before she did. "Try not to scream too loudly. I need my sleep."

"Yes, you do!" I shouted as she left the room. Once she was gone, I gripped the covers and pulled them up to my chest, then nestled into the comfort and warmth, searching for something, anything. Everything felt so empty.

For a second, I wished Alex hadn't left. She, like everything else, was a welcome distraction. Nighttime was the worst. Goose bumps spread along my arms.

I looked at the open window. The moon was barely a slit of a crescent white against the sky. The oil lamp Alex must've lit when she came in flickered oranges and yellows onto the black-and-purple damask wallpaper and reflected off the large, framed mirror on top of the rosewood-and-walnut dresser. I eyed the glass case, which had been invented to be used as a floating garden. It was the perfect home for my babies.

My thoughts floated to Elijah. He hadn't been as repulsed by Ebony or Buttercup as I'd expected, but I hadn't thought one of them would pop out of my pocket like that. They usually slept when I walked. It had been a risk taking them out, but they hadn't been anywhere yet and had been cooped up in their cage for days.

I would take them with me tomorrow. He'd promised me a walk around the grounds, after a little nudging. It was exhausting pretending to be so nice, but it was working. Cas was working his way into the church community, via his new friend, Priest Montague's wife. Our plan was underway, yet I couldn't find happiness in it—or even a sense of accomplishment. I felt... nothing, only sedation to the fury licking through me like flames, knowing I was avenging Ember.

Dark magic lingered long after morning came. I tried to eat breakfast, but nothing tasted good anymore, not even those apples, though they'd been the one thing to come close. I forced myself into a bath, got dressed, and picked up the charm I'd grabbed from the shop that Ember had made. I kissed it for good luck.

Yesterday I had come close to seeing Damian. I'd diverted my way to his bathroom to find something of his to use in a hex bag, but I'd almost been caught. Elijah had seemed distracted, but his staff was not. I couldn't risk it again, which was why Alex and Cas would place the hex bag in Damian's bed at the ball.

I painted my lips dark red before I brushed down the front of my blouse and blue skirt. These dresses were the closest compromise I could find between the fashion in Redforest and my own. Free-flowing skirts were comfortable, not too tight, but the blouse's collar reached up to my throat, which was a little annoying. Fortunately, I had my charm to lure Elijah. After all, he had invited me back today to spend time with him, so something was working.

I grabbed a bag and placed my babies inside of it. I made my way out and headed into town. I was going to pick up some items from the bakery first and check out the progress of our shop.

I opened the front door but grabbed my jacket when I saw the gray sky. Storm clouds rolled to the west, and a thunderous boom landed over the distant forest. At least the weather matched my mood.

Thirteen

Elijah

I draped my arm over the back of an armchair, kicking my legs up onto the coffee table, as Charles grabbed a cigar from the tray. "Want one?"

"Already had one." I angled my head at my best friend. "Your sister knows the Kapps guy, right?"

He nodded once. "Why?"

I glanced down, then brought my stare back to his. "He owes me dramair."

"He rob you?"

"Something like that." The memory of Corbin sitting behind the apothecary, off his head on opium and with his pockets empty, flitted into my thoughts. Those so-called friends of his had robbed him blind and could have killed him in the process. I'd let them off before. It was my brother's responsibility, after all, and he was just as bad an influence as they were, but they'd all gone too far this time. "What do you know about him?"

He shrugged. "His parents have *some* wealth, I suppose, nothing worth bragging about."

I leaned forward, holding out my hand. He handed me his cigar, and I took a puff, then blew out a circle of gray smoke into my bedroom. "Find out everything you can about him, will you?"

He raised an eyebrow. "I'm not your investigator."

"No, but you're better than any in this town. You can find things out about people, and you're the only one I trust."

He took back the cigar and leaned against the wall. "I'll ask around."

Morning light seeped through the crack in the floor-length drapes, illuminating wisps of dust and smoke in the air.

I nodded. "There's another one too. Jackson Thompson."

"He rob you too?"

I didn't answer. "They're friends."

"All right, I'll find out what I can. You gonna beat them down?"

I clicked my tongue. "They're nineteen, men now. They'll get punished as such."

"Do you want me to get them alone?"

The corner of my lip curled upward. "The Kapps guy, yeah. He's their little ringleader."

He kicked back against the wall, walked to the ashtray, and pressed the cigar into a pile of ash. "You got it. Right, I'm heading out. Work doesn't end. Got to meet the boys down at the docks. New shipments came in."

"Did the cigarettes come with it? They've become popular at the club."

He checked his pocket watch. "Yep, and we've got the best gin from up north."

"Deliver everything to Bernie. He'll be working at the club tonight."

Charles grabbed a scotch before he left. "See you this evening."

I stood and poured myself a water. I needed to talk to my father about not becoming a hunter. The training would begin soon, with my birthday approaching fast. I could no longer hide from my destiny. I had to make a choice, and I knew what mine was. My interests lay in business, not in hunting, politics, or the church. If I could make him understand how my ventures would be beneficial to us, he may understand. I could grow our wealth, leaving him financially free to continue carrying out his purpose. I'd be able to bring Corbin into the family business. There was room for more than just the club. I wanted to expand and open more gentlemen's clubs throughout Salvius, aimed not only at businessmen and the elite but ones for the working class, where they could make connections. Only a few would have access to liquor. I didn't want to risk being shut down.

I inhaled sharply as I walked to his study, which adjoined mine. I fixed the collar of my shirt and knocked twice.

"Good morning, son." He was standing across the room, his eyes bloodshot. "I hope you'll be joining me for my sermon tonight. It's the first one since I left."

"Good morning. I wouldn't miss it. I know it's important we show a unified front."

He leaned over his desk, sighing. "If only your brother understood those values. I don't believe he's set foot in the church since he was ten."

"He struggles with his faith."

He snarled. "It's in his blood; that's why. If he were stronger, he could fight his demonic tendencies."

I white-knuckled the back of the wooden chair tucked on my side of his desk. "He isn't demonic."

"You should be leading him too. He won't listen to me, but he will you."

"I try, but he struggles. He gets upset."

He rolled his eyes. "Weak."

I clenched my jaw. "Don't."

He waved his hand dismissively, gesturing for me to sit. He had no idea how much I tried to get Corbin to stay on the straight and narrow, but my brother was as stubborn as my father, a shared trait neither would admit existed. There had been no *punishments* for some years, but I knew that both the memory of them and the threat he still loomed over Corbin affected him. I would intervene if Father pulled out his whip again, but the last time I'd stopped him from hitting Corbin, we'd both lost so much. The loss was so painful, it still ripped through my nightmares some nights.

I shook my head as if to scatter my thoughts. I couldn't think of it anymore. He tried to keep us on the right path, in his own warped way, and while it wasn't okay, I couldn't hate him. He'd given up so much for us, time and time again, and he always looked out for us. His health wasn't what it had been. Some nights I heard him coughing up a lung until the early hours. He kept up appearances well, however, by managing his symptoms with remedies made up by the family doctor, but I didn't know how many years he had left with us.

"I need to talk to you about something," I said tentatively and lightly touched the book of Zerheus lying on his desk. "I've been wanting to discuss it for some time."

He gestured for me to sit. "What is it?" He placed down a paper, with a list of names.

To find:

Terra Vineroot

Mary Vineroot
Elliot Vineroot
Lily Amberwood
Cassian Amberwood
Victoria Amberwood
Alexandra Amberwood
Richard Blackwood

"The ones who escaped me," he explained, seeing my expression. "Fear not, my boy. We can find them together after your training."

I took a seat, clearing my throat. "That's actually what I wanted to talk about. I don't believe that witch-hunting is my destiny," I said, cutting to the chase.

His expression hardened, but I continued, keeping my tone as calm as possible.

"It's a noble career, but I enjoy running the club, and I'm looking to expand into other businesses. I find great joy in it, and I can continue to build our wealth while you work and Corbin studies." I placed my folder of prepared numbers on the wood surface between us, moving his glass paperweight. "Profits have tripled at the club. I know you don't agree with all the practices there—"

"The only reason I have allowed your club to remain open," he said, interrupting me, and pushed the unopened folder back to me, "is because it gives the men in this town a safe place to go for the evening, where they can practice debauchery and I can have eyes and ears on their activities because people will always sin. I admit, I'd rather you run it than someone I can't control, because those Zerheus-forsaken places will always pop up in every town, but if you think I will allow that house of sin to come between you and our family's legacy, then you are sorely mistaken. I would rather hand it over to another than to see you turn away from your true purpose. Son, we are anointed, blessed by Zerheus and Celeste to rid this world of evil."

I gripped into the side of the chair, scratching at the wood where he couldn't see. "You were anointed, not me. It's not something that aligns with my skills. It would be a waste of my talents. Grandfather imported cigars and tobacco. That was his legacy. This is yours. I will create my own."

He laughed and rolled his eyes for a second. "Come on, Elijah, we both know it takes no real skill to run a club or something like that. It's not a legacy. Do you know what is? Hunting. You'll see in your training."

"No."

His expression dropped, his thick eyebrows pulling inward, creasing the scar around his eye. "After everything I have done for you, for your brother, and you will humiliate me like this?"

"I'm not trying to."

"But you will." He slammed his hand on his desk, and I noticed the curved scars running around his fingers and up to his wrist. "Everyone knows the first son takes over the family business, and if you go rogue, everything I have built will come into question. They will wonder why my loving son doesn't want to follow in his father's footsteps. They'll see it as I cannot manage my household."

"They won't see it like that. It's not unlike anything you did before, with your own father." I shook my leg, barely holding my temper from taking over. "Times have changed."

"That was different." His eyes glossed over. "Don't you see? There are dark forces at work all the time, pulling us in with temptation. I have even fallen victim from time to time—we all have—so I do not judge you for being enticed by dramair and power, but it is not what you were placed in this world to do. You were always the good son, the one I could count on. Don't let temptation steal you away."

"It's not temptation!" I stood, scraping the chair backward.

The muscle in his jaw feathered as he stood slowly. "Have you been in contact with any unruly women recently? Perhaps someone spelled you to—"

"I am not under a spell, or anything like that," I spat through gritted teeth. I hated his fucking superstitions. Everything had an answer. "I am still a man of Zerheus."

He shook his head and took a step back, knocking into his chair. "You have been led astray. I don't want to do this, son. I truly don't, but it's the only way."

My eyebrows shot upward. "Do what?"

"I'm only looking out for you."

"What are you going to do?"

He sighed, muttering something under his breath. "I will have my men find out who you've been seeing while I've been gone. If it's not a woman doing this to you, then it must be your brother. No matter, they will be punished. You don't see it now, but I'm doing what's best for you and this family. Someone is tainting your mind, and I will get to the bottom io it."

I growled under my breath. "Don't you dare." I dug my nails into my palms. "I am not under the influence of anything dark. I just don't want to be a hunter. This is insane."

He looked down, shaking his head and pressing his lips together. The corners of his eyes crinkled when he climbed his gaze back to mine. "You're not acting like yourself."

I inhaled deeply and held my breath for a few seconds before I exhaled. My rage wasn't going to convince him otherwise. I had to calm down, before I did or said something I would regret. His hands were slightly trembling, but he hid them behind his back when he saw me looking.

Corbin would get the shit for this. Or Amber, or maybe even the new girl to town, Victoria. It wouldn't be the first time someone else got the punishment for my actions. "Please, Father, I am not under any spell. I promise you."

"We have nothing more to talk about tonight."

I pressed my fingers against my forehead. I couldn't go against him and the church. They were stronger than even the monarchy in this kingdom. "I'll train to become a hunter, but I want to continue running the club too."

He hesitated, bringing his hands together into a clasp. After thirty seconds of silence, he nodded slowly. "I still feel I should look into anyone who may have been in contact with you recently."

"Please." I hated the sound of the words as they left my mouth in a plea. "No one has done anything. You're right; it was a moment of temptation. I want to follow in your footsteps. I also worry about our dramair."

"We have enough wealth left by your grandfather, and priests do not pay taxes on income. You need not worry about such material things. We are the richest household in Redforest."

He wasn't wrong, but we wouldn't stay that way with the amount he spent on the community and events. "The club can be a part-time project," I said, with a lump in my throat.

"As long as it doesn't distract you from your true calling, I will allow it. You have managers who can do most of the work."

"Yes," I said sourly but kept my tone light. "I must go attend to some matters, but I will see you at the sermon this evening."

"Son," he said as I turned to walk out. "If you ever feel your soul darkening, you must always come to me."

I closed my eyes. "I will." I walked out, and as soon as the door clicked shut behind me, I hurried down the corridor, ignoring a question from one of the maids.

Once I reached my room, I let my anger spill over. "Fuck!" I shouted, punching the wall next to the mirror. The glass shuddered and fell to the ground, shattering seven years of bad luck across the carpet. Unclenching my fist, I saw the red around my knuckles and hissed through my teeth. He wouldn't listen to reason. Everything was fucking witchcraft. I was tired of it, but I couldn't fight it without him thinking I was under a spell or some stupid shit. Someone else would get hurt, a repeat of what had happened four years ago with our nanny, Sandra. She was the only woman to ever come close to being like a mother to us.

She'd protected us, nurtured us, and read us stories in the evenings. Her affinity with healing ointments was incredible too, and she'd often healed our father of his wounds when he returned from executions and the crowd had gotten a little wild, or if a witch had fought back. I still didn't know if she was okay. I'd sent out feelers through a guy I trusted and found out she was living far north, away from anyone. At least she wasn't dead. I couldn't risk sending word to her. I worried it would be the last notch in her noose if I did.

A memory floated back easily. Perhaps it was the alcohol or rage, but my mind was an open book for a moment. It was late evening when father had finished whipping me, then moved on to Corbin. I'd watched, helplessly, for years as he beat the demons from us, mostly my brother. I wore the scars on my back with fear, hiding them always.

I'd had enough.

It was the first and last time I'd raised a fist to my father. I hit him, four, maybe five times until he was on the ground, covering his face with shaking fingers. Corbin picked up the whip, but I stopped him before he could do any real damage. I thought it was the end of it. I had turned seventeen a week before that night, and I wasn't going to go into adulthood fearing him anymore.

Sandra came to us as always, healing ointment at the ready. She treated Corbin's marks first; they were always worse than mine. She treated the bruises on my hands and then the cuts on my back. She sang Corbin to sleep, and I decided to sleep in his room on the floor.

The next morning, I'd come out to faint shouting coming from the lower levels of the mansion. When we'd rushed down to see the commotion, I felt like I was going to die. Sandra was shackled with the same ones they used to restrain witches. They had the ointment bottles she'd used on us in a bag, as evidence.

He appeared with his face bruised, but he never said a word about what had happened. It was only when she was on trial that he presented his so-called evidence, saying she was influencing us to act out in violence. He couldn't detect magic on her, but it hadn't stopped him from finding her guilty of creating "potions" by replicating witchcraft. She was exiled, one of the few who weren't killed under his capture.

We never saw her again.

I worried if I pushed him too far, he'd do it again. I was helpless to become like him, without inciting his and the church's wrath. I couldn't risk the people around me. Grabbing a half-drank bottle of whiskey I'd forgotten about from a side table near my dresser, I took a swig, then another and another until I didn't feel like I was drowning.

Hazily, I opened my eyes as a knocking sound protruded through the room like a pounding in my skull. "What?" I shouted.

"Excuse my interruption, Mr. Shaw, but I have a Miss Weathermore here."

"Tell her to leave," I spluttered, finding the bottle empty next to me. "I'm busy." Waves of nausea crept through me as I tried to make sense of what was happening. I couldn't let her in.

If she was seen, she could be determined as the "witch" who was influencing me. I didn't put anything past him.

"Mr. Shaw, shall I fetch the doctor?"

"No," I growled. "Get out and tell her to go home and to not come back."

She gulped, then left quickly, closing the door behind her. I blinked slowly, my eyes half closing as sleep lulled me. I barely climbed onto my bed when blackness enveloped me.

***

That evening, Charles had sent me the location of where to find the little thief. I needed an outlet for my anger anyway.

"Don't fuck with me, Kapps." I tightened my grip on his ash-brown hair, pushing his face against the wall in the dimly lit alleyway. "Where is it?"

"P-please." He struggled against the brick, so I pushed back. "I don't know what you're talking ab—"

"Stop fucking lying." Landing a fist to his side brought me far more satisfaction than I'd thought.

He whimpered, like the little rat he was.

"You stole the dramair out of my brother's pockets. You could have killed him." I brought my lips to his ear, my teeth bared, and spat, "Did you think you'd get away with it?"

"Okay, okay, please," he said between heavy breaths. "I have some left."

"Some?"

"I spent half on the horses."

I growled, pushing on the back of his head until blood trickled down his temple. "Get me what you owe me by week's end, or I'll leave a more permanent reminder." I flicked my knife from my pocket, ensuring he caught a glimpse of the silver before

I stashed it away again. "If you or your friend ever go near Corbin again, I'll make sure you don't have any fingers left to steal with."

With a final shove, I let him go. He collapsed to the floor, and my bodyguards stepped out from the shadows of the narrow alley behind the gambling den known as The Viana. I pulled out my silk handkerchief and wiped my hands. "Add an extra ten gold dramair too."

He paled. "Ten? I can't—"

"Ten," I said, cutting him off.

With an amused smirk, Charles walked out from behind my men, pressing his thumb against his chin when he looked at Kapps. "Good evening?" he asked me.

I ran my hand through my blond waves, pushing back strands that had curled on my forehead. "Thanks for the tip, and for getting him here alone."

"It was easy. I came as quick as I could, but I see you've already taken care of him. Did you get your dramair back?"

"Not yet, but he'll get it to me. He knows what will happen if he doesn't."

"What about the Jackson boy?"

"He'll know not to fuck with me again once he sees this little shit." The corner of my lip curled upward. "Let's head out. Boys, clean him up and get him out of here," I said to my bodyguards.

We walked to the end of the alleyway. The stench of urine mixed with liquor hit my nostrils. "Did the shipment arrive okay?"

"Yes. So I heard through the grapevine your father's back in town." He lifted an eyebrow. "I'm sure that has nothing to do with your sudden need to beat up that Kapps guy."

"Fuck off," I said, glaring ahead as we emerged into the emptying town center. "Where's your girl?"

"We broke up."

"You two were never a good match anyway."

"You don't think so?"

I shrugged. "Nah." The truth was, I always thought she was with him for his money, but I didn't want to say that. "I have to go to the church."

"Ah, that's why you're acting like more of a dick than normal."

"It's just one sermon."

He paused. "Did you talk to your father about not being a hunter?"

The gas lamps illuminating the sides of the street in a yellow hue flickered as we strolled. I glanced at the starless sky, then at the three-story houses with wraparound porches. My mind was drifting when he nudged me.

"Eli."

I shook my head to scatter my thoughts. "Oh, yeah. He said no."

"There's more money in The Black Horse. Didn't you show him the numbers?"

"He doesn't care about that. He sees it as we have enough wealth, and we are blessed because we're carrying out Zerheus's will."

"Do you believe that?"

I grimaced. "No, but fuck if I know what I believe anymore. Look, I got to go. I'll stop by tomorrow."

Fourteen

Victoria

"I look like a porcelain doll." I looked at the peach frills on my dress and turned to my side to see the reflection of the back. "It even has a tail."

"It's not a tail. They're ruffles, and it's all the fashion," Cas said with a smirk.

I shot him a look. "I understand we have to fit in, especially after what happened today with Elijah, but did you really have to get me a dress that looks so ugly?"

"Yes." He spun me around. "You could almost pass as a lady."

"Almost."

Alex sauntered in, wearing emerald green. "Ew."

"I know. Your dress is at least half decent. Cas is playing favorites again."

Cas shrugged. "She doesn't threaten to put snakes in my bed."

I smiled in the direction of my vianas' cage. "I should take them."

"To a church? I'm sure the priests will appreciate deadly snakes being at their sermon."

I made a sour face. "It's the hunter's sermon."

Alex guided me to sit in the chair in front of my dresser. "You're already flushed at the thought of him. Can you keep it together if you see him?"

I bit the inside of my cheek. "Yes."

Cas rolled his eyes. "Sounds convincing."

"Don't be sarcastic," I snapped. "Are you feeling overjoyed at seeing our sister's murderer again?"

Alex pulled a silver hairbrush through my strands, pulling them up into a silky bun. "None of us are," she answered for him. "We're just focusing on the plan. He will suffer more."

"I know." I tried to keep the anger lacing my words at bay, but it was hard. It was my plan after all, and I was being treated as the loose cannon. "I'll focus on seeing Elijah. He turned me away today, and I want to know why. I doubt he'll even notice me in this curtain."

Alex finished my hair, leaving a couple of strands on either side to frame my face. "It's not that bad. You'll blend in, which is a good thing, with the hunter watching."

Cas grinned. "Besides, we're not entirely certain you can even walk into the church without bursting into flames yet, so you may not even have to worry about the dress."

"Says you." I laughed. "Aren't you seducing a priest's wife?"

He picked a piece of lint from his gray vest and straightened his tailcoat. "I see it as I'm doing a service to their god and goddess. She is ever so bored with her life; I don't think her husband services her in the bedroom at all."

"You're disgusting," Alex said.

He rustled her hair, and she batted his hand away. "Sometimes you have to do what you got to do. At least I've made more progress than our dear sister."

My mouth set into a hard line. "I'll make it right."

Cas sat on the end of my bed, shrugging away from the snakes' cage. "You need to charm him, sister."

I stood. "I can charm him fine."

He stood too. "Fine, fine. Let's go before we miss the start of the sermon. I for one am riveted to hear what the bastard has to say."

I balled my fists at my sides. "Me too."

Silence befell the room. Alex looked up, tears glossing her eyes. "I know we haven't spoken much about her, and it's easier to pretend sometimes that things are normal, but…"

I squeezed her shoulder. "We will avenge Ember. I promise. Everything we are doing is for her, and for our cousin."

"And for every witch who's been killed by him," she said. "She would be proud of that."

Cas shook his head. "We all know Ember wouldn't like any of this. She'd want us to move on and forgive or whatever. She always was far better than us."

I looked at Alex. "Not all of us."

Alex shrugged. "No, he's right, but it's okay. She was the nicer of us, to Damian's detriment. She may have forgiven them all, but I won't. None of us will, and in a way, I'm glad she's not here to see this—to see what our family has turned into."

Cas placed his hand on hers. "We're still a family."

She looked from him to me, tight-lipped. "Barely. We don't eat together anymore, unless it's a plotting breakfast. We don't do anything together, and I get it. I know why we're here, but I miss it sometimes. Without her and Mama, it feels like we're just three strangers trying to live together."

Her words hit me like an arrow to the heart, but I didn't dare show a flicker of pain, not when it could hurt her to see it. Instead,

I looked at Cas, who only sighed. We'd let Alex down. "We'll have dinner tonight, after church."

Cas nodded. "I'll even cook."

She smiled. "I can make cookies for dessert."

My stomach dipped. Ember was the one who made cookies. "Sounds good."

Cas cleared this throat before opening the front door. "Once he's dead, we can go back to normal. We'll go back to Mother and build a new shop there. I can sell the one here."

Alex nodded and I forced a small smile, but I didn't agree. I couldn't imagine an *after*, not without our sister. Besides, I wasn't even sure if I was going to get out of this alive. If it came to it and our plan turned on its head, I would be the one to put myself in the line of danger, to protect them, and there were a thousand things that could go wrong.

We walked out into the matte-black night, then into our waiting carriage. An oil lamp inside the carriage flickered as we traveled along a bumpy road, toward the little church of Redforest.

I grimaced at the sign when I stepped out of the carriage. Redforest – May Zerheus Bless Our Town. Witches Be Warned.

Someone had added to it since we arrived. I assumed Damian was responsible.

Cas stepped up to my side. "I'm going to greet Maria Montague."

"Do what you must."

"Can you keep it together?"

I bared my teeth. "Stop. I'm fine."

"You could've fooled me. Keep an eye on her, Eva."

I reminded myself to use their aliases. One slipup could cost us greatly. Perhaps I should have been using their aliases at home, so I could get used to them. I tucked away the idea for later when I saw the back of a blond head.

He turned, and the oil lamp hanging over the doorway to the church flickered light to one side of his face. His pointed, glacier-blue eyes focused on whomever he was talking to. He shoved his hands in the deep pockets of his gray coat, nodding as he and the other man conversed, but there was something different about seeing him now. His shoulders were tensed, his jawline hardened.

Trailing my gaze over his face, I saw his father, and my stomach dipped. Every time I saw him, he reminded me of that night, of a face warped with anger as Damian held the heart of my sister, ripping her soul from this world as if she had been nothing.

"Tori," Alex whispered, gently touching my balled fist. "We don't have to go in. Cas can manage."

"No." I exhaled slowly. "Let us go in."

We stepped forward, and Elijah flicked a glance in our direction when we passed, then looked back once he realized who I was. Patting the man on the shoulder, he excused himself and walked in our direction.

He stopped a few feet ahead of me, and I noticed eyes on us. "Good evening, Miss Weathermore, and the younger." He glanced at Alex. "How's your day been?"

My nose wrinkled as I reined in my annoyance. He was acting as if turning me away this morning was nothing. Had I been too nice to him? I saw him in the club that night with those women. He wanted a challenge, and I had failed.

"Mr. Shaw." I turned on my heel. "Excuse us. We must find our brother." Grabbing Alex's hand, I pulled her with me into the crowd lingering outside before he could say anything else.

She stopped me once we were out of earshot from anyone. "What was that? I thought you were trying to win him over?"

"I am." I gritted my teeth. "Trust me, I know what I'm doing."

She rolled her eyes. "Of course you do."

I nudged her. "Where is Cas?"

She looked around. "Must be inside already."

"Okay. Follow me."

She grinned. "Good. We can test if you really will burst into flames."

My eyes widened, glittering with anticipation. "I'd love to see their god try."

She smirked. "So would I."

We were the last to walk inside. The outside gave no justice to the interior, where stone walls were nothing without the fractures of light falling through stained-glass windows depicting scenes of gods, angels, and goddesses. Rich tapestries were draped behind the altar. At the entrance, two pillars of rock narrowed toward the hundreds of wooden chairs standing on an uneven stone. Two veiled women stood on either side of the walkway leading to the altar. Both bowed their heads, not looking through the white, thin net.

"It's impressive," Alex admitted, lifting the skirts of her dress and sitting on a chair two spaces into the left side. "If not a little dramatic."

From a distance, Cas spotted me, sitting at the front with the wives of important men to the church. He winked and turned his attention back to the front.

That was when I saw him. He appeared, robed in red, the colors only worn during sermons, or so I had heard. I'd never bothered going into one of their churches before today.

His graying-blond hair tousled when he removed his hood. His blue eyes widened, reflecting the light of the oil lamps hanging from beams above as he looked out upon the crowd. His gaze found everyone but no one, addressing each of us without truly stopping to look.

His thin lips stretched into a smile as he clasped his hands together over the altar. The top of my lip twitched, and my nostrils flared. Even his scars seemed softer under the hue of the church. What an ironic mask to wear, one of a priest who loves his people, when hiding below the surface was the face of a true murderer, the one I recalled every night since he'd killed her. Darkness coated his expression, flames from the townspeople's torches illuminated his scars against that night, and his blue robes were laced with the blood of innocents. That was what I saw when I thought of him. Not this… façade.

"Welcome, cherished ones, to this sermon we have been blessed to deliver on such a beautiful autumn evening."

Every person, except the three of us and Elijah, leaned forward.

He continued, his lips curling tighter at the corners. "As I look out upon each of your faces, I am reminded of what must be protected. As many of you know, I have been away in another town." He paused briefly. "Your priests do not keep secrets from you, so I will tell you of our results. We were led by the light of Zerheus to a place plagued with witches. There, a dark club of black magic was found, where, unfortunately, good people like yourselves were found sacrificed."

Many gasped. I didn't flinch.

"We were too late to save them." He looked down, as if lost in grief. I repressed the urge to roll my eyes. "But we saved countless others. We found and executed seventeen witches, sending the demons back to the underworld."

My stomach sank when they cheered, and some excitedly chattered with each other. Behind the crowd, I spotted a face I swore I recognized, but he was gone before I could blink. I was seeing things. Fantastic.

"It has been several years since we have had so many witches in one place. They are forming their own communities."

The building silenced.

"They know they are stronger with numbers, and we have seen through these trials that there are more witches out there than we realized. Families of them are in hiding, some even having relations with humans. As we hunters have become more skilled over the years, so have the demons. We must become more diligent in our detection of their witchcraft and dark ways."

One of the other priests who sat in the front angled his head at Damian.

The hunter caught his eye, and his expression shifted. "However, worry not, for we continue to protect Redforest above all, so before I begin the sermon, I have some celebratory news." He gestured toward where Elijah sat. "My son will be joining us in training beginning in two weeks. He is committed to the cause and wants to follow the path carved out for him by Zerheus."

The room erupted in applause. Elijah stood, smiling as he nodded in the direction of those congratulating him.

So he really was *just* like his father after all. Committed to the cause... *murdering people.* I couldn't focus on anything else; he looked so damned pleased with himself that I wanted to run across the church and boil his and his father's blood, but I knew better.

Damian spoke, and the words passed through my ears, but I couldn't take in anything he was saying. Hearing them all cheer for my sister's and the others' deaths solidified the part of me screaming for vengeance. It was easy being around people, seeing them as good and harmless, like they appeared to be back home, but tonight I was reminded of the way of humans, how easily they had turned on Ember as soon as she was labeled as a witch. All her friends, neighbors, and acquaintances who had known her since she was a baby watched as her heart was pulled from her chest, and they fucking cheered.

Fury lined my gaze, a cloud of red filling it as every rage-fueled memory shot to the surface of my mind. A woman screamed, snapping me out of my trance. She fell to her knees. More screams erupted, and Alex grabbed my hand, pulling me back.

"She's bleeding."

My jaw slacked. I pulled my hand from Alex's, pushing her back, and fought my way toward the dead woman. Her eyes were red, her blood still wet from trickling down her face. Her tongue was swollen, hanging out of her mouth, and one of the priests, whom I quickly realized must have been her husband, touched her arm but recoiled quickly.

"She's as hot as fire," he said.

I glanced at Cas, whose wide eyes found me. He tilted his head, gesturing us toward the door. I followed quickly, especially when words of witches and demons surfaced.

Once we were outside in the brisk air, he pulled me to a corner, his voice low. "What in the underworld were you thinking?"

My breath hitched. "I don't know. I didn't mean to do it; I was just so angry. I swear, I didn't even know I could do that. I didn't even look at her."

"How else do you explain that? Get your emotions under control."

My stomach swirled. I still couldn't process anything when Alex appeared and whispered something to Cas. Before I could say anything else in my defense, I was being pulled toward one of the carriages waiting on the street. The cries from inside the church accompanied us outside. She was dead. I'd killed her, and the worst part was I hadn't even meant to do it. I'd lost control.

Fifteen

Elijah

"She had a disease," I explained because I was the only one in the room making sense. "Besides, the doctor said she wasn't dead after all."

Father paced in a circle in our living room. A priest, Father Montague, sat in front of the cracking fire, which let out a hiss when he poked the logs with iron. "She may not survive. She's been taken to the hospital, but—"

"Those houses of death," my father spat. "She won't last the night."

"It wasn't a witch," I said. "I didn't see anyone there who was acting suspiciously."

He gritted his teeth. "This is retribution, for taking out seventeen of them."

"We don't know that."

"Her blood had been boiled!" Priest Montague stood, wiping beads of sweat from his forehead. "I felt her body. She was hotter than a candle."

I shook my head. "She had a fever accompanying her disease. Perhaps one in her blood. Let us wait for the doctor to finish looking at her before we—"

My father slammed his fist against a wall. "I'm going to find who did this."

"No one did this," I said again. "Witches wouldn't dare come here, and we've known these people all our lives."

"Then look for any newcomers to town, or women who look... out of place."

A lump formed in my throat. Victoria. Naturally, he'd think her a suspect. His paranoia always went asylum-worthy when he talked about witches. It was the Blackburn Witch Hunt all over again, where the small town had gone into a frenzy some fifty years ago and killed hundreds of innocent women, believing them witches when the plague had come to their town. "I'd seen Lady Abor coughing before the sermon tonight, and I may have seen some blood from her nose a week ago when she out walking."

"Are you certain?"

I looked at my father. "Yes. I believe she's been unwell for some time, probably afraid to tell anyone."

Priest Montague placed his hands in his lap. "Women are known to come to hysterics when they are sick."

"We will investigate. In the meantime, we must have Father Abor checked for the same symptoms. It could be contagious."

Father Montague nodded. "Let us pray tonight, Lady Abor recovers well."

"Indeed."

I let out a tense breath. "I'll pray for her."

"Get some rest, son. Your ball is tomorrow."

I'd hoped tonight's events would have at least postponed it. It marked the beginning of my new journey to becoming a hunter, but how could I become one when I'd just lied to save anyone from being accused of witchcraft?

I hurried upstairs, pulling at my collar and undoing three buttons before I slumped onto my bed. The clock chimed midnight from the corridor, its faint rings deafening against the silence. Happy birthday to me.

***

Music erupted from the ballroom. I picked a piece of lint from my waistcoat and inhaled deeply. "Brother."

Corbin had surprisingly made an effort for tonight.

"It goes without saying, but you will have no liquor tonight. Half the town is coming, and the priests will be in attendance."

"I'll behave."

I lifted an eyebrow. "I'm grateful you're coming."

He grinned. "I wanted to celebrate your birthday; besides, I may have my own selfish reasons for attending."

"What would those be?"

He pushed back his dark hair. "More like a who."

"Someone from school?"

"Yes." He fiddled with his bow tie. I clicked my tongue, leaned down, and fixed it for him. "Thanks."

I nodded once. "Are you ready?"

"Are you?" His eyes narrowed. "You don't have to do this. I heard what happened at the church, and not to that awful woman, but Damian announcing to the entire town you're going to be a hunter."

Goose bumps spread along my skin. "I have no choice."

"You do."

I held his stare, warning flashing in my expression. "I don't. I won't hear anything more on it."

He looked away. "It's your life."

I swallowed thickly. It was my life, but it was also everyone else's. I was protecting him and anyone who would be hurt if I didn't follow in his footsteps. He was never going to let me own my own businesses. He had the church behind him, and my wanting to do anything but the god's work was suspicious. "Smile, we're about to enter."

"I'm not you. I'm not going to smile for these people."

The doors opened, and Corbin kept to his word. He frowned his way through the crowd while I was announced. I wanted to leave the second I'd entered, but I was already crowded with people either wishing me many happy returns or congratulating me on becoming a hunter.

"Amber." I sighed with relief when I saw a familiar face. Her painted lips stretched into a far-too-welcoming smile. "I apologize, Lady Smith." The last time I'd seen her, she was wrapped in the sheets with me. Tonight, she was hanging off the arm of her husband. "Good evening, Sir Smith."

"Mr. Shaw." He bowed his head slightly, looking from his wife to me. "Congratulations on your announcement."

"Thank you." I cleared my throat. "I hope you enjoy yourselves tonight."

"The peaches are divine," Amber said, her big eyes fixed on mine.

I smiled in response, but her husband filled the awkward silence. "I hear you will be titled."

"Yes, I am honored."

Amber licked her lips. "Let us know when we should begin addressing you as Sir Shaw."

"I believe it would be from tonight."

Her cheeks pinkened. "Then happy birthday, Sir Shaw."

I loved the way that sounded from her. Her husband, clearly, did not. "Come, let us go see Thomas and his wife."

"Yes, let us not keep the lady waiting," Amber said, looking over my shoulder.

I turned, and my eyes widened when I saw her.

"Miss Weathermore." I furrowed my eyebrows. Between sending her away and the chilly reception at the sermon, I hadn't expected her to come. "You're here."

"I wouldn't turn down free food." She picked an oyster from the tray of a passing server.

I couldn't help but smile. "Then I shall thank the chef."

"No need. I probably won't stay long."

I trailed my gaze along her dress, which was a far cry from the peach thing she had been wearing last night. Purple lace wrapped around her chest and cinched at her waist, then it spread into a wide skirt at the bottom. When she swayed, light glittered the gems on her dress, making her stand out among the rest, but then again, she didn't need diamonds to do that.

"It's rude to stare." She smiled saucily. "I do believe I have a dance scheduled with someone on my card." She waved it in front of me.

"Will you be saving me a dance tonight? You did promise."

She extended a gloved hand. I took it, then moved my fingers from hers to her lower back. She leaned in, her breath hot against my ear. "You also promised to meet me the other morning, so I owe you nothing." She pulled away, smirking, and disappeared into the crowd.

"What the—" I spotted Corbin with Victoria's sister, dancing. He twirled her around and was smiling—actually smiling. I couldn't believe it. "I guess there's a thing about these Weathermore girls," I said under my breath before heading to the drinks table.

The small talk was killing me. I waved off another couple, then ducked before Father Montague and his wife saw me. From what I'd gathered, Lady Abor had recovered enough. The doctor believed it to be tuberculosis. He had seen a few who had strange symptoms from the disease. She had been shipped away to some hospital in quarantine, and so had her husband. It was all anyone could talk about. I was grateful they'd proven it to not be the work of witches, because the last thing I cared for was more trials in the town center.

"Son." Father tapped me on the shoulder.

I turned slowly, forcing a smile.

"Have you spoken to Father Montague yet? He will be the one training you."

"Not yet." I looked around for him. "I've actually spoken to my bartender and—"

"I've already made arrangements for your club. Charles has agreed to take it over for a good price."

"My friend Charles?"

"Yes. I spoke with his parents just yesterday."

My smile faded. "I was supposed to continue running it. We had an agreement."

"I don't want you to have any distractions. After your ramblings that night, I made a decision."

"You can't sell my club."

"It's under my name. So I assure you I can."

Before I did something I'd regret, I pushed my way through the party. Fuck Charles. Fuck Father. Fuck everyone. I was done. Everything I had built had been for nothing. It was only in his name because I'd been too young at the time, but everyone knew it was mine. I'd built it from the ground up when it was nothing but a rundown, back-alley building.

Ignoring a man I recognized from the church and his wife, I stormed into the study and rummaged through cabinets until I found my remaining cigars and my best bottle of scotch.

"Oh, apologies." Some women tripped into the study. "Sir Shaw."

Closing my eyes, I swore under my breath. I couldn't get any fucking privacy.

It was pitch black outside when I emerged into the gardens. I forced my way through those gathered outside, past the fountain, along the path waving through the flowerbeds, and down a secret walkway until I reached my favorite spot. It was fenced in with one small opening. Trawling ivy covered the crisscrossed wood, large bushes covered the area in darkness, and a rose garden had been allowed to grow wild. I sat on a white metal bench and swigged the scotch.

I couldn't have been in there for another second. I felt trapped, like a bird stuck in one of the priest's gilded cages. Goose bumps spread along my arms, standing every hair erect, when I heard shuffling from the walkway.

"Elijah."

I recognized her voice. The dark mass of her dress and wavy hair silhouetted against the indigo. "Victoria?"

"Yes. I saw you run out here. I was talking with my brother, and you seemed upset."

I took another drink of scotch. "You don't need to come."

"I don't *need* to do anything. I followed you in here because I wanted to."

"Why?"

"Because I saw you had a bottle of something I'll assume is liquor."

"It's scotch."

"Well, pass it over." She took a seat next to me. "I'm having a bad evening too. I also need some space from being in there."

"I didn't take you as a scotch girl."

"I'm an 'I'll drink anything right about now' kind of girl."

"What happened," I asked, taking back the bottle as she coughed, "for your evening to be so terrible?"

She shook her head. "It's not just tonight. I've had a bad run of things lately."

"Right." I was an idiot. "Your parents dying, of course."

She fell quiet.

"Do you smoke?" I asked, to fill the silence.

"No, but feel free to."

I pulled out a cigar and lit it with a match. The temporary illumination of her face made my heart skip a beat. "Have you been crying?"

She wiped the skin around her eyes. "No."

"Sorry, it looked like it."

"I haven't been." She kicked her shoes off, curling her legs up against her chest. "Why has your day been so terrible? I heard about your new *career*."

"Yeah." I held my breath, then took another swig of scotch. I didn't want to talk about it, no less with her. "Where are your snakes tonight?"

"Right here." Hissing sounded, and something touched my leg. I jolted back. "Shit."

She laughed, leaning forward and sucking back a couple of breaths. "It was me. They're at home."

I chuckled, then laughed harder. "I won't pretend I wasn't scared."

"At least you didn't scream."

I put a finger up. "I was close."

I couldn't see her expression, but I wished I could. "You looked beautiful earlier. I should have said."

"Thank you."

"Seriously, I've been thinking about that dress ever since."

"Only the dress?"

Was she playing with me? "I was trying to be polite."

She hit my arm, then laughed and pulled the bottle from my hand. I took another puff of smoke from my cigar, closing my eyes for a moment. "We can just stay out here all night if you want."

Her tone softened. "Why do you want to skip out on your own ball? Don't get me wrong, I get it—I hate parties—but you don't seem like the type who does."

I paused, swallowing thickly. She wouldn't understand even if I did tell her, and what good would it do if she did? Nothing was going to change my situation. "It's nothing to worry yourself about."

"I want to listen. I'm bored, and you make for okay company."

I smirked. "You're relentless."

"A little."

I tapped the ash from the end of my cigar to the ground. "I'm stuck doing something I don't want to do."

"Do you mean being a hunter?"

She was quick. "Yes."

"Why are you stuck?"

"I expected you to question me on why I don't want to become a hunter."

She shrugged. "Why would I question that? It's barbaric."

My forehead wrinkled. "You're the first person to say so in this town."

"I don't like the idea of murder, no matter the justification."

I sucked on my cigar, then blew out a circle of smoke. "I don't condone murder either, but witches aren't exactly people. No matter, that's not the reason I don't want to do it. It's just not my calling, and I think sometimes innocent people get tied up in these trials, even people who aren't witches."

"I see your point," she replied with a strained tone. "Why can't you choose to do something else?"

"It's my father's legacy."

"So he wants you to follow the same path," she stated.

"Exactly."

"I assume you have a good reason for not just saying 'no.'"

"I'm glad someone understands." I sighed. "It's complicated."

"Have you tried changing his mind?"

I nodded. "It was a mistake."

"I think you shouldn't give up so easily."

"I wish it were so simple."

She touched the side of my cheek, and I turned to look at her darkened features. "There's always a way to get what we want; we just need to want it bad enough."

My lips parted. "I expect you're the type who always gets what she wants."

She blinked twice. "If that were true, then I wouldn't be here."

"What do you mean?"

She pulled back, hesitance in her voice. "I mean, if my parents hadn't died, I wouldn't be here."

I drank a few gulps of the scotch, sucked in a fiery breath, and handed her the bottle. "It seems we both need a drink."

She took hers, then wiped her mouth. "Why did you abandon our plans the other day?"

"Would you believe me if I said it had nothing to do with you and everything to do with me?"

"Yes. I don't see why I would be the problem."

I laughed. "Have you heard of the word humble?"

She nudged my side. "Yes, but what I have is called self-worth."

"Can I get some more of that scotch?"

She tinkled the bottle. "I think it's empty."

My eyes widened. "We finished it already?"

We both snickered. I finished my cigar and stood. I hadn't expected the alcohol to hit me so hard. "Would you like to dance, my lady?" My words began slurring at the ends.

"Are we going back inside?"

"If you'll have me."

She pressed a hand against my chest. "We can go, but you better find some more of that scotch."

"I think we've had enough." I leaned down, but she danced away before I could do what I'd thought about the whole time we were sitting there.

"Come on then."

The chandelier flickered the light of a hundred diamonds onto every surface. Lamps lit up the alcoves, while candles melted down at tables lining the back wall, bringing the tapestries above them to life. I took Victoria's hand and pulled us past a pale-blue pillar and into the main dancing area. She gazed at the curved ceiling made of sprawling art, then lowered her eyes to meet mine.

I looked over her shoulder, nodding at the quartet at the side of the room. James caught it, and a new melody slipped between the strings of the violin, cello, and harp. The pianist to their left fell into the tune as if she had expected to come.

"A new song," Victoria said with a surprised smile. "It's perfect timing."

"That it is," I replied, not wanting to ruin the magic of the night. My head may have been swirling from the scotch, but I kept myself straight, unwavering when I slipped a leg forward, nudging hers back. She smiled when our knees touched, and the music grew louder, resonating throughout the hall.

Tentatively, her fingers danced down my arm and stopped at my bicep. "You're a good dancer."

My heart palpated. It must have been the music or the liquor. Every worry and fear coiled inside me was untangled, loose. My inhibitions shot to the wind as I carried her with each step. Placing my hand on her side, I lowered my fingers an inch. Her gaze swallowed me, her cupid-bow lips parting. I'd never seen anyone with such big eyes or such kissable lips. Her bronzed skin glowed under the low lights.

I swallowed thickly, then pulled her closer until there was no distance between us. She closed her eyes, and I inhaled deeply, breathing in the scent of jasmine and rosewater. Flickers of touch ran between us, a brush of an arm, a hazy touch of fingers against my neck, a carefully timed lean inward on my part. Her hand moved over my chest, splaying over where my heart raced. I didn't care to think, to feel anything, but I allowed myself to be swallowed by the moment. The music slowed. I thumbed her chin, lifting her face. Her lips were inches from mine. I could almost taste how they would feel. I leaned down when I caught my breath. She pulled away, turning out under my arm and curling herself back into me. It was either poorly timed or well timed.

Was I wrong to assume she liked me? She had searched me out, although I had invited her twice.

She laughed, and everything else melted away. "Everyone's looking."

I blinked twice, glancing around. For a moment, I'd forgotten we weren't the only ones in the room. "They're envious of your dance moves."

She pressed her lips together, suppressing a smirk as she tugged my hand. "I think I'm all danced out."

I wasn't. I hadn't felt so present in... well, for a long time. It was a welcome break from reality. I wanted to live in it for as long as I could before I had to wake up. I guessed balls did that. It was a night promised of magic and stars, of moments and possibilities. Everyone loved a party; I'd just never experienced what others had gushed about until now.

"Would you like a drink?" I asked as she looked at me with raised eyebrows.

"Yes, I'm rather parched."

Charles found me from across the room, shooting me a knowing smirk. I glanced at him, shaking my head. I was mad he was buying my club, but I figured I'd talk to him another day about it. Right now, I only wanted her. I slipped my arm under hers, taking her at my side toward the back of the room. I walked us past the drinks table and to the grand staircase. She brushed her thumb along the back of my arm, which she held as we walked. An accident? Maybe.

"I thought we were going to get a drink?" she asked.

"We are." I licked my dry lips. "Not from in there. That lemonade is for the guests. I have the good stuff in my study."

She bit her bottom lip, bringing my attention to them. "I shouldn't be unaccompanied with a man for too long," she said, but there was a slight tease in her tone.

"I think it's a little late for that."

She smiled in response, and I led her toward the study. When we reached the door, I paused. "I have something that will surprise you."

"Top shelf liquor, I assume."

I grinned and pushed open the door. "Not quite. As much as I enjoy you for a drinking partner, I believe we've both had enough to last us the night."

She followed me inside, and I walked her to my coffee station. "Now you're just showing off."

"Only the best for my finest lady."

She raised an eyebrow. "I'm *your* lady now, am I?"

My breath hitched. "You're here with me, I mean."

"Right." She leaned over the coffee station. "I've never tried it."

"It'll help with the liquor."

She placed a hand on her hip. "What if I don't want help with my liquor? I quite enjoy feeling this free."

I touched her hand, and the connection buzzed through me. "Then we can skip the coffee."

She searched my face. I wasn't sure what for, but I did my best not to let anything through. Usually when women chose to be alone with me, it wasn't long until we were fucking, but she seemed uncertain. Perhaps I had misinterpreted things between us.

I must have been staring for too long because I swore, if just for half a second, I saw a flicker of something dark cross her features. If I didn't know better, I'd assume it to be a look of hatred, but she had no reason to feel that way toward me.

I shook my head, scattering my thoughts. I was too inside my own head. The liquor was getting to me. Bringing her to get coffee was a bad idea. "I'll get you out of here, Miss Weathermore. We can find your brother, and you can go home."

She cleared her throat. "Right, yes." She stepped back, stumbling.

I only closed my eyes for a split second and missed her hand reaching for mine. A loud crash sounded through the room when she caught hold of the side of my drinks' globe, tumbling the entire thing to the ground. Glass had shattered around us, shards pointing upward in warning. I leaped forward, dropping to her side to try to shield her head, but it was too late. The dull thud sent a shiver down my spine.

The door to my study opened, and my father looked down at us, anger lacing his expression.

"Victoria." I touched the back of her head, which was hot. When I pulled my fingers away, they were soaked with blood. "Oh god."

"Elijah." Father called to someone I couldn't hear.

Her eyes rolled to the back of her head.

"What have I told you about bringing young women alone?"

My stomach fluttered. "It wasn't like that. We weren't—"

"It doesn't matter. Her brother, Ambrose, is a friend to my priests. This could look bad on us."

A maid returned with our doctor, flushed in his tux and still holding a glass of lemonade.

Father spoke first. "The young lady fell. She must have come in here looking for something, although I do not know what for."

The doctor knelt by her, touching the back of her head. "It looks worse than it is," he explained.

I didn't let go of her hand, not once. She squeezed lightly. I was grateful she was responding at all.

"I will get her cleaned up. Can someone fetch my bag? It's with my wife."

I jumped to my feet. "I'll go," I said, needing to do something helpful. It was all my fault. I'd given her the scotch and brought her back here. I wasn't usually so irresponsible, not in my own home. At the club, everyone knew what they were doing, but Victoria was with me. In my house. She was new to town and didn't know anyone. "Fuck." I ran to the ballroom, searching out the doctor's wife, hoping Victoria's head wouldn't be too bad. I spotted her brother standing with Lady Montague in the corner, laughing. I'd only briefly met him at the church, but he reminded me of Charles and my other friends: arrogant, self-centered, and likely would be furious if he knew his sister was back there, bleeding.

Sixteen

Victoria

Slipping into the bedroom adjoining Elijah's, I couldn't help but smile. He'd hesitated in the hallway for five minutes, then went back to his room after deciding against knocking. I couldn't play him along for too long. My head was still throbbing, but it had been worth the fall, though admittedly I hadn't expected to make myself bleed.

Elijah felt responsible for me, which grew our connection beyond the mere sexual encounter he'd been planning all night. I knew the look. My stomach knotted at the thought of it—me with a human—but I had to do what needed to be done. For Ember. For Jackson. For every person who'd been hurt by the Shaw family. Damian had said I could stay the night—insisted actually—so they could keep watch over me and stop any negative talk about my getting hurt and being alone with his son. They'd had to get permission from Cas first. It was laughable that Cas would have any say over what I did or didn't do. It was only a shame the doctor was staying too, in a room up the corridor from me, so he could check in on me in the morning.

I thought back to the study. A part of me was glad I had been semi-unconscious when the hunter was in such close proximity. I couldn't bear the sight of him. Even his spiced, leather scent made me nauseated.

I pulled at the neckline of the boxy nightgown they'd given me, then spilled my lemonade onto it, soaking it against my bare breasts. "Oops." I ran my hand through my hair, loosening the strands from the tight bun it had been in all day.

It took him less than three seconds to open the door after I knocked. "Victoria," he said with a hitched breath. "Your gown."

I bit my bottom lip. "It's probably side effects from the concussion. The doctor said I might experience some dizziness."

"I'll call to have another brought up."

I placed my hand on his bicep through his shirt. "Please, I don't want to be a bother."

"You can't wear that to bed." His gaze lingered over my chest for a long moment. "Here." He grabbed a shirt from his closet.

"That's perfect."

"How are you feeling?" His light touch grazed the back of my head, and it took every ounce of restraint I had not to punch him for it.

"It still hurts, but it's only a surface wound. It looks worse than it is. I feel okay." I paused.

Worry lines curved his frown, crinkling the corners of his eyes.

"Really. I feel good." I held up his shirt. "I should change."

"Of course." He gestured to walk me back to the room I was staying in, but I but stepped into his room instead. His eyebrows flicked upward.

I stepped inside his closet and pulled off the nightgown, wondering if curiosity would tempt him enough to peek through the gap I'd left in the open door. Just in case, I peeled the fabric off slowly, keeping my back to the door, then pulled on the shirt, leaving the top two unbuttoned.

"You're sure you feel well, Miss Weathermore?"

I gritted my teeth. I was Miss Weathermore again? Fuck. "Perfectly fine. Truly. I wouldn't lie." I turned and stepped out. "How do I look?"

His gaze undressed me, and he landed his bedroom eyes on mine. "It looks better on you than me."

I ran my fingertips down the front of the shirt, paused at my navel, and danced my fingers down a beat lower. "It's so soft, almost like your shirt is hugging every part of me."

"Careful." His eyes flashed as he leaned back against the wall, setting a glass of scotch on the side table. "I might think you're trying to seduce me."

I fluttered my eyelashes, placing a hand on my hip. "If I were seducing you, Mr. Shaw, the result would already be apparent." I glanced down at his pants and smirked when I saw the slight bulge.

"Don't worry, Miss Weathermore, you are not disappointing." He looked me up and down. "You know, now that I think about it, you are creasing my best shirt. Perhaps you should take it off."

I arched an eyebrow. "Your best shirt? I must be special." I twirled around. "As you said, it looks so good on me, so I'll keep it on."

He closed the distance between us. My heart palpated. He pressed his thumb under my chin, bringing my gaze to meet his. "It would look better on the floor."

I brought my fingers to his, then brought them to my lips. "If I didn't know any better, I'd say that you're the one trying to seduce me. Not the other way around."

"You don't need to play games with me. You've already won." His stare intensified, and he pressed up against me. I bit the end of his finger lightly, and any control he had snapped.

Before I could catch my breath, his lips were on mine, his fingers hesitating at my hair. His length throbbed under his pants. I pulled away an inch, but he tugged me closer, his groan lost in my mouth as he pressed me against the wall, his hand protecting the back of my head with a tenderness I didn't expect. He slowed his breathing, pushing proof of his desire between my thighs. Satin slicked between my legs, to my surprise. My body was reacting, though my mind knew better. He rocked his hips, and I moved in rhythm when sense kicked in.

I couldn't become another conquest.

I pushed him back onto the bed, moving on top of him. I brought my lips to his ear and whispered, "I'm not going to be a one-night thing." I went to pull away, but he pulled me back toward himself, whispering back in my ear, sending tingles down my spine with each breath.

"I never expected this to be a one-night anything."

"Then what?"

"We can do this as many times as you want."

I closed my eyes. He didn't see it as serious. My objective was to make him fall in love with me, not lust, although it was a good place to start. "I should go to bed." Before I got off him, he sat up, so I was still straddled around him.

"What did I do?"

"This is a bad idea," I said, though my body was betraying me, still tangled around him, want running through my veins with startling desire. "I should go home."

"It's three in the morning." He looked at the night sky hiding behind a crack in his drapes. "It's dangerous this late, and the doctor wants to see you in the morning."

"I let the scotch go to my head," I lied. I'd only meant to seduce him, to allow him one kiss, not anything to this extent. It was important to leave him wanting more.

He moved me off him, gently laying me on the bed at his side. "If I was too forward, I apologize. I must have misread this evening, apparently."

He hadn't. I was the one who'd let it go too far. "No, you didn't." What could I say? I didn't want to appear anything less than the seductress he believed me to be, but how could I get out of this gracefully without ruining things? "I'm just feeling a little nauseated from the alcohol."

"Do you need some mint tea?"

I shook my head. "Maybe I'll stay, but I'll go back to the other room." I paused once I walked to the door, placing my hand on the handle but not opening it. "It was a good kiss," I said.

I hoped I hadn't put him off me. I needed the plan to succeed. I'd almost let my instincts ruin everything. I wasn't a fucking animal. Perhaps it *had* been the scotch. Yes. It had to have been, because there was no way I wanted him in that way. He was a human who wore the face of my enemy. I hated him, yet I'd almost enjoyed our kiss. It wasn't meant to be. It was never part of the plan. Kissing, touching, anything it took to make him fall for me was meant to be hard, to be painful to endure, not enjoyable.

I had swizzled too much. I wouldn't let it happen again.

On a positive note, at least I was in his house. I took a deep breath in, slowing my racing thoughts. Focus, Victoria, think. Every part of our plan had worked so far, except for that. I'd seduced him and hurt myself so I could stay in his house. It had been Cas's idea, and I was shocked it had worked, but my brother had gathered more information about Damian and how he would react than I had. I smiled. Alex had been successful in placing the hex bag under Damian's bed while the kerfuffle—me—was happening. I just needed to map out the house better now that there wasn't anyone around.

Dismissing the ache left by him from between my legs, I crept out of the room with no oil lamp, in complete darkness, and headed down the corridor. I found Damian's room; I presumed because it was the only one locked and Alex had said it had a blue door. I made a mental note of where it was, looking around and taking in my surroundings. Dark-brown beams ran down the length of the cream walls. Quietly, I made my way down the next corridor, careful not to hit too many squeaky floorboards, until I reached his study.

After an hour of searching the place, I'd mapped the most important rooms in the house and found a collection of beautiful dresses hidden away in a room separate to Damian's. It was dustier than the others, as if no one had gone in there in a long time.

They must have belonged to Elijah's mother, and while it was not above me to wear a dead woman's dress, it felt wrong. I loosed a sigh, then pulled on the boxy thing, hoping Elijah wouldn't see me. I couldn't go outside dressed all in my black clothes. The people of this town already looked down on me for my fashion tastes; I had to at least look somewhat respectable when meeting Damian. How else could I gain his trust?

I walked out, breathed in deeply, and headed to the gardens.

***

Damian stood with his hands clasped behind his back, overlooking the vast gardens and toward the slow sunrise. I wondered what was going through his mind. Angling my head, I took him in. His blue robes rippled against the gentle breeze, and as the sun coated him, he raised his chin as if he were being covered in light by his god.

I picked up the skirts of my dress, my eyes narrowing at the white lace. It frilled around my neckline. My hair was tied into a silky knot at the back of my head, and I was grateful Elijah was still asleep, giving me a chance to change before he'd see me.

I made my way downstairs, only passing one male servant along the way, which was fortunate as I was sure some of the maids would report to Elijah.

I stepped in front of Damian Shaw as the sun rose gently in the sky, casting light around me. His eyes widened as he looked me up and down. I placed one hand over the other and glanced coyly at the ground, then slowly climbed my gaze back to him. "Mr. Shaw, I must apologize for intruding on your morning prayers."

He cleared his throat. "No intrusion at all, Miss..."

Typical. He'd already forgotten my name. "Weathermore."

A ghost of a smile crossed his lips. "I am surprised to see another soul up this early."

I stepped out of the way, placing myself at his side. "I did not expect another to be up either. I enjoy strolling the gardens, to see the beauty of the world before the noise fills it, from others." I knotted my fingers. "It is the most intimate time, I believe, to pray to Zerheus and Celeste."

He inhaled deeply, then let out a long exhale. "It seems you and I are in agreement, Miss Weathermore."

"Please, Mr. Shaw, you can call me Victoria." As expected, he didn't recognize his late wife's dress, though I could still smell a hint of lavender among the dust.

"Where is my son?" he asked, looking over his shoulder, as if suddenly aware of our being alone.

"Sleeping still, I assume. I didn't check, but I stopped by his door on the way here."

He licked his lips, his expression hardening. "He should be awake."

I forced a smile, one that balled my cheeks, to pretend as if I couldn't hear the contempt in his voice. "It may be my fault for his being up late, with what happened."

"Late nights are no excuse." He turned toward me, as if suddenly remembering I had gone through something awful. "Do you feel better?"

"Yes. Thank you for your generosity and for allowing me to spend the night in your home."

"Of course. The doctor will check on you again before you leave today." He paused. "It seems my son is rather fond of you."

I closed my eyes for a heartbeat. "I am fond of him too."

He nodded slowly. "I thought so. He's been known to bring women back to his rooms before, although he thinks I didn't know." He smiled. "But he seemed worried about you, which is unlike him."

My stomach flipped.

He continued. "You should be made aware, Miss Weathermore, my son has responsibilities here. If he were to find a woman who he wished to court, he would still need to put his work first." He watched me carefully, anticipation bright in his blue eyes. He really was an older, more scarred version of Elijah, but the biggest difference was their eyes. Damian's was dulled of the twinkle that made Elijah's eyes stand out.

"A man's purpose must come before worldly desires," I answered, quoting a line from his sermon—one of the few lines I'd listened to the other night.

His eyebrows flicked upward. "I am pleased to see my son is finally making good choices when choosing a wife."

My cheeks heated. "We're just getting to know each other."

He swirled his hand dismissively. "He must take a wife sometime. I only want the best for him." Approval swam in his eyes, and in that moment, I'd earned exactly what I'd wanted.

"Thank you, Mr. Shaw."

"I must prepare my writings for today's sermon. Good morning." He lowered his head in a slight bow, then turned and left.

Once he was gone, my smile fell into my usual frown. I looked up at the windows on the second floor. I needed to get dressed before anyone else saw me.

Elijah knocked on the door. I awoke, my eyes burning as they opened to the pouring sunlight. "Good morning."

"Ah."

"I thought I'd let you sleep in."

"What time is it?"

"It's almost ten."

I sat upright. I couldn't say I hadn't got much sleep; else he'd know I'd been up all night and most of the morning. "Thank you." I stretched, closely watching his expression. "How are you feeling?"

"I was going to ask you the same thing."

I rubbed my forehead. "A little bit of pounding in my skull, but otherwise, I'll be okay."

He stepped forward and exhaled slowly. "About last night."

"Please don't." I put a hand in the air. "We both had too much to drink. It was a mistake," I said, to save him any embarrassment of my hightailing out of there as soon as things had got steamy.

The muscle in his jaw ticked. "A mistake?"

"We were both heavily intoxicated."

He nodded slowly, disappointment hardening his sharp features. "Right. Well, I came to ask if you'd like to accompany me to my club tonight, but if it was a mistake…"

Fuck, everything had messed up. "It's not like I didn't want that to happen." I paused. *How can I fix this?*

Something brightened in his eyes. "It was only a kiss," he said, and my stomach turned to lead. "Some harmless fun. Nothing I regret."

Harmless fun?

"The club?" I questioned.

He scratched the side of his neck. "You don't have to come. It might be dreadfully boring."

"Well, if I'm not there, then I worry it will be."

He smirked. "In that case, you better turn up."

I smiled, grateful for the playfulness that returned as if last night hadn't happened. "I may. It depends, will there be more scotch?"

"Only the best; however, after last night, perhaps we should stick to lemonade."

I chuckled. "I can handle it, Elijah."

"Back to Elijah, are we?"

My chest tightened. "As long as I'm no longer Miss Weathermore."

He grinned. "No."

"I'm bringing my snakes."

He laughed. "You might give my bartender a heart attack."

"Fine. I'll take them out today instead." My mouth dried. "You can accompany me to your orchard, if you like? I can let them roam around there."

"You aren't worried about them escaping?"

I rolled my eyes. "Never. What would they be escaping from? They're well fed, loved, and too lazy at this point to do anything for themselves."

He chuckled. "You are a mystery, Victoria."
I licked my lips. If only he knew how much.

Seventeen

Victoria

Elijah met us at the orchard, as he'd said he would. Alex came with me, wanting to taste how good the apples really were. She had a day off school and said she wanted to spend quality time with me. I think she just wanted to be involved somehow and was bored.

We'd only just sat when a storm thundered in the distance, rolling clouds of dark gray swirling on the horizon.

"I feel the first splashes of rain," I said, holding out my hand. "I didn't think to bring an umbrella."

Elijah pulled off his jacket and handed it to me. "Here."

Alex side-eyed me. "Ever the gentleman."

"You both can cover your heads with it."

Ebony slithered through the blades of green, and Buttercup knotted herself around a fallen apple.

Elijah leaned back. "We should get going."

I stroked Buttercup's head. "It's a shame. They were enjoying themselves."

Elijah reached out. "They're quite sweet really. Nothing like I expected." His finger slightly touched Buttercup's scales, and my heart palpated.

"No, not her!" I warned, but she'd already struck, sinking her fangs into the side of his thumb.

"Oh, gods." Alex stood as the storm blotted the sky like ink, fizzling the sun to nothing.

I attempted to grab Buttercup, to stop her from biting again, but she'd already slipped through my fingers and was gone. One bite was bad, but two wouldn't have given us a chance.

Rain lashed down, soaking his shirt and clinging it against his toned muscles. If he died here, both our necks would be inside nooses.

Elijah laid his head back against the grass, his bloodshot eyes finding mine as the storm clouds darkened the gardens. I dropped to my knees at his side, grabbing his wrist in my fingers. His blood was seeping through the fabric, veining out in warning. I pushed his sleeve up and gasped. Buttercup always had been the bitch of the two, but I could never have expected this.

I ran my thumb around the two prolonged punctures, swallowing thickly when I saw the blackening under his skin. The venom was spreading.

"Fuck!" His scream shattered through my brain, forcing me into action. "Ale-Eva, run to the house. There's a bottle of purple liquid in my dresser. It has a black stopper." I looked at her through blurred eyes. "Hurry!"

She nodded, closing her slack jaw, then turned to run.

A groan escaped his lips as he bit back a third scream.

"It's okay." My breath hitched. *Think, Tori, think.* "I'm going to need you to sit up. Can you do that?"

He tried to angle his body forward, but he groaned through clenched teeth, dropping back. I needed his arm to be lower than the level of his heart.

"Lean against me," I said, moving until I was behind him.

He groaned as he pushed his back up against me.

I moved my legs to either side of him, taking his weight until the back of his head was resting against my shoulder. "That's enough."

I glared at the bite. I'd never seen firsthand the result of a black Salvian viana, but I'd heard stories of those who were bitten. Rarely any made it out alive. Soon, if the stories were correct, he'd begin convulsing. If the shock didn't kill him first. He wrapped his fingers around the bite and moaned.

"You're going to be okay." I squeezed his shoulder.

His eyes rolled back.

"You need to stay calm. Eva will be back soon. I have a remedy that will stop the venom. I usually keep it on my person, but I left it at home…" I shook my head. "I know it hurts, but soon the pain will subside. I need you to stay awake and as calm as you can be. Can you say something? Anything?"

I wrapped my arms around him as shivers ran up his back, then down his arms. Splaying my fingers over his chest, I felt his heart racing against my fingertips. Every few seconds, it would skip a beat.

"W-where is the snake?"

I breathed in deeply. I had no idea where she'd gone. I eyed the grass, panic setting in momentarily. I was mad at her, but I couldn't lose her. "Safely away," I lied.

He was fading away, his eyes closing.

No, no, no. "Elijah." I grabbed his shirt. He was sweating even under the rain. I unbuttoned it, and he flinched. I peeled it off him and used it to wrap around the area. "Your back." My eyebrows pinched in the middle. Long, jagged scars ran the length of his back, zigzagging across each other, some pinker than others. "What happened?"

"Don't." He groaned, trying to turn away.

"Did you have an accident?"

He shuddered. "It-it's nothing," he said through chattering teeth. His temperature was all over the place. I needed a distraction. Clearly he didn't want to talk about the scars, so I made a mental note to bring them up later, if he survived.

"Tell me about your mother," I said quickly, remembering him bringing her up once.

He scoffed a laugh. "Y-you want to t-talk about my mom… now?"

I pressed my lips together. "Yes." I scrambled around my mind for questions. Anything to keep him not focused on the pain. "Did she look more like you or Corbin?"

"Corbin," he said, shaking out a short exhale. "I-I hate she never had a chance to meet h-him." His breaths shallowed as cold seeped through. Even I was shaking, and I didn't have venom forcing its way into my veins.

Where in the underworld was Alex?

"How did she meet your father?"

I hugged my arms around him tighter, willing all my body heat to go into him. I knew a spell, but I couldn't do it without him knowing. "S-she me…" He trailed off, then convulsed.

"No, no. Elijah!"

His body jolted against mine. Thick raindrops slicked my hair. I pushed my black strands out of the way, then wiped the water from my face. He was going to die if I didn't do something, but if I did and he remembered any of it, I'd be putting myself and my family in danger.

There was no way he could know I was a witch.

I laid him down away from me, swallowing thickly as a lump formed. His face had drained of color, and the whites of his eyes were showing as his arms and legs jerked, his body shaking violently against the grass. Black slithered up his arm, creating pathways under his skin, branching out like veins of ink.

Ember's face floated into my mind when I placed my hands over Elijah's arm. Rage seared through me. His father had done that. He'd squeezed her heart in his hand as if he hadn't destroyed everything. If Elijah died, it would be justice in one way—not the revenge we'd planned, but payback nonetheless.

Blood spurted from his lips, and he stilled. I listened carefully to his shallow breaths and looked at his discarded jacket on the grass, the one he'd given me to keep me dry instead of him.

I bit my lip, then swore. "You better not make me this regret this."

I unsheathed my dagger and slid it across my leg, then bit back a howl as the cut ran deep. I pressed my fingers into the blood, letting the rest drop onto the ground. "Take this blood as payment," I whispered, pressing my hand with the blood against his bite. "With this blood, take my payment. Remove the darkness in his veins and put them in mine. Allow me to share in his pain and sickness."

I closed my eyes as the transfer spell took place. It was dark magic, one that would leave a mark in my mind, but it worked. Searing heat ran up my arm, and fang marks appeared in my skin. I collapsed back, praying Elijah would remain unconscious until Alex returned with the antidote.

It felt like flames licking against my veins, and it forced a cry from my mouth, a sound I didn't recognize as my own. If this was only half the venom, I couldn't imagine how much pain Elijah must've been in.

I shut my eyes to the gray light of the world, finding calm in the blackness. I couldn't react. I had to stay still. I gritted my teeth so hard, I was surprised they didn't shatter. My arm swelled, and heat prickled to my fingers. Numbness reached my shoulder, making its way to my chest. Slumber came for me, stronger than the madness splintering the corners of my mind, pulling me into nothingness.

Someone was shaking me. I opened my eyes and saw my sister. "What did you do?" Her black hair was slick around her face, her eyes wide as she looked from my face to my arm. "Take this."

"What ab—"

"You first." She forced the liquid down my throat until I choked. Within a minute, I felt relief. I turned my head, rolling it against the ground, watching as she force-fed the antidote to Elijah. She looked back at me once the bottle was empty. "You better hope he thinks all this blood is from the bite." She clenched her jaw, lowering her voice to a whisper. "Why would you do this? A bloody transfer spell, sister? I know you want him alive to hurt Damian, but his life is not more important than yours." She peeled back his eyelid, examining him. "We're lucky he's unconscious, but just in case, we should erase his mind."

"No." I managed to sit upright. "Mother did that, and she never recovered. She's slowly dying because of it. I won't have it happen again."

She clicked her tongue. "I wasn't planning on me doing it. You're the one who messed up. You should do it."

I ran cold. She really did have a vengeful streak, not unlike me. We were both the furthest thing from Ember, who would have sacrificed herself in a second for any of us. "He won't remember."

Her pointed stare promised pain. "He better not. Don't try to kill yourself next time." She stood and threw the bottle on the ground. "Idiot."

My eyebrows raised. "I'll take care of him."

"I'm sure you will, seeing as he means more to you than your own family."

Her words were arrows to my heart, and tears welled in my eyes. I was thankful the rain covered evidence of it. "That's not true," I snapped because it wasn't. "I don't even like him."

"I can't understand why else you'd save him, at the risk of revealing yourself. Of us. What if I hadn't come back in time with the antidote? You could have died. Do you not care?" She placed her hand on her hip. "I'm going to find Buttercup before he or someone else finds her and kills her. This kingdom isn't kind to snakes."

Once she was out of sight, searching behind some trees, I let a tear roll down my cheek. I turned toward Elijah. Why had I saved him? I should have let him die. It was punishment enough. Now my sister hated me, and when Cas found out, he'd hate me too. Because it's true, I risked us all. If he remembered anything, we could all find ourselves like Ember.

I had to know for certain. After a few minutes, he opened his bloodshot eyes and coughed.

The mixture of rare herbs and oils had been infused with two spells Cas had mastered.

"Victoria?" He spluttered, then slowly sat upright.

I held the dagger tight in my grip. If he said anything, I'd have no choice but to slit his throat.

"Where's the snake?" he asked, and I loosed a sigh.

"Careful." I climbed to his side and helped him to his feet.

He wobbled, drooping his head forward. He'd had it ten times worse than me.

"Let's get you back home." I eyed him carefully. If he did know anything, he didn't show it.

***

Once we arrived back at the mansion, I slumped him into an armchair in front of a crackling fire.

A maid approached us. “Oh my goodness.”

“Get him something sweet and some tea, please,” I ordered. “He’ll be fine. He’s just in shock.”

She nodded, wringing her hands against her apron. “Tea. Yes.”

“Hurry, he’s not well,” I said when she didn’t move.

After a minute, he rubbed his head, exhaling a tense breath. “Whiskey.”

I gave him a look. “Alcohol? Is that a good idea?”

“Please.” He coughed, holding out his healthy arm.

I poured him a glass from the decanter on the side table, then passed it to him. He drank it in one gulp, then rolled his shoulders back. “I’m going to kill that thing.”

The corner of my mouth twitched. “You don’t need to.”

“It almost killed me.”

A shudder ran the length of my back. “She’s already dead,” I lied. I’d need to keep her hidden.

He arched an eyebrow. “You killed her?”

“No. Eva did.”

He raised his eyebrows and sighed. “Good.”

He didn’t even say thank you for saving his life. Fucking prick. I took the seat across from him. “You were passed out there for a bit. How are you feeling?” I prodded tentatively. “It looked as if you were hallucinating at one point,” I said, in case he did remember anything.

He shrugged. “I don’t remember a thing. I guess I should be glad.”

Relief lightened the heaviness in my chest. "Yes, you bled a lot." I pointed at the blood on his shirt. I mean, some of it was indeed his, but some belonged to me.

"I need something to eat."

"The maid will be back in a minute."

He paused. "I should thank you."

I suppressed a scoff. "You should."

"I'd be dead if you weren't so… proactive."

I opened my mouth, then closed it again. "It was my duty," I finally said. "It was my snake that bit you."

"You didn't know it would happen." He looked me up and down. Fortunately, my dress covered the cut on my leg, and the black hid the blood, but I could feel its burning presence with each movement. "You're soaked."

"As are you."

"I can have dry clothes brought for you."

"So kind of you, but you should rest right now," I said, trying and failing to keep the contempt from my voice. It wasn't his fault I'd saved him and my sister hated me for putting my life at risk, yet every time I looked at him, I saw my failure.

"I should see a doctor."

I opened my mouth to speak, but the maid returned, interrupting my thoughts. She placed a tray between us on the low table. "Sir, is there anything else you need?"

He barely looked at her. "No."

"Hey." I snapped my fingers. "Recovering from a bite doesn't excuse you from having manners." I looked at the maid. "Thank you."

He chewed the inside of his lips and leaned across the table to grab a piece of fudge. "Thanks, Adeline."

The maid smiled and opened the door and left. Once she was gone, I grabbed a handful of blackberry bonbons from the white bowl, then poured myself and him a tea. I needed the sugar too. I felt terrible.

"I'm going home," I said at the last sip. "I have dry clothes there. No need to inconvenience yourself."

He hunched over, not touching his own tea. "Victoria..."

"Try to rest," I said and stood. "I won't be attending the club with you tonight, but then I don't think you should go either."

His lips parted when I stepped past him, but he didn't speak. I walked out and toward the courtyard to get a carriage home. I was drained and worried about my snakes, and my head pounded as if something was trying to force its way in.

***

I awoke unable to breathe. Grasping fingers were at my throat, and my eyelids flung open, my bedroom empty. My heart raced, skipping every other beat as if it knew it was about to beat its last. That's what this was. Death.

A slither of air passed through my lips, then another, but it wasn't enough. I pressed back, arching my back against silk sheets. I silently choked, unable to alert my brother or sister. Had I been poisoned?

After a minute, I slowed my shallow, fast breaths. After another, my heart rate slowed, and the waves of numbness subsided.

Sitting upright, my eyes bulged. I inhaled deeply and reached around my bed, but nothing was out of the ordinary. What had I been doing before this happened? Dreaming. Yes, that was it. I had dreamed of Ember. Fond memories surfaced simple day-to-day stuff, stuff I'd discarded then, before I knew they'd become an important part of my collection of her life. Like how she'd always make me tea when I couldn't sleep, or when we'd laugh about something Cas did… whispers in her bedroom as we played with the snakes, not wanting to wake Mother, and Ember going on about girls at the academy.

A shudder snaked through me, running me cold. She was gone, and nothing could bring her back. The reality hit me like a ton of bricks. I couldn't save her, and she really was dead. She wasn't going to come home sometime. She was no more. How could I accept that? She was my sister. We grew up together. We shared secrets, laughs, and so much more. She was so many things, and she couldn't just not exist anymore.

The truth of her being gone had been in my head since that night, but it was numbed. A wall of blackness covered the stark reality as if my mind were trying to protect itself. Conversations from when we were just kids, staying up all night when we shouldn't or sneaking out to the woods to look for rabbits, resurfaced. I couldn't take it.

Suddenly I couldn't breathe again, but I understood why. It was her. The dark magic had pulled out the grief I'd buried deep inside, forcing it to the surface. In saving Elijah, I'd fractured my mind even more, and this was the consequence.

I made a noise I'd never heard myself make inside my mouth, keeping my lips firmly pressed together. It was bigger than me, the emotion too powerful for my body. I gripped into my pillows until the material ached my palms. I dug in my nails and screamed again, unable to keep it in like before. Each one resonated inside my mouth, chattering my teeth as my tears fell thick and fast. I held onto everything and anything, sheets, pillows, blankets… anything to keep me grounded to this world.

The grief was going to kill me. I only wished it would hurry. I wanted to shout and scream at the crows sitting on my windowsill, for no other reason than just existing. I hated everything and anything. The world wasn't allowed to continue, but it had.

All I wanted was to go into the kitchen, in my own home, to make myself a tea and stare at the chair where Ember sat. To go to her room and look at her things. It was all gone. Our house was gone, and all our things with it. I was here, enacting out some ridiculous revenge plan, allowing myself to attend a ball and drink as if the worst thing hadn't happened. I should march into their mansion, take a knife to Damian Shaw's throat, and spill his blood, delighting in the seconds I had to watch him choke on it until I was likely executed shortly after for murder.

I mean, hadn't I done that to the woman in the church? I'd somehow murdered her without even meaning to. That was how much my emotions were fucked up. I couldn't control them, and since that hex, my mind had become a sliver more unhinged than before. Maybe the hunter was right in one regard: witches could be dangerous.

I threw my pillow across the room, at the door, then screamed aloud, until my scream dried out. My door flung open, and I didn't bother to hide my emotions.

Alex's eyes were tearful, matching mine, her lips pressing together. "I know."

Cas appeared behind her. "What's going on…" He trailed off, his stare fixating on me and hands wringing. "Oh, sister."

I expected anything but this. They both climbed onto my bed, Cas sitting upright against the headboard. His hand was on my back, and Alex curled up next to me, lying on my hair.

Midnight fell into the morning hours, and I cried more than I knew was possible. Cas had even shed a tear, though I knew he was trying to keep himself together for us.

"She's still with us," he said into the darkness of my room, his words meant for himself more than us.

"I remember when we'd make potions in the bathtub, when Mama would bathe us together," Alex recalled, laughing through her tears. "Not real potions. They were from soap and bathing flowers and herbs."

I let out a small smile. "That's probably where she got her inspiration to make perfumes from."

Cas chimed in. "Do you remember when she made her first perfume?"

I recalled the small explosion in the fireplace. She had been twelve. We all laughed, carrying her memories until the sky lightened to pinks and morning greeted our tired, blotched faces.

I wiped the last of my tears, sniffling into the back of my sleeve when I was done. "Who's hungry?"

Cas patted my back as I sat up. "What do you want to eat?"

"I can cook," I said.

Alex laughed, then sniffed loudly. "What and now you can cook? Gods save us."

"I can make egg fritters," Cas said, standing. "With haddock."

Alex rubbed her stomach. "I'm not going into school today."

I squeezed her hand. "I don't think any of us should do anything today."

Cas nodded in agreement, then left my room and headed for the kitchen. Alex waited until he was gone before she spoke. "What about Elijah?"

I shrugged. "We can take a day off."

She looked at the bed. "Can I be honest with you?"

I yawned. "Always."

She shuffled uncomfortably. "I don't want to drag Corbin into this. He's not the same as his father or brother."

"I thought you didn't like him." I arched an eyebrow.

"I don't not like him."

"Mmhmm."

"He's not an awful person, that's all."

"Just be careful, Alex. Please." For a second, I heard myself, as if I were reciting the same thing I'd said to Ember. Everyone had gone at me for being controlling, and even if my advice could have saved her in the end, it was the same control that had created a rift between us. Had we not argued because of it? "He's human."

"I know." She crossed her arms over her chest.

"I trust you," I said slowly, realizing I should have said the same thing to Ember before she'd die. Even if her mistakes had cost her greatly, maybe she wouldn't have gone so hard against me if I'd loosened up a little.

Something changed in her gaze. "That means a lot to hear."

"I wasn't going to have Corbin involved. He's just a kid."

She nodded slowly, hesitating. "What about Elijah?"

"We both know he's a part of the plan."

"So you really don't care for him?"

I made a face. "No."

"He is planning on being a hunter too, so he's just as bad as his father."

My lips parted, and before I could explain what he'd told me, how he didn't want to become one, Cas reentered the room. "One of you make the tea, please. Maybe you can set the table, Tori?"

"Coming." I cleared my throat and looked at the cage. I was grateful for Alex saving Buttercup and bringing her back here after what had happened. "I'll feed them after, but I'm still angry at Buttercup."

Alex rolled her eyes and stood. "So you do care a little about him then."

I placed my hand on my hip. "She could have ruined our entire plan."

“About that.” Her eyes darkened. “If it ever comes to you and him or the plan again, always choose yourself. I can’t lose another sister.”

My heart palpated. Just like that, I had a reason to not be so discarding of my life. “I won’t. It was a mistake.”

She nodded and followed Cas downstairs. I hugged my cardigan around myself, one that Mother had knitted for me one Noelle, and for a short second, I actually missed her too.

Eighteen

Elijah

I hesitated outside her front door. I wanted to say thank you, or anything really, but I was humiliated. She'd had to kill her pet because I'd been too forward, thinking I could touch a deadly snake, when in actuality I had been trying to connect to her. Then she'd seen the scars. I remember that much. She'd have questions, ones I didn't know how to answer.

I could tell she was mad at me when she left. I considered having someone bring flowers, but it felt too impersonal. I'd at least send some to her sister, whom I recalled running home to get the antidote.

I ran my finger along the bite marks. It had mostly healed, which was remarkable. I was sure when it had bitten me, I was dead already. I imagined her brother had made the serum. She had harked on about how talented he was in the medicinal field, and while I wouldn't usually put much weight into an apothecary—not when I had the best doctors in town on call—but if he could cure a bite like that, then he may do well on our staff.

Perhaps she would see that as a thank-you, if I helped her brother.

I paced in a circle, finally encouraging myself enough to knock. I heard shuffling inside before it opened. Her hair was loose. It fell like silk around her shoulders. I couldn't help but smile when I saw her in a simple dress, with no powder on her face. She was breathtaking. I loved the blacks, but seeing her in light blue softened her sharp features. It brought out the warmth in her skin and the glow in her eyes.

"I need to talk to you, about earlier."

She inhaled sharply. "I'm actually busy."

"Don't do that." I placed my hand on the door. "Let me at least say what I came to say." I paused, noticing the faded red around her eyes. Had she been crying? Shit. "I want to apologize for touching her, and I'm sorry she's dead."

"You're right; you shouldn't have touched her. I did say before, but..." She placed a hand on her hip. "What's happened, happened. I shouldn't have brought her around you, so it's just as much my fault. How are you feeling?"

"Okay, considering. Still a bit weak."

Her eyebrows knitted together, creasing her forehead. "You were bitten by the most venomous snake in Salvius, and you're only feeling a bit *weak*?"

"Whatever you gave me worked really well. I was surprised."

"Why? Because it was made by an apothecary, or because I administered it?"

"Neither." I sniffed the air. Was that haddock I was smelling? "Can I come in?"

She fumbled with her necklace. "We're having a family day."

I nodded slowly, looking around her, down the dark passage. "Of course. Another time?" I thought back to the way she had run her hand through my hair when I felt like I was on fire, how she spread her fingers over my chest and talked to me about my mother. How she held me tightly when the venom and cold had become too much.

She paused for a moment before her smile fell back into the frown I was accustomed to. "I don't know."

I took a step forward, closing the distance between us. Something had changed in her since yesterday. I couldn't place my finger on what, but it was significant, like I was seeing her truly for the first time. "You were right about me being an asshole to my staff."

"I know."

I sucked in a deep breath. "I wish none of this happened. I understand if you hate me."

She exhaled slowly, then shook her head. "Buttercup's not dead. I just said that because I was afraid you were going to hunt her or something."

My lips parted, then closed. What could I say? I felt different now. I was the fool for prodding the creature, and it had reacted as was expected. "It wasn't the snake's fault. I'm fine anyway, so no harm done."

She licked her lips, looking at the ground. Seconds ticked into a minute before she spoke again. "I think it would be better if you and I didn't hang out together anymore. It's not you, it's me, mostly, and… just understand."

I inhaled calmly, my heart slowing. No woman had ever got under my skin before, but she had settled there without me even realizing it. I barely knew her, yet being around her felt so familiar. "I do."

She gently closed the door, but I couldn't let it stop like this. I placed my hand on the painted wood, pushing it back open. "I'll admit, I haven't cared to get to know anyone much before, but…" I gazed into her eyes, and I swear I could see them soften. "I want to know you, even if just as friends."

She shook her head. "Sorry, but I'm not interested."

I watched her in the doorway, my stomach sinking. I couldn't push her, but there was one thing I hadn't mentioned yet. "About the scars on my back."

She shook her head, looking away. "It's not any of my business."

I believed she wouldn't tell anyone. She didn't seem like the type. "It was good knowing you, Miss Weathermore."

She closed the door, leaving me standing under the graying sky. The cold had crept up on Redforest, baring the maple trees and adding a cold nip to the breeze. I walked into town, kicking rocks on the way.

The town was emptier than it should have been for a Thursday afternoon. Small shops closed their doors to the harsh winds gushing down the main street. Shoving my hands deep in my pockets, I walked uptown, stopping in front of the new apothecary. It hadn't opened yet. I wondered if they'd all be working together. A part of me envied their closeness. I couldn't remember the last time, if ever, that Corbin, Father, and I did anything together.

"Look what the cat dragged in," Charles said in greeting, approaching me from behind. He slapped his hand on my shoulder. "I saw you at the ball with that pretty little thing. I assumed you'd still be wrapped up with her."

"It wasn't like that," I said. "She was no one."

"It didn't seem that way." He ran his hand through his tousled hair, then straightened his tailored jacket. "The night went well, anyway. Your dad was cold as always, but he was talking to mine about raising funds to fix up the gallows."

Bile rose in my throat. "Why would he need to do that?"

"Right?" He scoffed. "He has enough dramair to pay for it himself."

"I mean, why bother refurbishing them? They're fine, and we seldom have any executions here anymore. Even witches know not to come here."

He flicked a piece of lint from his sleeve. "Mine agreed to donate anyway. You say witches in this town, and everyone's ready to hand over their coin to help fight them."

I looked around and recognized a few faces.

Witches just didn't come here. They had to know a trial here would never end well. Not that it should, for real witches, but after my father made accusations about me being under a spell just because I wanted to be a businessman instead, and with Sandra being sent away, it made me wonder how many innocents we had condemned too.

Charles snapped his fingers in front of my face. "Elijah? You drunk or on something?"

I shook my head, pressing my fingers to my forehead. "Neither. Distracted."

"Let's go to the club. We can open early, have a drink, something to eat?"

I needed a pick-me-up. I wasn't sure if it was lingering effects from the bite or the meeting with Victoria. I felt bad for what had happened, her snake was gone, and I was at her door apologizing. The more I thought about it, the angrier I got. She was flipping me off for what? I'd been a bit blunt after, but I had been weak. If she couldn't be understanding, then why should I be? I shouldn't care that she doesn't want to see me anymore. We hadn't fucked. We hadn't done much together at all, so I shouldn't have cared. I didn't want to. "Let's do it. I need to talk to you anyway," I said, wanting to push her as far from my mind as possible.

"You're paying, although I guess soon, I'll be the owner, so maybe I should treat you," Charles said, and I climbed into a carriage with him. He never did care for walking. "So you're becoming a hunter."

"Yes, and that's what I wanted to talk to you about." He was taking over my club soon, and while the thought made my hand curl into a fist, I reminded myself it wasn't his fault. If anyone was going to take over the club, I'd rather it be him. "I start in a couple of weeks. He wants me to go away to train with other recruits."

"You'll pass in no time."

It wasn't that I was worried about. "When I first heard you were buying my club, I was angry. It's why I haven't come to see you, but the more time I had to think about it, I guess I'm glad it's you instead of someone else."

"Why do you think I opted to buy it when I heard? I know what it means to you. I won't let just anyone run it."

"Take care of it."

He knew how it worked, and he was proactive. He always had been. "I will, and you can come in anytime if you need a break from your family."

"So come in every day then?"

He laughed, and I rested my head back on the seat and sighed. The carriage gruelled to a halt, and I smiled. A nice whiskey and some roasted beef would brighten my mood.

Nineteen

Victoria

Cas, Alex, and I had enjoyed ourselves for the first time in a long time. We'd played board games, and Cas and Alex had listened to me play the piano. Cas had given it a go, but he didn't possess the same musical talent. We'd walked into town, checked on our store, and went to bed early. It was the first night I hadn't had any nightmares.

Cas sat at the breakfast table, swirling his tea, reading a newspaper over his eggs. "Good morning." He shot me a genuine smile. "How did you sleep?"

"Remarkably well." I grabbed a slice of toast and sat across from him, digging my pointed nail into the crust. "How about you?"

He blew on his tea, then took a sip. "Very well. Alex must have too. She's still out. I didn't want to wake her."

I waved a hand. "Let her sleep."

He exhaled slowly, placing his teacup back on the table. "I know emotions were high yesterday when you sent Elijah away, but I am assuming you wish to continue our plan."

I hadn't thought about it much since I'd told him we shouldn't meet up anymore. A part of me yesterday wanted to let go of it all, to kill Damian right then and get it over and done with, but a good night's sleep had changed things. I couldn't give up now. I had let my feelings, my grief, get in the way, and I'd made a mistake. "I'll get him back."

He arched an eyebrow, putting the paper down. "I hope so. If not, this was all for nothing." He leaned forward and squeezed my empty hand. "Not that I'm not without compassion. We were all upset yesterday."

"I shouldn't have reacted so rashly," I admitted. "I'll go over there today. I'm intrigued to see how the hex bag is working on the hunter. I hope he's having a terrible time sleeping."

"I'll see if I can find out anything from the priests. They have grown rather fond of me." The glint in his eye made me smile. "So have their wives."

"*Cas.*"

He shrugged back. "They have, and I've got them wrapped around my finger. There are so many rumors about him."

"Like what, and why haven't I been told?"

"Because they're rumors, and you know how people like to gossip. I wanted them confirmed before I spread them myself."

I gripped into the wood of the table, leaning forward until my stomach dug into the edge. "I want to know anyway."

He licked his lips and leaned in. "Most wouldn't say a word against him, but after my being in the inner circle for long enough, certain people would let out their thoughts on him. I've heard whispers that he hits his children."

"Like with a cane? It's not unheard of."

His eyes widened. "With a whip, apparently."

My mind flashed with the image of the scars covering Elijah's back. They crossed each other, some thicker and newer than others. "I believe it. Elijah's back was covered in scars. It was vile. There were hundreds of them, some stretched so wide, I wonder how deep the original wound must have been."

He shook his head. "Fucking monster."

"No wonder Corbin is the way he is."

"With the opium?"

"Yeah, and the alcohol. Even Elijah drinks a lot, although I'm sure he doesn't think it's a problem."

"No wonder, with a father like that. Although, it seems like Elijah wants to be a hunter too, so we can't feel too bad for him."

My lips parted. I wanted to tell him he didn't, but I couldn't let Cas think I felt bad for him—or that I might back out of our plan. "He hates witches too." That part was true.

"Who doesn't in this town?" Cas scoffed. "At least, from what I heard yesterday, it appears he likes you. A lot."

"Yes, and we can move on to the next part of the plan."

His eyebrows flicked upward. "We can even add in a new part."

"Which is?"

"We shed light onto those rumors about his whipping his children."

"If it's already gossiped about, why bother?"

"Barely." He put his index finger in the air. "We can find evidence, spread it around more. We can really turn his own people against him."

"And turn Elijah against me," I stated.

"No one will know we started it. I'll have to figure out how we're going to do it first. Give me a few days to think on it."

I felt nauseated. "It might mess Corbin up even more."

"Since when did you care?"

"Alex cares."

He sighed. "We put the focus on Elijah."

My chest somehow felt heavier. "I'm going to focus on the next part of our plan instead."

"Yes. Turning Elijah against his father."

I nodded. "I have an idea on how to do it too."

"You need him to trust you first," he said. "While you earn back his trust, you can add another hex bag. If he's tired, he'll be in a bad mood, but if we can give him a sickness or ache in his muscles too… maybe some good old-fashioned diarrhea."

"It needs to be subtle. How about the hex of itches?"

He grinned, leaning back in his chair. "You are cruel. It's a small hex, but effective. Imagine having an itch you couldn't scratch."

"I'll prepare a bag this evening after the opening. He hasn't found the one under his mattress yet. As long as I hide them well enough, I think we can get away with it for some time."

Alex chimed in, stepping into the kitchen. "I've heard the hex of unquenchable thirst is even better."

We both turned to look at her. "I worry about you sometimes," Cas said, looking from her to me. "You're far too much like Victoria."

"What's that supposed to mean?"

He rolled his eyes. "An affinity for cruelty."

Alex placed her hand on her hip. "I'm not cruel… against those who don't deserve it." She smiled a little too sweetly and grabbed an apple from the bowl. "I'm late for school. I'll get the cane, but don't worry, I have a hex bag for the bitch."

"Alex!" I stood. "I told you, you're not to be using dark magic. It takes its toll on the mind."

She shrugged. "It's just one—and a small one. It'll turn her next meal into worms."

I extended my hand, wiggling my fingers. "Hand it over."

She gritted her teeth and looked at Cas. "Seriously? Tell her to let me."

"She's right, for once," he said. "Give it to her. I don't want you using dark magic."

"So Victoria can, but I can't?"

"She knows what she's doing," he explained.

"Whatever. Here." She threw it to the ground in front of me, missing my hand. "Have a good day." With that, she stormed out the door. After it shut, I looked at Cas incredulously. "She's got an attitude on her."

He chuckled. "She's seventeen. You were worse."

I picked up the bag. "I wasn't using dark magic."

He huffed out a breath. "We will deal with this another time. We need to get to the shop to open it. I've spread the word among the church community."

"Elijah said he would be there, but I doubt he'll come after yesterday."

"No matter." He grabbed his jacket from the coat stand. "It's chilly outside."

I nodded, grabbing my coat. "Tell me more of these rumors about Damian on the way."

"There's not many more." He opened the door, and the harsh cold air hit me when I stepped outside, watering my eyes. "Apparently he sent away a human for doing witchcraft some years ago. His children's nanny. Oh, and he's terrified of disappointing the high priest who comes to town annually. He was Damian's mentor, and he's after the job. He'd do anything to become high priest, but there can only be one."

We reached the gate, and I hugged my coat tighter around my black-and-red dress. "Anything else?"

"I did hear something from Lady Montague. She said the maids at the mansion have said that Damian has some kind of sexual suppression, that he punishes himself when he feels anything down there." He cleared his throat. "Mental case."

"That is a huge rumor!" I said. "We can use it."

"How? Are you going to torture him with seduction? I don't think you could or should have to stomach that."

I clicked my tongue. "Absolutely not, but I will find a way to incorporate it into our plan. We vowed to do anything to make him suffer."

He lowered his gaze to the carpeted ground of skeletal leaves. "I know. We've lost so much. I've heard news that Mother's health isn't any better. She's worried about us."

I closed my eyes for a moment. "She's safe away from all of this."

"She's heartbroken." The lump in his throat moved. "I've written to her. Once we're done here, we will go back to her."

The hairs on the back of my neck stood erect. I forgot there was an after to our plan. Would I be able to move on? An image Ember's fear-laced eyes from that night swam in my mind, palpating my heart. I squeezed my fingers into a fist. How could we go back to being a family when we were one missing? A hollow feeling followed me down the road as I followed Cas into town. I wished we'd ordered a carriage, but the walk ended up being good for my head.

"We have an audience," Cas whispered when I stepped up beside him, approaching the curved windows of our shop. The painters had coated the exterior in dark green, making it stand out from the two, with flaky paint, on either side. Above the first curved window was our name, Weathermore, and over the second window, the lettering "Apothecary." Pillars of dark green lined either side of the door, with gold embellishments curling around it. In the dimly lit windows, bottles and vases stood on the polished mahogany shelves behind the glass crossed with lead.

Cas shook the hands of those in the small crowd, all members of the church community who'd gathered to support us. He opened the narrow double doors and pushed back the curtains covering the arched glass on them to let in some light. "Welcome."

I followed in behind him. I noticed he'd added some charms for the superstitious—a clever move in this town, I had to admit—and some Noelle decorations on the shelves filling the three walls.

Behind his counter were cabinets, over them, the word Dispensing. I checked the time on the clock on the wall between two shelves. It was only ten in the morning. The day was going to be long. I'd almost forgotten how work felt, it had been so long. I opened some of the drawers, rolling the bottles filled with various powders and herbs, and blew out a long breath. It was a long stretch from our colorful shop back home, but I was still proud of Cas. His last shop had been falling apart with waning supplies. Now, he had enough to last him a year. He'd opened the business he'd always wanted.

My heart ballooned when I saw it, the perfume stand in the corner. It was an odd addition to an apothecary shop, yet it fit perfectly. I hadn't known he was having one fitted, a nod to our Ember. I swallowed thickly and found him talking to two customers. He pulled out two teas, rose mint and sweet thyme, both his own signature, and handed them in pouches to customers.

I moved to another section. Sweet-smelling herbs replaced the more earthy smells, with a hint of spice. The bell tinkled all day over the door as more people came and went. We sold more than expected, and Cas was grinning ear to ear. I replaced two bottles of lavender and sage and restocked the soaps.

"Victoria." Fingers tapped my shoulder, jolting me. "It's only me."

I turned slowly. I knew his voice. "Elijah. I am surprised you came."

"I know you want me to stay away." His expression hardened. "But I said I would come, and I wanted to thank your brother in person for saving my life. It was, after all, his antidote which helped the snake bite."

And my sharing the bite, I thought bitterly, then shook my head, snapping myself out of it. "I was upset yesterday."

"Say no more." He turned toward where my brother was standing at the counter. "I will go say my thanks. I also have a business proposition for him."

I reached forward, my fingers lacing against his. "Elijah, wait."

He stopped mid-step. "What?"

Was he angry? "I shouldn't have said what I did yesterday."

"It doesn't matter. You were right."

"I was right?"

He shrugged. "We let this go too far already. It didn't really mean anything."

"I'm sorry." I touched his back when he went to walk away a second time.

He flinched, his eyes narrow when he turned to look at me.

"I opened up to you yesterday," he whispered, "and you turned me away like I was nothing. I don't take to that lightly."

"Look—"

"I think you're just afraid of anything real, and you push people away."

I balled my fists. "That's not true. I'm not afraid of anything."

"No?"

"I'm not," I stormed. "Yesterday I had a bad night. So when you came, I wasn't thinking straight."

He searched my expression, and I did my best to soften it. "Why do you even care to know me? It was so easy for you to turn me away yesterday."

Fuck, fuck, fuck. "For the same reason you wanted to get to know me, I imagine."

He shook his head. "I wanted to *fuck* you. Your company was secondary."

I laughed sharply, forgetting myself. "You really are an asshole."

He ran his hand through his blond strands. "And you run hot and cold."

I hitched a breath. "You are so used to getting what you want, you can't stand it when someone tells you no." I pointed a finger to his chest. "Don't stand there and act like you know me. You know nothing, prick."

The intensity in his gaze matched mine. We were at the back of the store, fortunately away from everyone else, when he grabbed my arm. "You think you can talk to me like this?"

"What are you going to do about it?" I asked in challenge.

He leaned toward my ear. "I'll make you regret it. Don't forget who I am."

I leaned back, tiptoeing slightly and dancing my fingers up his chest. "I'm not afraid of you or your threats, and you'll do well to remember who I am too." I moved my lips away from his ear, brushing them against his cheek, moving them toward his lips. I whispered against them, "Are we going to start over? Or would you prefer us to be enemies?"

He held his breath.

I glanced down at his pants and the hard length bulging outward. "I think you'd rather be friends."

He tangled his fingers in my hair and pulled my lips back to his, almost touching. A jolt of energy shot through me. "You're impossible."

"Oh, admit it," I said, smiling, enjoying being only an inch from his lips. "You couldn't stop thinking about me after I turned you away. You're a masochist."

He blew out a whistle. "You know, I'm starting to think I'm not the only one."

Who knew it? He preferred the real version of me? "You'd be surprised."

Challenge glinted in his eyes. "I'm taking you out, tonight."

"Are you now?" I asked, pushing myself against him. "Where are we going?"

"Just be ready at nine. I'll pick you up from your house." He let go of my hair, pulling back a couple of inches. "I'm glad I came here after all."

I glanced at his pants. "That was fast," I said teasingly, but I knew what he meant.

He almost smiled but hid it. "Speaking of, are you going to do anything about that?"

"There's a restroom at the back if you're desperate." My heart raced. "You can take care of it yourself."

He undressed me with his eyes. "You drive me crazy."

I shrugged, although my cheeks heated. "It's not as difficult as you think."

He smirked and turned away from me. "Don't be late tonight."

I went to throw back a quip, but he was already at the other side of the shop, looking at some shelves—maybe waiting for his dick to go soft again. He shoved his hands in his pockets, his white shirt bunching at his hips. What was I doing? Was I really checking him out? I didn't do that, not to a human—especially my enemy.

I hurried to the counter. "Cas, I'm heading home. Can you close?"

"Yes, you've been a great help."

I nodded and quickly left, not looking back. The cold air was welcomed against my hot skin and flushed face. I hated that he had an effect on me. It had been a long time since I'd been with a man. That had to be it, because there was no way I wanted Elijah Shaw.

A raven flew into me, jolting me back against the shop's wall. I splayed my fingers over my racing heart, looking up as the inky bird flapped away, against fierce gusts of wind. I leaned down, picking up a lone feather. It reminded of my friends who'd fled persecution and went to the kingdom of the white sea, a voyage unreachable from our lands. The Ravenwoods were a raven-sorcerer race who could turn into ravens at will.

I pocketed the feather. I could use it in our next hex bag, which I'd have to put off, as Elijah was picking me up tonight. I gazed upward, wondering where he'd be taking me. I was surprised he wanted the real Victoria more than the slightly nicer version I'd shown him. I guessed the entire family was a glutton for punishment.

A flurry of white circled in front of me as I stepped out into the street. Snowflakes caught in the winds, catching in my black strands and on my coat. I pressed my chilled lips together, inhaling the icy air, and decided I'd be taking the carriage home instead of walking.

Twenty

Elijah

Father yawned, cracking his neck to the side. His bloodshot eyes landed on me, and he assessed my outfit. "Going somewhere nice?"

"I'm meeting someone." I tugged at my collar. "You look tired. Bad night's sleep?"

He drummed his fingers against the coffee table. "It's nothing but a few nightmares," he said, leaning back against the cushions of the sofa. "The high priest will be coming to town soon, so I decided to postpone your training by a couple of weeks."

I loosed a sigh of relief. "I will make sure I'm there to greet him."

"Yes, you will." He closed his eyes slowly. "Where is your brother?"

I had no idea, but I didn't want him getting in trouble. "Upstairs, I believe."

"Tell him I want to talk to him."

"Has he done something?" I asked.

"It is between your brother and me."

"I'll tell him."

"Good." He waved his hand dismissively. It was 8:15 a.m. already, but I couldn't leave without finding Corbin first.

I searched the house, then found our housekeeper. "Have you seen my brother?"

Her eyes widened. "He went out with the young Miss Weathermore."

I had seen them together at the ball. What was he playing at? "Thanks," I said and hurried back to the lounge, where I found Father snoring lightly. Thank Zerheus he was asleep. I wanted to be here when he and Corbin talked.

In the lobby, I stopped in front of a mirror and slicked back a lock of my hair that had curled on my forehead. I looked myself over one last time before heading to the carriage. I stopped Adeline before climbing inside. She brushed down her apron.

"If Corbin comes back before me, tell him to go straight to his room. Father Shaw wishes to talk to him, and I'd prefer to be here when he does."

She nodded in understanding. She'd been working for us for six years and knew how quickly a talk could escalate into something else. It had been years since any of his punishments, but I didn't trust him not to act out, especially when he was this grave looking.

"Be careful, sir."

I caught a snowflake in my gloved hand. "Make sure the fire's lit for when I return."

"When will you be back?"

I looked up at the sky. I honestly had no idea. "It depends. Hopefully tomorrow morning, but we'll see."

She nodded, and I climbed inside, blowing out a fogged breath. I rested my head back against the cushion of the seat, imagining my evening with Victoria playing out. It didn't take long for my dick to get hard. It was those fuck-me eyes and glances over her shoulder that got me. I loved the way she challenged me, and damn if she wasn't so smart. I opened my eyes. I hated how she had this effect on me. I just needed to fuck her once, then I'd stop thinking about her all the time.

The carriage stopped, and I pushed my erection toward my belt before I stepped out. She emerged from her doorway, dressed in black and white. Ruffled white covered her arms, reaching up to a collar where a cameo black broach pinned the front together. Around her waist was a black corset, used as a belt of sorts, cinching above where her skirt billowed out. Her black hair fell poker-straight down her chest, her dark-purple painted lips contrasting her dress. "Hello, love."

Her lips curved upward. "You don't look too bad yourself."

I brushed down my burgundy tailcoat, holding my cane in one hand. "Are you ready for the night of your life?"

"I don't have any expectations, considering our previous outings, so yes." She pushed past me and climbed into the carriage, refusing my helping hand.

I smirked and climbed in behind her. "Our previous outings haven't been official courtships," I said, defending myself. I glanced at the sides of her dress. "No snakes tonight?"

"Why?" She arched a dark eyebrow. "Afraid?"

"Honestly, a little."

She leaned back, suppressing a grin. "No snakes tonight."

Less than an hour later, we arrived. She stretched when the carriage gruelled to a stop. "This better be worth my aching back."

I opened the door and helped her out. "This is our family cabin, but I come for the view mostly."

She walked out to where the trees dropped off, clearing the view of a crystal lake and its reflection of pinpricked stars glistening like diamonds against an indigo canvas. The forest stretched into a sea of greens and reds, out to the snow-capped mountains towering into the horizon. Snow drifted down, icing the trees and frosting the leaves carpeting the ground. "I've never seen anything like this."

"It's my favorite place," I admitted.

"I'm sure you've brought many women up here to bed, but it'll take more than a pretty view for that."

My stomach knotted. I didn't want to tell her she was the first person I'd brought up here. "I ordered a fire lit, and some food and wine inside."

She looked back at the log cabin and angled her head. "Good. It feels more like winter than autumn."

She climbed the steps made from logs, holding onto the carved railing until she reached the door. The entrance was dimly illuminated by a hanging oil lamp. "I guess being rich has its advantages."

"Just a few."

She didn't need to turn for me to know she rolled her eyes. She pushed open the door and gasped, although she tried to mask it as a yawn. I stepped in behind her, breathing in the woody, smoked air. I'd missed it there. Corbin and I would come when we were kids, with Sandra. It was one of the few places where we felt relaxed and free. Father used it to stay in when we went hunting but seldom came anymore.

She ran her pointed nails along the beam in the middle of the room, which pillared to the ceiling. She stopped in front of the fire, and I smiled. They'd left everything as I'd ordered, and more. A rose, grown to perfection, stood alone in a vase on the oak table. Next to it sat a silver platter with oysters, cheeses, fruitcake, and bread from the town's bakery.

I opened the bottle of wine and poured us each a small glass. She eyed the piano in the corner, the corner of her lip curving.

"Do you play?" I asked.

"I do."

I gestured toward the stool in front of it and placed her glass on top of the rosewood piano. She placed her fingers delicately atop the ivory keys and closed her eyes. I took a sip from my wine, enjoying the crackling from the fire and heat of it on my back. The subtle nutty undertone complemented the spicy, dry taste.

The melody began slow and deep, with high notes lifting it into something masterful. Her fingers danced the tune, coaxing something smooth and beautiful from the keys. Her eyes were lost in the notes as she became one with the music. Each note weaved with the next, a song I both recognized and didn't. It was slow but mesmerizing. I became transfixed as if the song were a story, her story. Her fingers pounded, moving from light to heavier movements as the music loudened. My heart raced as it arched, then slowed to an end.

She wiped her eyes, then placed her hands on her laps, staring at the piano as if she hadn't just created something incredible. "That one's called Ember."

"Like an ember in a fire."

"Something like that." She picked up her wine and took a sip.

"You're a great pianist. I had no idea. Do you play anything else?"

"The violin, cello, and harp, but I'm still a novice at the harp."

I took another sip of wine, feeling somehow breathless even though I hadn't moved. "It was beautiful."

She didn't look at me. "The food looks good." She grabbed the platter and brought it down to the rug in front of the fire.

I kicked my shoes off and sat across from her, lying on my side. The fire's orange hue danced in her brown eyes. "How did you learn to play?"

She ate an oyster and placed the shell back onto the platter. "My dad taught me before he died."

"At least you have a piece of him with you."

Her eyebrows furrowed. "You're not wrong."

She glared at me, waiting, anticipation thick in her features. I didn't look away as our locked gaze intensified. I couldn't stop thinking about what happened at the shop, the way she'd pressed herself against me and whispered daring things against my lips. "Can I admit something?"

She shrugged. "If you care to."

"I couldn't stop thinking about you after I left earlier."

She tapped the side of her glass. "How awful for you."

"It wasn't that terrible."

"So I'm not a complete bitch then?"

"Oh no, that you are." I grinned. "But I like it."

She leaned forward. "Of course you would. Sadist," she teased.

"I thought I was a masochist?"

She rolled her eyes. "Well, now that you have me here, what are you going to do with me?"

My breath hitched. "Don't play with me if you're not ready."

She unbroached her collar. "But I like to play."

Fuck. "So do I."

She moved her hand to her top button and twisted it between her fingers until it fell open. She moved on to the next, and the ache in my groin increased, my erection growing until it was pressing against the inside of my pants.

She unbuttoned them painstakingly slowly, but I couldn't look away. Finally, her shirt fell open, revealing her cleavage. Before she could do anything else, I leaned across the platter, pushing it to one side. Her wanting eyes found mine. Nothing but sharp intakes of breath were between us as flickers of touch arched her closer. Running my hand into her silky strands, I pulled her toward myself, deepening our kiss. Her nips on my lip sent a jolt down my length. Her fingernails danced to my midsection, which rippled under her touch. She nibbled again, and my pants became tighter, rubbing against me. I thrust my hips upward, ripping her shirt all the way down to her corset.

"Take it off." I pulled back an inch, reaching my hand to her thick thigh and squeezing it under the skirt of her dress.

Her back arched under my touch, her lips as frantic against me as her fingers. I traced mine under her skirt but stopped at her thigh. She flinched, so I paused, looking into her eyes. She closed them, then kissed me harder. I took it slower, moving kisses up her neck to her ear.

She groaned inside her mouth, unaware of how much it made me want to spill into my pants. I kissed down to her navel, and she pulled off her skirt. Her rosewater scent lingered. I moved my fingers further, until I felt the slick wetness between her legs. I wanted to feel her come. I pushed my fingers in slow and deep, biting the inside of my lip when her ass lifted from the rug.

She leaned forward, pulling my pants down. When my length was in her hand, she caressed me. A shock of pleasure rippled through my stomach, and the pressure mounted as I felt an orgasm build. It built until I moved back, pressing her against the rug. I wasn't ready to finish yet. I wanted to feel all of her, on me.

I'd never felt this before. She was incredible, so forward and unafraid.

I couldn't help but admire her as she climbed on top of me and enveloped us as one as she sat on top of my length. She moved slowly at first. I wanted to go faster, to finish inside her, but at the same time, I wasn't ready for it to end. I steadied my breathing, watching her bounce. I grabbed her thick thighs and pulled her down, pressing myself in as hard as I could, my eyes rolling into the back of my head.

"Oh gods." She moaned, rocking her hips.

I pulled her into me. "Victoria," I said, her name a caress on my breath. Her body shook against mine and she groaned, her teeth pressed against my shoulder.

I thrust into her faster, feeling my orgasm rock through me. My hips locked and my toes curled against the rug, and I rushed, erupting inside her until my grip loosened and the orgasm finished with pulses and jolts.

I ran my finger along her back and stopped at her waist. I couldn't catch my breath, intoxicated by the way her body moved. She rolled off me, panting against the rug with her back arched.

"Wow," she said breathily, and I couldn't help but smile.

I pulled her close, not ready to let her go quite yet. Her hair poured over my chest, and I played with the strands.

"Do you come here often?" she asked after a few silent minutes.

"Not too much anymore, but I used to come here with Corbin and our nanny."

She paused. "Of course you had a nanny."

"She was more like a mother to us," I admitted, enjoying the feeling of Victoria's warmth against me.

She shuffled, twirling her hips between my legs.

"She was a kind woman."

"Was? Where is she now?"

Victoria never missed a trick. "I have no idea. Somewhere safe, I hope."

"Is that like a rich people thing? The nannies get sent away at a certain age?"

My throat felt somehow tighter. "It's complicated."

She turned around, looking me in the eye. "The best stories are."

"This is a sad story."

She turned back around, laying her head back on my chest. The fire flickered warmth over us, covering us both in a hue of orange. I continued playing with her hair. "She was sent away for dabbling in witchcraft."

She jolted. "So she wasn't a witch then?"

"You don't miss a thing. No, she wasn't. She made ointments, much like your brother, and they thought she was mixing them with spells. She wasn't," I assured her. "She was just very good at what she did."

"I'm not surprised. A talented woman who's good at something. She *would* be branded a witch." She rolled her eyes. "Fucking men."

"How do you know it was men who sent her away?"

"Was it not?"

I blew out a long breath. She wasn't wrong. "It was my father."

"Oh my."

"He's just stuck in his beliefs. He thought he was doing the right thing."

"Don't you get tired?"

"Of what?" I asked.

"Of defending him?"

I lay my head back, watching the orange dance on the wall. It reminded me of the witch I'd watched burn when I was a boy. "Sometimes, yes."

Twenty-One

Victoria

I trailed a fingernail along his chest through his chest hair and lifted my eyes to meet his icy blues. I could still feel the ache between my legs from the night before. I was grateful I'd remembered to take my special ointment this month, despite not expecting to have sex. I didn't want any surprises, and it helped the monthly pains.

I couldn't believe I'd fucked him. I knew eventually I'd have to, especially if I was going to earn his trust, but I'd enjoyed it… and the worst part was I wanted to do it again.

He was the son of the man who'd murdered my sister, he wore his face, and he was a human. Yet there I was, lying on him, wishing he'd kiss me again because despite all that, he wasn't the worst. I thought about what he'd said last night, about his nanny. He didn't condemn her even though his father had. That, coupled with the scars on his back and the rumors accompanying them, told me he'd had a bad run of things too.

He nudged my ear, then stroked my temple. "Morning."

"Is it?" I asked, looking out at the gray sky. It was difficult to tell what time of day it was since we were under a constant cloud cover. "I should go to the shop."

"You're already late." He nibbled on my neck and kissed the area when he was done. "Last night was amazing. I've never had anyone ride me like that."

I'd never ridden anyone like that either, but I wasn't going to tell him. "You weren't too bad yourself."

His fingers trailed down to my navel, feathering touches lower until wetness gathered. He lowered his mouth to my ear, sending a shockwave of pleasure down my spine. He pressed a finger against the top of my groin. "I want to taste you next time."

My breath hitched. "Who says there will be a next time?" I asked all too unconvincingly.

He merely smirked in response.

I moved out from under his touch, unable to stop myself from wanting to climb on him again. "I really should bathe."

He relented, lying back against the pillows. "I'd be happy to join you."

I smirked. "I'm sure you would."

"It must have been difficult, to have grown up with a priest for a dad," I stated, desperate for a topic change.

He shrugged nonchalantly. No answer.

"I assume he wouldn't approve of our activities last night."

The corner of his lips curved, releasing me under his grip. "No, he wouldn't. He thinks sexually wanting women are succubi in human form."

I lifted an eyebrow, feigning confusion. "What's that?"

A playful smirk played on his lips. "Female sex demons." He trailed his finger up my neck to my hairline and tucked a lock of hair behind my ear. "You don't need to worry about those. One wouldn't dare come near this town. My father's not just known for hunting witches, you know."

"He hunts demons too," I realized aloud.

He shrugged again. "They're the same thing. Witches just hide their true natures better."

Rage simmered under my cool exterior. "Supposedly."

He shrugged.

I blew out a tense breath. "How does he hunt these succubi?"

"He traps them inside cursed objects, which are hard to come by in Salvius." He half laughed, then sat upright. "You know, I don't really fancy talking about my father while I have a gorgeous woman lying at my side." He leaned in, trailing a kiss along my collarbone. "I'm not sure I want to do any talking at all."

I pressed a finger against his lips, stopping him mid-kiss. "Humor me," I pleaded. "Tell me, how do you know witches are demons? I've heard they're not demons at all, but the result of ancient gods and humans having children together."

He laughed softly. "Rumors created by them to hide their true natures."

"I've read it in historical textbooks dating back centuries. I doubt it's all a blanket lie. I mean, it doesn't explain why there's an entire land of witches to our east, and they even created a barrier to protect humans."

His forehead creased. "I… They don't want us hunting them again."

"Surely if they're demons and there are hundreds of thousands of them, then couldn't they easily beat us? I don't see why they'd be afraid of us."

"A century ago, we burned witches at the stake, and in turn they killed us, even binding their grimoires with our skin," he explained, though I already knew all of it.

"Strange." I paused, and his blond eyebrows flicked upward. "How so little has changed since then. Witches are no longer hunting us, and yet here we are, in a town with gallows erected, and witches aren't even given a fair trial."

"They shouldn't be in our kingdom." He sat upright against the blue headboard. "If they had any sense, then they'd go to be with their own."

"Maybe they have a good reason for staying."

"Like what? Are you a sympathizer or something?"

"No." I swallowed thickly. I'd pushed him too far. "I just like to question things. I don't see why I, nor anyone else, should accept anything as truth without digging a little deeper."

He loosed a sigh, then kissed my temple. "Calm down." The small act tensed my shoulders.

He was treating me like a fucking idiot. I always did have a hard time controlling my temper. "I won't. I'd rather have my own mind than just follow the herd." I climbed out of bed, doing my best to shrug off my annoyance. "I assume you've arranged for a carriage to come."

He put his hands in the air. "I'm not attacking you. You're right. It is good to question things, and yes, I have sent for a carriage." He watched me scramble for my clothes, scoop them into my arms, and run into the bathroom. There was little point in hiding my body from him now. He'd seen and touched every part of it.

Once I was back in my dress, I emerged from the bathroom, tying my hair up. "Good."

He'd dressed too and was pushing back his hair. "Except the carriage won't arrive for a couple of hours yet."

"Fantastic."

"I'll make you some breakfast," he said quickly.

I chewed it over. "It better be good."

A hint of a smile crossed his expression. "Yes, your highness."

I almost laughed, but I caught myself.

I looked at him over my eggs after he finished serving us. "When do you leave for training?"

"In a few weeks. My fathers pushed the date forward. The high priest is coming soon, and everything stops when he comes to town."

Interest piqued, I leaned in. "When exactly?"

"I can't recall. I'll know once I go home though. Every preparation is being made for it, so I'm sure it'll be soon."

I scratched my nail against the surface. "You don't like this priest…"

He shrugged. "I don't hate him, but my father gets so uptight when he arrives."

"How long will he come for?"

"He usually stays for a week, sometimes ten days. He never lingers too long. I only wish my father wasn't so ready to lay his life down for the man. Next to Zerheus himself, he sees him as a saint."

"He is a priest," I said, smiling. "He's been taught to idolize and not question those higher than himself."

His eyes narrowed, and he placed his fork next to his plate. "You sure do have a lot of opinions."

"And thank Zerheus for it, or this conversation would be extremely dull."

His lip wavered, then curled upward as he scoffed a laugh. "Please, tell me how you really feel."

I grinned, my mood lightening when compared to thirty minutes ago. "Surely you must have thoughts about the church.

You said yourself you don't want to be a hunter, and yet you're going along with it. I think you've been told you can't have your own thoughts so many times, you've grown to believe it."

His lips parted, then closed as he leaned back in his chair. "I do have my own mind."

"Then prove it," I said in challenge, and his eyes widened. "Tell your father no to becoming a hunter."

He exhaled harshly, leaning forward and picking up his fork once more. "I can't."

"Why?"

He played with his eggs, moving them around his toast. "It's complicated."

"Most things are."

He glanced up, then back at his breakfast. "It's not any of your business."

"I might be able to help you."

"How could you do that?"

I took a bite of egg and tapped my fork against my plate. "I don't know yet, but I'm pretty resourceful. If you don't tell me, I can't help you."

He stiffened momentarily. "I appreciate the sentiment, Victoria, but this is my business. I'm not being forced into becoming a hunter. It wasn't fair of me to place that burden of a secret on you, that I didn't want to become one. I shouldn't have said anything."

I reached across and grabbed his hand. The movement reeked desperation, but I didn't care. I was so close to getting him to open up, and Cas said I needed to get him to trust me. "I don't want to see you give up anything you don't want to."

His eyes searched mine, something changing in them. "Victoria..."

I prayed to Thalia. "Does this have anything to do with the scars on your back?"

He tensed, releasing my hand from his.

I knew I'd gone too far before I could take back the words.

"They're nothing." He pulled the napkin from his lap and dropped it on top of his plate, then stood. "I'm feeling a little unwell. I'm going to lie down until the carriage arrives. Please, feel free to play." He gestured toward the piano. "Or wander the area."

I stood, screeching my chair back as he walked to the room where we'd spent the night. "Elijah."

He didn't look back. It had been a gamble bringing it up. I wished I could show him I already knew the rumors and it didn't change the way I saw him. He was still the enemy, but it made me almost feel sorry for him. I closed my eyes, licking the salt from my lips, and downed a glass of freshly squeezed orange juice. It was all or nothing. We didn't have long before the high priest came to town, and we needed to make Damian as unstable as possible until then.

I drank a glass of wine for courage. I had to succeed. He needed to trust me completely, to feel something more for me, so when I pulled out the final puzzle of our plan, Elijah would be on my side, no questions asked. He had to see his dad as the monster.

I blew out a shaky exhale, then walked to the door, clearing my throat when I entered. He was lying on his back, one leg bent and the other straight, his hand resting over his forehead.

"I'd prefer to be left alone."

I swallowed my pride and everything other emotion that simmered under the surface. It wouldn't work if I saw him only as a Shaw. Compassion couldn't be faked, and I wasn't unfeeling. I closed my eyes, finding solace in the darkness as I searched for that part of myself, the one I didn't show anyone, not even my family. Maybe occasionally Ember.

My heart skipped a beat when I opened my eyes. Elijah wasn't the worst person there was. He was a little ignorant and acted like an asshole on occasion, but it was an act. I was certain of it. Underneath it all, he was a man who was hurt and trapped doing something he didn't want to, forced to take care of his brother who was going off the rails.

I sat next to him, looking up at the ceiling. "When I was younger, something happened." I slowed my breathing, although my heart raced. "My mother almost died because of something I did. I'd put my whole family in danger, and I never could correct it. After that, I spent years feeling utterly powerless."

"What did you do?"

I dug deep. I couldn't tell him how she'd used a dark magic spell to harm another and it had come back thrice upon her. "I accidentally gave her some rare poison when I was playing doctor with a friend. I got into Cas's apothecary kits and found some unlabeled liquids."

"Who's Cas?"

Shit. My eyes bulged, and I ran cold. "An uncle. He was the one who got my brother interested in medicine."

"Oh, well I'm sure she forgave you. She was your mother."

"She did, but it didn't change anything. Her health slowly deteriorated, until she died. She lived in misery—I know it—and I couldn't do a thing about it."

"How old were you?"

"Eleven when the incident happened," I said. "Old enough to know better."

He stared up at the ceiling too. "You were just a child."

"It doesn't take away from it. I spent years feeling helpless. I was trapped in a house I didn't want to be in, constantly confronted with the physical result of what I had done." I dug my nails into my palm, leaving half-crescent marks, and the pain sparked through my fingers. "I did everything I could to look after my family, but in the end, I couldn't save them."

"You seem like a good sister to me."

I thought about Ember, and my heart hurt. "I could be better."

"I feel the same way, about Corbin, but there's only so much we can do."

"Perhaps, but it doesn't stop me from feeling like a failure."

His hand flinched in my direction, but he didn't reach out. "I feel the same way."

Silence hung between us as thoughts flickered in my mind. "Whatever is going on, with your scars"—I grabbed his hand before he could distance himself—"and the real reason you're agreeing to be a hunter even though you don't want to, I want you to know you're not alone. I may not be the strongest person, but I can withstand a storm or two."

His fingers trembled, and I swore he was going to pull away from me, but he stayed still. "I see that."

"You don't have to be strong around me." I turned my head to look at him, and the compassion in my eyes was real. "You can let yourself just be. I'll never judge you, and nothing you tell me will change how I see you."

He glanced at me and back at the ceiling. "I'm not trying to be mysterious." He pressed his lips together until they turned white, his fingers jolting under my touch. "The truth is just layered."

I looked at the clock on the nightstand. "It seems we still have some time until the carriage arrives."

"Stop."

I sat upright, placing my hand on his chest, the other on his face. "Okay," I answered breathily.

"Why do you care anyway?" he asked, his jaw tensing. "You run hot, then cold and expect me to believe after one night you suddenly give a fuck about me."

I didn't loosen my grip. He was fighting back. His eyes glittered fear, the crease between his brow deepening. "I do care."

Is that what he needed to hear?

"I care about you," I said.

"This is ridiculous," he said, this time with a crack to his voice and a gloss to his eyes.

"Don't push me away," I begged as he sat upright, moving me off him. He was angry, and I knew it had nothing to do with me. "Help me understand."

"Victoria, drop it," he warned, and normally I would, but this was my mission. I had to get him to fully open up to me. I hated pushing on anyone's boundaries, but feelings didn't matter in the grand scheme of things. "You know what, it's good with me. Keep pushing everyone away, be alone forever." I grabbed my jacket and moved toward the door. "Stay in here and keep your secrets. You are so afraid to let me in, and don't pretend it's just me, because I've heard rumors about you, Elijah. You've slept with many of the women in this town, eligible or not, and refuse to marry, refuse to commit in any way."

"And you think you're the one who could change that? How naive on your part."

"No, I didn't think that, and I didn't expect to like or care about you but here I am, although you're making it easy to regret that."

"You should regret it."

"Well, I don't." I crossed my arms over my chest.

"You're relentless."

I chortled. "You're no picnic, you know."

"Last night was a mistake."

Ouch. "Why? If you don't care about me, then it shouldn't be a mistake." His fingers flexed at his side.

"It was a mistake," he said, turning slowly, "because it isn't worth this hassle."

"You're the one who wanted to bring me up here," I said. "I only tried to get to know you, and I may have pushed a little too hard, I know..."

"Why do you keep pushing me?"

My chest tightened. If this was my anxiety, it had a knack for showing up at exactly the wrong moment. I clutched my chest, my eyes glossing with tears.

"Victoria?" His suspicious tone drawled out my name. "What's wrong?"

"Get away from me." I pushed his hand away when he reached toward me.

"I shouldn't have shouted."

Voices filled my head. I closed my eyes to shut them out, but they were stronger than ever. Reality distorted and fragments of our conversation lingered, but only threads, nothing tangible to hold onto.

"Victoria." His voice sounded distorted in my ears. I dropped to my knees. "I'm sorry."

I pressed my fingers against my temples. "It's..." I was breathless, unable to form a sentence. I searched my mind, but it was broken, and then as if nothing had happened, everything snapped back to normal.

My eyes bulged, and my breath hitched. What the fuck was that?

"Victoria." His panicked stare landed on my watery eyes. "I'm getting you out of here. I'll carry you if I have to."

"No." I swallowed hard, tracing a finger down my throat. I found my balance and let out half a breath between my barely parted lips. "It was nothing."

"Don't." He white-knuckled the back of a chair. "I went too hard on you."

I realized I could use my sudden sickness to my advantage. "I feel unwell sometimes, and stress can exacerbate it."

"Here." He led me back to bed and helped me sit. "I'll get you some water."

"Thanks." I lowered my head as he hurried from the room. Was it the insanity coming back in bursts from the hexed bag and sacrifice in the forest? I'd been tampering with dark magic more than I ever had, and I knew the toll it took, but I hadn't thought it would be this sudden.

Elijah returned with a glass of water and some bread and cheese. "Here."

I ate some of the bread, but my appetite wouldn't allow for much. I placed them on the nightstand and touched my cheeks. My face was deathly cold. "Do you ever feel like you're going insane?"

"No."

"Yeah, that'd be crazy."

His eyebrows knitted together. "Maybe you're not fully recovered. Do you want to lie down?"

"No. I'm feeling much better, really."

He sat next to me, dipping the bed. After a minute, he clicked his tongue. "About earlier, I do care about you, and it's been a long time since I have cared about anyone in this way…" He entangled his fingers. "You make me nervous, if I'm being honest, and I only got defensive because I don't want to talk about that part of my life. Not yet."

"I make *you* nervous?"

"You're so forward and open-minded. You call me out on things, and you're funny."

"I've never met anyone like you, and I'm terrified I'll mess things up. The people I care about have a habit of her getting hurt."

"How so?"

"Let's just say no one has lasted long in my life, except for my brother and father, and those relationships are nowhere close to functional." His shoulders dropped back. "I don't want you getting hurt."

"Can you let me worry about that?" I couldn't help but smile. "I can handle my own, believe it or not."

"Oh, no." A ghost of a smirk played on his lips. "I believe it." He gazed up as if lost in thought. "When you played for me yesterday, that song… it was like I heard it before. I kept thinking throughout the night of where I'd listened to it before, then it hit me. I hadn't."

I nodded slowly. He couldn't have because I'd created it.

He continued. "It spoke to the emptiness in me, showing me feelings I knew all too well, and now I understand why. You have the same pain in you. From what you said. I didn't want to admit it before."

"I shouldn't have pressed you about the…" I was afraid to finish the sentence.

"Don't be. You're curious. Anyone would be, and it's why I never take my shirt off around anyone but my brother."

I stayed quiet, biting at the inner lining of my lip.

"Don't pity me," he said quickly. "I'm not the one who should be pitied. There are those with far worse scars."

"Like Corbin?" I asked.

He looked at his feet. "Yes, like Corbin."

Twenty-Two

Elijah

The servants had already begun hanging decorations for Noelle, though I was sure the early display had more to do with the high priest coming to visit rather than Father being in a festive spirit.

Adeline found me as soon as I returned from taking Victoria home, her fingers shaking as she attempted to clasp them together. "Thank Zerheus you're here."

"What is it?"

She gulped, and a shiver ran down my spine, making my skin crawl. Her eyes crinkled in the corners, and her blue eyes glossed. "I'm sorry."

Had someone died? "Adeline, tell me."

She breathed in deeply, her voice barely a whisper. "It's Master Corbin."

My throat closed over.

"He came back early, looking for you. He said he had news, but Father Shaw found him first, and they went to his study, and

I'm not certain what happened, but he's been in the bathtub since. No one's been allowed to go into his room."

Vomit climbed up my throat. We both knew what had happened. I hurried past her and up the grand staircase.

I should have been here. I shouldn't have gone to the cabin, knowing Father was looking for my brother, but I assumed with him asleep on the sofa and Corbin being out late like normal, they wouldn't cross paths. They usually didn't.

Bracing myself for what I was about to see, I held my breath, creaking the door open. The bathroom door, connected to his room, was slightly ajar. Water seeped under the crack. I swallowed thickly. "Please don't be dead," I whispered under my breath, shakily pushing the door open.

He was as white as the sheets crumpled on the ground next to the free-standing tub, where watered-down-crimson puddles surrounded it. He wasn't moving, and my heart stopped before I could take another step.

Goose bumps spread along my arms, every hair erect as my heart sank into my stomach. This couldn't be happening. I forced one foot in front of the other until I was at his side, grasping his hand in mine. He was warm enough, which told me there was blood still pumping through his body, but I reached up to his mouth to make sure and sighed when I felt his shallow breaths against the back of my hand.

As I pulled him up and out of the water, my jaw slacked, horror creeping through my veins, turning my blood to rage. Thick, deep cuts were slit across old scars, and chunks of skin were missing.

"Brother." I shook him, but he didn't respond. He could die. Sandra was the one who'd taken care of us before, but now, with his wounds this many and deep, I didn't have anyone. Our father would never allow for the doctor to come, else he'd have called him already. No one could know about this, except for those he deemed beneath him. It didn't matter if the servants guessed.

I searched my mind, panic seizing every part of me. There was still someone I could send for—someone I could trust, because Zerheus knew how long my brother had.

***

Victoria arrived with her brother, holding an apothecary kit, a little over an hour after I'd sent for them. Eva came in behind them and gasped. I didn't expect her to bring the younger sister, but it didn't matter. They were here, and that was what was important.

I held my brother in my arms, having moved him to the bed. I'd tried everything to keep him awake, but he'd barely let out a grunt. In all our punishments, I'd never seen one half as severe as this.

"Help him," I begged, my voice cracking. I cleared my throat and Victoria looked at me, holding her fist to her mouth.

Ambrose sank beside Corbin, working with Eva on pulling out various ointments and leaves and placing them on his back. He administered a needle, while Eva fed my brother sips of water.

"Can I do something?" I asked, wringing my hands.

"Not right now," Ambrose said, wiping the sweat from his forehead on the back of his sleeve.

Victoria rested her hand on my shoulder, sitting next to me on the sofa as I watched them. "Thank you for coming," I said, my voice still shaking. I no longer cared if she knew—although none of them asked how this had happened—and Victoria had already guessed as much this morning.

She ran her hand from my shoulder down my back. "He's going to live."

I dropped my head in my hands. "I should have been here. What sort of life is this?"

"You shouldn't blame yourself, but I know that won't change how you feel," she said and hung her head. "Ambrose is going to want to keep watch on him overnight."

I ran cold. Our father would never allow them to stay with him. If he even knew they were here… No, I didn't want anyone getting hurt by him. I had to get Corbin away from here. Even if he cut us off for leaving and sold the club anyway, as he liked to shove in my face, it was all in his name. I could still make a name for myself. I was business savvy. Corbin was old enough to help. I'd find a way, and once he was out of here, I would come back and teach our father for ever laying a hand on him—on us.

"You can come to our home," she said slowly, as if she could sense my reservations. "We can take Corbin in a carriage once he's well enough to withstand the ride."

I looked at my brother, drooped over Eva's lap, her hands in his black curls. "If he will be. He's sustained a lot of injuries."

"More reason why we should get him out of here."

I couldn't agree with her more. "We will take him in a couple of hours, once night falls." I stood, balling my fists. "I'll make sure none of you are interrupted. I need to take care of something."

"Elijah." She grabbed my hand.

"I'll be back," I said, pulling my hand from hers. I did not look back as I stormed for the door.

***

It was an hour until my father arrived back at the study. I held the whip—still wet with my brother's blood—in one hand and curled my other into a fist. He walked inside, pushing his graying-blond hair out of his face. "Elijah." His gaze landed on the whip. "Have you come to hurt me?"

"You have some fucking nerve."

He shook his head, sighing as he poured himself water. As if my threat meant nothing. "I did what had to be done. Your brother will thank me one day."

I took a step forward, my jaw clenched. "Are you joking? You should see him. You could have killed him."

"You know better than anyone that my punishments always fit the crime."

"What crime was worthy of such brutality?"

"Witchcraft."

I froze, rage licking through my every vein. "I should have expected nothing less. What did he do? Cross paths with a black cat? Throw a dramair into a well for luck? Everything is fucking witchcraft to you."

His eyes darkened, making the scars around them more pronounced. "I found a hexed bag under my mattress. It had been there for some time." He scowled, pulling it out of a small wooden trunk on his shelf.

I looked at the pouch and then the contents when he poured it out. "What the—"

"Your brother has been practicing. Don't ask me for how long, but I know he has. A servant found a grimoire in his room. You're lucky a whipping is all he got. I could have put him on trial, even executed him for his crimes, but I showed him mercy. He is, after all, still my son."

I white-knuckled the whip. "You're insane, and that servant was mistaken. He wouldn't be involved with witchcraft, and even if he was, it doesn't mean anything. He's not a witch, so he can't do magic."

"He can call upon them, summon demons into this world. There are rituals in the grimoire meant for it."

"He wouldn't do that, and it doesn't matter. He doesn't deserve to be beaten to an inch of his life."

He slammed his fists against the tray holding his water jug. "He deserves what I say he damn well deserves. That hexed bag was meant to harm me. I've been getting nightmares every night—unable to sleep well. It's only when I slept downstairs and didn't suffer did I realize there was something wrong with my bed, so I searched and found the bag. It contained my hair." He drank his whole glass of water, gripping it so tight, I was worried it would break in his hand. "Your brother sought revenge against me because he thinks he's being singled out. How much further would he have gone? Corbin may have summoned a demon or harmed others. One taste of witchcraft can send a man crazy. That one hexed bag wouldn't have been enough. I told you he had these tendencies in his blood, but no one listened to me."

"You still can't know it was him."

"I know it was him. I wouldn't have beat my own son if I believed someone else might have been responsible."

"Bullshit."

"Watch your language."

"Or what? You'll punish me? You can fucking try." I squared my shoulders, challenge glittering my eyes.

"You're a big man now, is that right?" He laughed, taking one step closer. "I don't punish without good reason. If you hurt me, then you are the monster. I've done nothing wrong."

"You never do, do you?" I took a step, closing the distance between us. "Corbin could have died." I lifted the whip in the air, anger pulsing through every inch of me. "How would you like it? Being whipped to an inch of your life?" I swiped it through the air and it sliced against his face. I pulled it away, trailing my gaze along the wound bleeding from his eye to the corner of his mouth. He cupped his cheek, looking at me through wide eyes.

Before he could say anything else, I punched him in the nose, feeling his bone crunch under my knuckles. Blood spattered everywhere and he bent over, holding his face. "We're leaving." I threw the whip down. "Feel lucky that's all you got."

"S-son." The wobble in his voice paused me if only for a second, but I forced myself out the door, rubbing my knuckles as I ordered two carriages to be prepared.

I had no idea where we'd go after tomorrow, but we had a place to stay tonight. I didn't think he'd be stupid enough to hurt someone we cared about—though that list was short, for that reason—or send the church after us. The high priest would be coming soon, and he wouldn't want what happened to become public knowledge.

Victoria glanced at my hand when I reached the room. "I assume we'll be leaving now."

"I'll pack us both a bag." I looked at Ambrose. "Any news?"

He shook his head and again wiped the beads of sweat from his forehead with the back of his sleeve. "We've stopped the bleeding, and we're giving him water. He will recover, but it will take some days before he can stand again."

"Thank you, truly, for coming." I closed my mouth, not knowing what else to say. How else could I express my gratitude? I'd already propositioned Ambrose in his shop the day I went to see Victoria, offering for him to become a doctor and that I'd pay for all the training, but he'd refused.

Eva stormed over to me, pointing a finger at my chest. "Where's your dad? I know he's the one who did this. Corbin confided in me all his secrets. I'm going to hurt him and see how he likes it."

"Don't," I said quickly, a breath catching in my throat. I dreaded to think what he'd do to her if she threatened him. "He's been taken care of."

She bared her teeth. She was Victoria, but on cocaine. "*You* should have taken care of *him* a long time ago. This is your fault too."

"Eva." Victoria scorned, but I bowed my head.

"She's right."

Eva's face reddened, and her nails bit into her palms. "I know I am. Pray your brother recovers." She spun on her heel, her dark ponytail swishing behind her. "Or I won't hesitate to make sure your dad never hurts anyone again."

I watched her walk away, feeling smaller with each step. Despite all the hurt and anger, I was glad Corbin had found a friend who truly cared about him—even if she hated me.

Victoria stepped to my side, giving her sister a look. "Emotions are running a little high. Excuse my little sister."

"The carriages are ready," I said, changing the topic and wanting us to get out of there before things could get any more charged.

Ambrose and I carried Corbin down the steps, who'd at least come around enough he could help hold up his own weight. Eva and Victoria walked behind us, and I swore before we left the room, I saw them all exchange looks, and in them was something almost sinister.

Who wouldn't be furious after seeing what Father had done? I'd never felt so ashamed, mostly of myself because I should have put a stop to it a long time ago, instead of fooling myself into thinking it wouldn't happen again.

I'd been wrong. And it had almost cost me my brother.

Twenty-Three

Victoria

I waited until Elijah and Corbin were both asleep before creeping to the kitchen. Cas poured himself and Alex a tea, who tapped her foot against the ground repeatedly when she saw me.

"What are we going to do about Damian?"

"Not kill him," I said, holding my stare on hers until she relented. "We have a plan."

"Corbin could have died today."

"I thought you didn't care about him."

Her eyebrows flicked upward. "He's nothing like the rest of his family."

"Elijah cares about his brother."

She scoffed. "Oh yeah, you can tell."

Cas interrupted. "Now, now. Let's not argue among ourselves." He placed a tray of cookies on the table, and Alex snatched up two. "I think it's time to enact the next part of our plan."

I nodded. "It's the perfect timing. Elijah trusts me, hates his father, but there's only one problem. He won't be at the house to see it unfold."

Alex blew out a long exhale. "We'll need to find a way to get him there then."

"We don't want the church hunting us," I said. "Only him."

Cas licked his lips. "We make it personal, use his sons against him. We have them here, at our house. He doesn't have to know we won't hurt them."

Alex rolled her eyes. "Great idea, except *he* doesn't care about them… genius."

"He does," I replied, "in his own very fucked-up way. He will especially protect them against witches." I made a face, and she almost smiled.

"How will you protect yourself?"

"I'm going to make new jewelry. The spell on ours is wearing thin. He won't be able to detect my magic with them on." I grabbed a cookie and nibbled on the oat corner. "I'll boil his blood should he attempt anything, and threaten his sons." I gave Cas a creditable nod. "Now, we need to quieten our voices. We can't have them know anything, which means no practicing spells under this roof. We risked enough performing some on Corbin."

Alex held her stomach. "At least he'll survive now. I wonder if his dad knew how close his son was to death. He wouldn't have made it had we not intervened. I shouldn't have let Corbin take my grimoire…"

"Your what?"

Cas growled. "He took your grimoire?"

"Well, it's a long story but—"

"Does he know about us?" My eyes bulged, and Cas held his breath.

Alex licked her lips, slowly sitting at the table and entwining her fingers together. "He doesn't know we're *real* witches."

Cas took the seat across from her. "Oh good, just the fake kind then."

She rolled her eyes. "He knows I dabble with witchcraft. He caught me trying to hex my teacher, and I just told him I like to try to do these spells but that I'm not a witch."

I crossed my arms over my chest. "Alex, humans playing with witchcraft is just as punishable as being one. If he tells anyone—"

"He won't," she stated. "As I said before, he's not like his dad or his brother."

"Elijah isn't like his dad either."

Cas turned his attention to me. "Don't tell me you're catching feelings too?"

"No." I clicked my tongue. "But I'm not going to lump him in the same category as Damian. He's not a murderer and doesn't share the same hatred."

"Except for thinking witches are demons," Cas said.

"He doesn't know any better."

Alex shrugged. "Neither did Corbin, but he's open-minded."

"Good for Corbin," I snarked and grabbed another cookie. "I'm going to take a bath and after, go to the woods to perform the spell."

"No." Cas stood, screeching his chair back. "A lot of the humans are in the woods. It's hunting season, and many are gathering logs for their fires."

"I'll find somewhere else." I paused. "Somewhere closed off from everyone else."

Alex bit her lip, sucking it between her teeth, and sighed. "I know a place."

I arched an eyebrow. "Do tell."

"It's this abandoned house. It's so far out in the forest, I doubt anyone will be out there, and most of the people in this town are scared to go anywhere near there."

Cas tapped a finger against his chin. "You're talking about that haunted mansion, correct? I've heard some talk about it in the church community. A lot of murders happened there."

I dragged the pointed end of my nail down my chin. "It's perfect. Lots of energy to take from too. It'll help power my spell."

"Does nothing frighten you?" Cas asked.

I paused. "Only humans."

Alex looked down at her lap and then climbed her gaze to the ceiling, seemingly lost in thought. "I should check on Corbin."

I grabbed her wrist when she stood. "You better make sure he doesn't tell Elijah about your grimoire."

She ripped her wrist from my grip. "He won't."

We watched her leave, exchanging a look. We both knew the grimoire was the reason Corbin had almost died, but shoving it in Alex's face felt cruel, even for us.

"I'm going to the house."

"Now?"

I looked at the lead-paned window. The snow drifted down outside, swirling the horizon into a flurry of white. "It might be best to wait until morning."

"Finally, a good idea." He poured himself a tea. "I'll make you one." He handed it to me, and I breathed in the peppermint wisps of steam. "We're almost there, sister. Once you show the high priest how unstable he is and I begin filtering those rumors through the community, everything will come tumbling down. After, we can kill him."

I forced a smile, but my stomach was in knots. My heart a little heavier as I sipped on the tea. Ember. I couldn't bring myself to think of her most nights. It was too painful, and even though we were succeeding thus far, nothing felt good enough. We hadn't reached the end yet, however, and I knew that once I saw him break, it would be worth it. The hole in my chest will have been filled, and I could sleep at night, knowing we took him down. "There's still the townspeople who cheered as she was killed."

"One revenge at a time, sister. Besides, Damian is the one who actually took her soul from this world."

"You didn't see her eyes when she realized the town had turned against her, when she knew death was coming for her. She was so scared."

"I saw," he said slowly. "But then I saw you, and you collapsed to your knees, and the look on your face… I was worried you were going to burn the town to the ground, and Ember was already dead. I knew I had to get you out of there first."

"I never asked if you saw her die," I admitted, feeling a twinge of regret. I wondered if it haunted his dreams too.

"I just lost one sister; I couldn't lose you too. It's what kept me going and getting us back to our family. Our lives can't end with one of us. We still had Mother and Alex."

I swallowed thickly. "I never thanked you for protecting me that day."

"You may be a pain in my ass, but you're still my little sister, and I do… love you."

I made a face and then smiled. "I guess I love you too."

He chuckled. "Oh, the hindrance."

"Exactly."

His smile fell into a frown as he gripped his teacup. "Also, I screwed up with Ember. I encouraged her to get that job, and I didn't listen to you. I couldn't mess up things with the rest of you. She's dead because of me—"

"Cas, no, that's not true."

He scratched the side of his neck. "Don't tell me you haven't thought it."

I had, a couple of times, but I'd never let those thoughts sink in. Because the truth was that if I thought into it too deeply, I realized we were all to blame in some way. "Damian killed her. It's his fault. She was an adult, as much as I hate to admit it. She made her own choices, and her actions were her own. None of us could have known what would happen as a result of them."

"I'll try telling myself that tonight."

"You haven't been sleeping well?" I asked.

He shook his head. "Terribly, but we all have. You haven't noticed?"

I looked at the floor. I'd been so focused on our revenge and myself that I hadn't. "It looks like I'm the bad sibling."

"We're all trying our best." He ran his hand through his dark hair. "I'm going to lie down. I need to be up early to redress Corbin's wounds and make more ointment, then go to the shop."

I grabbed his hand before he walked out, and I pulled him into a tight hug, resting my head against his shoulder. "You're a great apothecary, brother, and an even better person. I don't always say it, but you're doing a good job with the business and looking after everyone."

He patted my back, then squeezed me tighter before stepping back. "If you're being nice to try to get out of your next shift, forget it." He winked and left the room. As soon as he was gone, I drank my tea and headed upstairs. Elijah was asleep on my bed. I reached into my babies' cage and pulled out Ebony.

"Hey, baby." She curled around my fingers, and Buttercup looked up at me. "I'm still mad at you," I whispered to the cage, and Buttercup curled up. I rolled my eyes and pulled her out too. She hissed at first but slithered up my arm and settled around my shoulders.

I suddenly felt the urge to play a song. My heart was full, and I had no outlet for the emotions tightening inside of me. My violin, which Cas had kindly bought me to replace the one I'd left at our old house, was downstairs, and there was an old piano in the living room, but some of the keys were broken.

A bath might be better instead. I put the snakes back into their cage, replaced their water, and undressed.

"Love," Elijah said softly, making me jump. I turned, holding my bundled dress against my front.

"You could have let me know you were awake."

"You were so happy, petting your babies, was it?" He suppressed a smirk. "Don't worry, as long as they're in their cage, I'm not worried."

"If you wait for them to come to you next time, they might take to you. More likely, Ebony will. Buttercup never lets anyone other than me and Eva hold her." *And Ember*, I thought. "Not even Ambrose can touch her. Why do you think he made the ointment against her bite?"

"Makes sense." He sat upright, maneuvering his legs over the side of the queen-size bed. "Your room is... interesting," he said, looking around. I'd barely done anything to it.

"I haven't made it my own yet," I admitted, although I doubted I ever would. Redforest wasn't my home, and even if we could stay after Damian's downfall, I doubted I'd want to.

"I was going to say, there's a lack of black."

"There's enough in my heart."

"Oh, I doubt that." He smiled, but I could see the sadness he was trying to keep from his features.

"There's been little change with your brother."

"I know. I went to check on him not long ago." I raised an eyebrow, concerned he'd been eavesdropping, but his expression gave nothing away.

"Eva's with him now," I said. "She's taking care of him."

"I'm glad he has her. He doesn't have many real friends."

I was pretty sure they were more than friends, and I wished I could agree, but a relationship between her and Corbin meant he knew Alex dabbled in witchcraft, and that could put her in danger. She was too trusting, like me as a child—and Ember. A lump formed in my throat. "Ambrose is going to redress his wounds in the morning and get some more medicine from the shop."

"Thank you for letting us stay."

I dressed quickly into my nightgown. "Elijah, about your father."

"Please, don't." He rubbed his knuckles. "What's done is done."

I nodded but didn't push him. "You did right by getting him out of there."

"I should have done it much sooner. Your sister was right about me."

I sat next to him. "It's not as black and white as that."

"You…" He slowed his breathing, holding my hand in his. "Are too good, Victoria."

He had no idea how wrong he was. He pulled me next to him and fell asleep at my side. I felt the steady thumping of his heart as I splayed my fingers over his chest and stared at his blond waves. Growing anxiety bloomed inside of me. I squirmed and felt his heart rate pick up, so I settled still.

***

I walked along the uneven, snow-coated ground, crunching flakes beneath my boots. Skeletal leaves reached through the white, covered with icy blankets. I was breathing slowly, fogging the air in front of my face, when I found the dark, three-story home beyond a flurry of white. Its two towers reached high into the sky, and the wraparound porch creaked and groaned as the wind gusted under the rotting wood and against the rickety fence. I could feel them, the undead. The humans weren't wrong when they called the place haunted. To them, it was a place for ghost stories and to grab a quick scare on a dull evening. For me, it was the perfect host for dark magic. Energies here would allow me to access stronger magic.

Tomorrow I'd show Damian the truth: I was a witch. I'd allow him to see a glimpse of my magic and feel the monster lurking within and would even allow myself to be captured. I'd admit to the hexed bags and everything else I had done, and when he was ready to take me to trial or out me to Elijah, I would feign confusion as to why he was accusing me of such atrocities.

I had to ensure he couldn't detect my magic once I was ready to make him appear as crazy as I knew he was. I needed to make jewelry again, this time four pieces instead of five. No doubt he'd send priests after Alex and Cas. Even if he didn't, I couldn't risk them. With us all protected, he would seem unhinged, accusing just about anyone of witchcraft. With Cas so deeply nested into the church community—and beloved by so many there—they may not believe it at first. Alex has Corbin, who is in love with her. He'd do anything for her; I've seen it in the look in his eyes. He seemed better this morning. He'd protect her against his father, even if things didn't go to plan.

I had to believe that.

As for me, people seemed to like me enough here, but my saving grace was Elijah. I wasn't sure how deep his feelings went for me. He'd never said, but in the touches, kisses, and late-night talks, there was something there. Was it enough to save me? I hoped.

I stepped inside, clutching my satchel with the three rings and a necklace. I would wear two, so if one was to be forced off or fell, I'd have another.

An herbal smell hung in the air of the dank entrance room. Leaves, shards of glass, and discarded newspapers littered the grand stairwell, a shell of white under a half-broken chandelier.

I could feel eyes on me, breaths of air hitting the back of my neck as I moved farther in. I pulled my hair down from its braid, letting it fall around my shoulders.

My satchel wriggled, squeaking and screaming from within. The rat had woken up. I thought I'd spelled it asleep for longer. No matter. I wasn't going to turn back now, not when death had become such a close friend.

I dropped to my knees at the foot of the stairwell on an empty space of the floor and made my markings with chalk against the floorboards. I reached inside my satchel slowly, then grabbed the rat before it could bite me. It angled its neck back before I could grab the knife in my other hand, and it bit me.

Pain seared through my hand, throbbing into the tips of my fingers. Instinct begged me to let go of the squirming creature, but something darker held on. He turned again to bite, but I was faster. I slammed it against the ground and plunged my blade through its center. It stopped moving. Blood sprayed my skirt and the floor and dripped between the boards. It was messier than I'd hoped, but he'd caught me unaware. Before continuing, I grabbed some of the aloes for my spell and spread them on the bite.

"At least you fought back," I said to the dead rat lying in the middle of my symbols.

I pulled black candles from my bag, lit them with matches I'd bought from a little match boy in town, and lined them around the rat in a circle. I placed the jewelry among the blood and began the ritual.

Half an hour had passed when I felt the magic take effect. Gripping hands reached up through the floor, black and smoky wisps of fingers clutching at the soul of the creature I had sacrificed. I moved back several inches. I hadn't seen this happen the first time, but I'd had my eyes closed.

Once they were gone, demons or ghosts from the underworld, which I wasn't sure, I breathed a sigh of relief.

I grabbed the jewelry and cleaned up the mess, then rubbed out the chalk so no one could make out what had happened here.

I took the blade from the rat and cleaned it with an old rag. When I finished, I placed it along with the candles back into the bag. I took the rat outside with me, feeling the eyes of the dead watching me leave. Only they knew what I had done here, and their judging stares bore into my soul.

I placed the dead rat on the ground and covered it in snow once I was far enough away, then I wiped my hands with the snow, melting it to get rid of the blood. I couldn't be seen with my dress like this. I had planned on wrapping the thing before killing it, but it had to have remained asleep for that to happen.

I pulled off my ring and placed it among the trees. A pulse of magic reached through my veins, unyielding and deadly. When I put the necklace on, the magic drained my energy. Each time I spelled the jewelry, I came closer to the edge of madness. I couldn't let it drag me over the edge, but I was so tired.

I rushed back home, my eyelids heavy when I reached the black door and heavy knocker. Alex threw the door open. Elijah was at the shop with Cas, I remembered, and she'd stayed to look after Corbin.

"Sister." Her eyes widened. "What happened?"

"Nothing." I tried to act normal, but my brain felt as if it might explode at any moment. "I just need to lie down."

"It's the dark magic, isn't it?" she whispered, her chest heaving. "Maybe this was a bad idea."

"It is done." I pulled out her necklace and Cas's ring. "Give this to your brother. I'm going upstairs."

"I'll bring you some food."

"No." I stepped onto the stairs, my knees feeling as if they would buckle under my weight. "Leave me to recover in peace."

I barely made it to my room when I dropped onto the bed, and the room warped in my vision. I imagined my snakes talking to me, the furniture moving as I gripped the sheets, trying to hold onto reality.

"It's just the magic," I said repeatedly, until a screaming started in my head—Ember's screams.

When I opened my eyes again, a man I recognized stood over my bed, his dark eyes fixated on mine. "Amberwood," he spat.

My heart hammered. Richard Blackwood, owner of The Black Card, was in my room, unless I was imagining it. "You."

"My family is dead because of you."

"Because of me? My sister is dead because of your family, not mine." I stood, steadying myself against the wall by my bed. "It doesn't matter, because you're about to join them."

Twenty-Four

Elijah

It was late when I left the apothecary. I hadn't expected working there to be so tiring. Ambrose had really had me climbing up to the top shelves all day, but I owed him. I wasn't sure how long we could stay at their house, or how we would make dramair, as we didn't have my father's wealth to reply upon.

I saw him before he could call out to me, sporting a bruise around his nose and a winging blackout under his eyes. The wound stretching down his cheek to the corner of his lip had begun to scab.

"Son," he said when I reached him.

I should have kept walking, but something kept me rooted to the spot. I wanted to ignore it and turn my back on him for good, but the sentiments of a lifetime of memories meant I couldn't quite let go, even after all the darkness and abuse.

I rolled my shoulders back when he approached me on the street.

"Can we talk?"

I hesitated. I really should get back to Corbin, the brother he beat until near death. The thought made my fingers curl my hand into a fist. "I have somewhere to be."

He placed his hand on my shoulder, his eyes crinkling at the corners. "Please."

"Why should I?"

"Because it's important." He looked to our left, then right and pulled me down an emptying street that led off to nowhere important.

I blinked away snowflakes, admiring a wreath of leaves, berries, and fruits on someone's door. "What do you want?" I stopped walking. "There's no one around, so spit it out."

"You're lucky I didn't send anyone after you. I gave you space, even after you *beat* your own father."

My lip curled. "Because you had *beat* your own son—almost to death, I might add."

"For his own good." He shook his head, running his finger along the fresh scar. He looked up in prayer, closing his eyes for a few seconds before opening them again. "I forgive you for what you did. You're not seeing clearly, and Zerheus teaches to forgive family. You aren't seeing clearly, and it's not your fault." He hung his head, the lump in his throat moving up when he loosed a sigh. "Are you staying at the Weathermore residence?"

Something felt wrong. He knew I was. He had eyes and ears everywhere, but his tone… "Why?"

"Where are they?"

My nose wrinkled. "I don't know. At home, most likely, and Ambrose is going to one of those church meetings this evening."

He sneered. "Ambrose."

"Don't you dare hurt them," I warned, as I'd seen that look before, "just because we left you. Don't hurt them because I hurt you, like you did to Sandra."

He grabbed my wrist, his stare latching onto mine, panic glittering with madness. "Sandra deserved what she got." He loosened his grip when my hardened stare found his. "Corbin didn't deserve all my wrath," he admitted. "Only some of it. I realized once you left and where you had gone who's behind all of this." A gust of wind swept between us, flurrying snowflakes into my vision. "The Weathermores are witches, an entire family of them. I believe them to be those who escaped. Victoria is Victoria Amberwood, and the brother, Ambrose, is Cassian. The younger sister is Alexandra Amberwood. It all makes sense now. They are the ones who got away, minus the mother who could be out hiding or dead. They are known to kill their own, you know."

I pulled my hand from his grasp forcefully. "They are not witches. You've gone mad."

He stopped me as I went to turn. "Believe me, son. Your brother got ahold of this." He lifted a grimoire. "The handwriting inside is not his. It doesn't say who it belongs to, but I'm certain it's one of theirs. Perhaps Alexandra's. Why else do you think they got so close to our family? They're seeking revenge against me."

"Why would they do that?"

He ran his hand through his thinning hair and replaced his black hat. "Because I killed one of their own."

"Who?" I asked, recalling how they'd said their parents had died.

"Their sister. She was the one who tipped me off to who would be at the club that night."

"Why would she tip you off, and if she did, then why did you kill her?" I took a step back. "None of this makes any sense."

"Because the Blackwood family was going to kill her brother, and I found out when I staked out their black magic club. She saw me. She knew who I was and panicked when I knew her name, all their names. I was going to kill her that hour, but she made a deal with me instead. She told me everything about the club, about the sacrifices they did and how to get in, the passwords and spells protecting the place… In exchange, I agreed to not harm her or her family."

My heart was racing. "What changed?"

"Nothing. She ran into the woods with her witch lover, one of the Blackwoods, that evening and thought herself safe when we took down the club, but I wasn't going to let her go. I don't make deals with witches. I captured them both and executed them. I was going to hunt her family next, but they'd already gone. Clearly, they were smarter than she was."

I pulled my gloves from my pocket and pulled them on as the winds picked up. "That may be, but my Victoria is not a witch."

"Your Victoria?" He closed his eyes. "Zerheus help us. You have fallen for the girl?"

"I… I don't—that's not important. I know her, and she's good."

"She's tricked you." Fury swallowed his expression. "She seduced you, as witches do, and her family has infiltrated ours. I should have seen it. She even played dress-up in white and came to me the morning after the ball, trying to win me over. I knew then something was off with her, but I thought it was desperation on her part to become a Shaw. Then I found the hexed bag—and the grimoire in Corbin's room—and you turned against me and moved in with them of all people. The timing of when they moved to town, their obvious aliases, aside from Victoria's… It all clicked into place after you left."

"Right there." I pointed out the flaw in his logic. "Why would she continue to call herself Victoria if she really was on the run?"

"I'm not sure." He wrung his hands. "But she's clever. They all are. Lady Abor's blood boiled in my sermon. It was not tuberculosis. The only difference that day was all three of that family were in my church. They did this."

"Father—"

"You have fallen into the arms of our enemies. They are using you to get to me, and you're letting them."

I shook my head, a lump forming in my throat. "I've heard enough. I'm leaving, and if you try to come after them based on your ridiculous superstitions, you'll have to come through me because they've done nothing but help me—and Corbin, who almost died."

"I made a mistake," he said carefully.

"No." I pointed a finger in his face. "People learn from their mistakes. You've been doing this for most of our lives. The only monster here is you." I turned away, my heart racing as I stormed down the road. There was no way he wasn't going to come after them if he thought they were witches, and I had to protect them—protect her.

Twenty-Five

Victoria

I unsheathed my pocketknife, feeling the grooves on the handle cutting into my skin as I gripped it with all my might. "You shouldn't have come here."

"I have nothing to lose," he said between gritted teeth. "My family are all dead. I wondered where you all had run to, so I came here, to finish that hunter myself, when who did I see but you, going around with his son. Traitor."

He was going to give us away. My mind wasn't working well enough to deal with this. Fractures of memories and words distorted my thoughts as I searched for the right thing to do. Why couldn't I get it together? "It's not like that. We're working against them."

"It seems like it." He spat on my carpet, the dirty animal. "Now I'm going to finish what I came here to do." He stepped forward, and I moved back against my bedroom wall. "Your sister's actions will not go unpunished."

"Ember?" I clarified.

"Yes, Emberly." He said her name with more venom than my vianas possessed.

"She died because of you and your son."

"No, no, no. She gave us away to the hunter. I found what she had written down for him the same day we were raided and my family murdered." Tears glossed his dark-brown eyes, so dark they could be black. "She sold out our club and our Chester, who only protected her, to save herself and all of you. The hunter must have found her when she was alone, because whatever he said or did made her spill all our club's secrets. She condemned her own people to save her own neck. Never have I known such cowardice."

I shook my head and backed into the wall. "Ember wouldn't have done that."

"No?" He arched an eyebrow, unconvinced. "Not to protect her family? To protect you?"

I held my breath, my mind swirling. Would she? Had she? If he was right, then she shouldn't be dead. "She was killed by the hunter. Why would he do that if they had a deal?"

"Because she was naïve. He was never going to keep to it. Any of us would have known it, but she was young, and because of it, we all had to die."

"Even if she did," I said, my thoughts a carousel of possibilities, "why would you come after us? He's the only one who killed your family, and she was only protecting hers. Wouldn't you do the same?"

He white-knuckled his own knife. Through the darkness, I caught sight of a trail of spit on his bottom lip, insanity lacing his gaze. "My family is dead!" he shouted, his voice drying. "They are gone, and I have nothing. Nothing. That's why I came here. I've been watching you all for a while. I'd hoped the hunter would finish you first so I could finish him, but even the little stunt I pulled in the church didn't make him suspect. So much for a renowned witch-hunter."

"What stunt?"

"With one of the priest's wives. I'm not sure if she died or not, but I really believed after that the hunter would be screaming 'witches' from the rooftops based on his reputation, but you all wormed your way out of it somehow." Insanity swam in his gaze. "I had enough of waiting, and now I'm here, to kill you all."

"Where have you been staying? How haven't you been caught?"

He gritted his teeth. "In the abandoned house in the forest. I saw you had come, and I followed you back here. I've been making trips, you see. I spied on your sister and the Shaw kid at their academy. She told him all about you and your family, and I was sure he would tell his father, but he didn't. He accepted you."

My heart hammered. "No, she just told him she dabbled in witchcraft, not that she is a witch."

"He took her grimoire; I saw it. A day later, when he left to meet up with her again, I broke into their house and found it in his room. He hid it well, but I made sure to leave it out in the open for the servants to find. I thought at least it would get the hunter's attention, and yet here you all are, alive and well—until now."

"Do you really think you can kill me and get out of this house alive? I have family here."

"I don't care anymore. I've already lost everything. What's more dangerous than a man with nothing to lose? And look, I have dark magic on my side." He flicked his wrist, and darkness danced up from his fingers.

I mirrored him. "You're not the only one."

He bared his teeth, growling softly. He was going to give us away, if Corbin hadn't heard his ranting already. He'd kill me and then who? Alex? Cas? The hunter for sure… and Elijah and Corbin. He had the same dark glint in his eyes like mine, but worse. How much dark magic had he used? He had already embraced the madness, and an unsettling reality hit me; I had to kill him. He would kill all of us.

I caught a glimpse of myself in the standing mirror. My hair stuck outward, frenzied. I had a knife in my hand and murder in my eyes. I could hardly recognize myself.

"Tori? Who are you tal—" Alex's voice echoed through the house as she entered my bedroom. She fell into the wardrobe when Richard ran at her, knife in hand.

I wanted to fight, to plunge my blade into him, but I couldn't move. Every part of me froze, including my voice. I watched as he raised the knife to her throat, and the memory of watching Ember die flooded back, rocking panic through me. My mind split into pieces, and Alex's cries for help were lost to some void I couldn't see inside of myself. I couldn't focus on any coherent thought. No sounds penetrated my mind, and my world gave into blackness as I collapsed to the ground.

I was not sure how long it took me to wake up. All I knew was when I opened my eyes, the world had turned blood red, and my sister was probably dead.

Cas cupped my cheek, shaking me with his other arm. "Sister." The word cracked somewhere in the middle, and I couldn't breathe. He sat me up, and I managed to pull in a breath. "Sister?"

"Cas." I barely exhaled, and my body froze up again. "Alex."

"Alive," he said, assurance thick in his tone. "Richard's dead."

"How?"

He didn't answer at first, and his silence told me something was very, very wrong. "Cas?"

"I came back to dress for my church meeting when I heard screaming." His tears came thick and fast, trailing down his bronzed cheeks. "He cut her throat, and she was bleeding. I grabbed the poker from the fire and stabbed it through his back and stomach." The color drained from his face. "I saved Alex, but she can't talk. He cut her vocal cords. She's bandaged. Corbin was awake—he might have heard everything—and Elijah is probably on his way here." He pressed his fingers to his temples. "Everything's gone wrong. What did he knock you unconscious with?"

Oh gods, he thought I had been knocked out. I had failed to help yet another sister in her time of need. I was useless and didn't deserve the family I had. "I fainted," I admitted and quickly changed the subject. "Give Corbin something to make him go to sleep." A plan was somehow formulating in my muddled mind. I couldn't fail them again. "Look after Alex. I'll deal with Elijah."

He gestured toward Richard's corpse and the crimson-soaked carpet. "What about this?"

"I won't let him up to my room."

"We should run," he said, stilling me into silence. "We will flee to Istinia. Grab Mother along the way like we should have done to begin with."

"W-we can't just go. Your shop…"

"Is nothing without my family," he stated.

My chest ached. "I know."

"Fuck the hunter and all of this."

"If we leave, this will all have been for nothing."

He rubbed his forehead, shaking his head. "I can't argue with you about this. I'm leaving with Alex. I can't force you to come with us."

"I've already lost myself, Cas," I said. "I don't know who I am anymore, or who I am without this to hold onto. I agree you need to go and so does Alex, but if Corbin tells anyone, then the hunter will come after you. I won't let that happen. I'm staying. I'm seeing this through to the end."

"He'll kill you."

"Let him." My heart skipped a beat. "It's how I expected it to end anyway."

His jaw tightened, a muscle feathering under his eye. "You want to die? After everything we've lost, you're going to let yourself get killed. What about me? Mother? Alex? Don't you think we've lost enough?"

"Don't," I pleaded. "I can't go on."

"None of us want to, but we do okay. Please, Victoria, I beg you, as your brother, come with us." He held my hands in his, but I felt nothing. My mind warped and bent, and I realized it was too late for me. Dark magic had already infiltrated my brain and diseased my thoughts. It wouldn't be long until I was gone, and if the last thing I could do was help rid the world of the hunter, then I would. "Don't worry, Cas. I'm going to kill him."

A knock sounded at the door. I ran cold. "Elijah?"

"Make sure he doesn't come up here."

I nodded and hurried downstairs, brushing down my hair on the way so I didn't appear so disheveled. I reached the door, and Elijah's hardened stare met mine. "We need to talk. You're in danger."

My stomach knotted. He walked inside, and I had him follow me into the kitchen, praying Alex wasn't in there. She wasn't. "Why?" I asked... barely.

"My father believes you're all witches, some escapee family of someone he killed. I tried to talk him down, but I'm worried about what he's going to do. When he gets something in his head, it's difficult to have him see sense.

"Thank you for letting me know." I looked to his left. The winter land of white swirled near the black iron gates and small houses, spinning around me. I grabbed the sides of my head, willing for it to stop.

His fingers were on my cheek, his eyes frantic as he searched mine, but I couldn't see straight. What was happening to me?

His voice echoed into my mind as if he were talking underwater. "Let me take you to your room."

Room. My room. Where there was a dead body. My mind ticked over the words slowly, and I managed to stop him before he could half carry me up the stairs. "No," I blurted, tugging him back toward the kitchen. "It's a headache," I lied, and the world warped again. Flashes of seeing Ember dead, mixed with Alex being attacked and a body on the ground, swarmed through my mind, and the darkness inside of me, taken from the magic I'd been using, was latching onto those painful memories. "Please," I pulled him again, struggling to keep ahold of his shirt.

"Calm down, love." He wrapped an arm under mine, and I collapsed against his chest. He held me tight, lifting my feet from the ground, and carried me into the living room. "I've got you." He placed me on the sofa and kneeled in front of me. "Victoria, can you hear me?" He stroked strands from my forehead, tucking them behind my ear. "Should I get your brother?"

"No." He couldn't go upstairs. That much still made sense to me. I pulled him closer, resting my forehead against his. "Stay with me."

"Okay." He stroked the back of my head, holding me tight. "I won't leave you."

It was dark outside when I awoke. Only black rippled between the cracks in the drapes. The pounding in my head was gone, and the room wasn't spinning, so that was good. I looked around, expecting Elijah, but instead spotted my brother half-asleep on the armchair. I rubbed my eyes, sitting up slowly. Had I ruined everything? Had Elijah gone upstairs? Oh gods, Alex… the dead body.

Cas looked at me, bleary-eyed, and straightened himself. "You're awake."

"Did I mess up?"

He lowered his head in his hands and shook them before he looked back at me. "No. It's me who has."

"What happened?"

"I should have seen it before. I've been so focused on our plan that I lost sight of my family."

"What do you mean?"

He swallowed thickly, wringing his hands. "You're losing your mind, aren't you?"

I let out a tense breath. "It's nothing, just a few headaches here and there."

"Don't lie to me."

I fell silent. He knew. I knew. I couldn't hide it, and he was smarter than I liked to think. "Alex."

"Is okay. She's healing."

My heart ached. "Good. Where's Elijah?"

He paused, running his hand through his dark locks. "He's gone."

"Where?"

"I don't know, but he has friends here. He can take care of himself. He's a big boy."

"Damian knows about us. Elijah came to warn me. It takes away our element of surprise."

"I know." He looked at the floor. "He told me before he left. I kept him away from your bedroom until I could cloak Richard Blackwood's body. I performed dark magic, and well… after, my head wasn't right for a bit. I couldn't think straight, and I realized that with you doing dark magic, paired with all the trauma you've been through, you're not okay. You passed out upstairs, and now down here." He lifted a glass jar with only a bit of amber residue sticking to the sides. "I've been working on something new, to help those in asylums who lose time and memories."

I hazily recalled drinking something at some point. Had he awakened me? "Thank you."

"You should have told me. You don't need to take on all the burdens on your own. We're your family; you can lean on us and, at the very least, lean on me."

"I'm used to doing things on my own."

"I'm well aware, sister." He exhaled heavily. The orange hues from the fireplace danced against his skin, flickering in his brown eyes. "I'm taking Blackwood's body out to the woods shortly."

"I thought you said it wasn't safe."

"I don't have a choice. I need a place to bury him. I've cloaked his body from sight. It's my saving grace while the spell lasts."

"I'll help." I tried to stand, but his tortured gaze stopped me in my tracks.

"No. I want you resting. I have some more of this." He waved the jar in his hand. "You should drink it and take it easy. Alex is sleeping, and Corbin didn't let on he'd heard anything, but I'm not entirely convinced. We'll keep him here until we know for sure."

It was pointless arguing. "Be careful."

"Always am." He stood and left the room, not looking back. Whatever he'd made had worked, well enough anyway, that I could think without fractures of the past interrupting my thoughts.

I found my violin on top of the piano and placed it under my chin, closing my eyes and relishing the feel of the wood against my skin. I had so many worries, too many fears, but when I held the instrument, it all melted away—temporary but effective.

As I grazed my fingers along the horsehair bow, I breathed in the polish and let the magic in my veins move my fingers into song, streamlining each stroke. The sound was complicated but beautiful, deep with high notes sliding with each other into a dark, somber melody. Each note pierced my heart, pulling a piece of my soul and putting it into song. In it, I played my grief for Ember, my anger for the hunter, my heartbreak for Alex, and the joy I'd found in our family. I poured out every part of myself until I had nothing left and closed the tune with a final stroke.

Clapping emerged behind me, slow, building. I turned and saw Corbin sitting in the armchair Cas had been in not long before. He stopped and placed his hands on his lap. "Your sister never told me you play. It's masterful really. I've always found such beauty in music."

I placed the violin back onto the piano. "Did I wake you?"

"No, I've been awake for some time."

It was incredible how different he looked than Elijah or his dad. His dark waves curled around his forehead and the tops of his ears. His skin was a couple of shades darker but still far lighter than ours. He was shorter than his brother, not much taller than me at maybe five foot seven, if I had to guess. He also didn't hold the same posture as the rest of his family. He slumped over, his hands relaxed, never fidgeting. "Have you seen—"

"Eva? Yes." He licked his lips. "Her throat has been cut."

"Yes, about that—"

"You don't need to play games with me. I'm not my father or my brother. I don't care about what happens in this house or what you all are. I love Eva, or should I say Alex."

My heart skipped a beat, numbness gluing me to the spot. He *had* heard everything, and Richard Blackwood had been right. Alex had told him everything.

He searched my expression and sighed. "Alex told me," he explained. "I've known for some time."

I opened my mouth but closed it again. What could I say? Was he the one who had told his dad about us? It was unlikely, as he did hate him, unless he was pretending to be close to Alex to learn our secrets.

I swallowed hard, but the lump forming in my throat didn't budge. "I don't know what she's said..."

"She showed me more than she said. I took a beating for researching it after."

I thought back. The grimoire. Alex's grimoire. She'd lied to us about telling him. I was furious, but she had just been attacked, so I couldn't be too mad with her. Not right now anyway. "We're not as bad as you think we are."

"I don't think you're bad people. Alex has a good soul. She's beautiful in every way, more so than all the people in this town combined. She explained to me about the gods and humans having children and the truth about witches. I always knew something was off with what my father said. He always did have a flair for the dramatic."

I almost smiled at the boy. What in the underworld was going on? A small part of me wanted to believe him, only because it would be easier, but I knew what humans were really like. I'd trusted my friend when I was a child. We'd cared for each other deeply, and she had still gone to condemn me to her parents. "Not entirely. We are capable of some unworldly dark things."

"If that's a threat, there's no need. I won't tell about any of you, nor would I ever do anything to hurt Alex."

"If you do, I *will* kill you."

He smirked. "I don't doubt it. I really wanted to thank you, for saving my life. Twice."

"My brother was the one who saved you the last time."

"You helped me, both times. Thank you."

"I know how it feels, you know, to feel so utterly out of control." I sat on the sofa, crossing my legs. "I just mean, I don't judge you for taking the opium; however, I don't want you influencing Alex."

"I don't touch that stuff anymore," he said with promise. "She's changed my life."

You're only seventeen, I wanted to say, and that they couldn't know love yet, but I kept my mouth shut. If his infatuation was the only thing preventing him from telling anyone else our secrets, then so be it. Alex's infatuation, however, could cost us everything if she wasn't careful. "Has she spoken yet?" I asked.

He shook his head. "Whatever your brother gave her sped up her healing, but no words, not yet. I'm confident she will."

"If she can't?" I asked, shuddering at the thought of my baby sister forever losing her voice.

"She will manage. She's a lot smarter than any of us."

I should have taken that to heart. It was sweet, and he was right. "You must understand why we've come here."

"To destroy my father. Yeah, I know, and I don't care. He's as evil as they come, and if I said I hadn't thought about killing him at least a dozen times, I'd be lying. Elijah's the one you should worry about. He may hate him now, but he's always been loyal to our father."

"He hit him for you."

He shrugged. "He loves him. Damian was actually a father to him, unlike me. Elijah looked up to him until the beatings started. Granted, it did pull them apart, but not enough."

I bit the inside of my lip. "Elijah wants nothing more to do with him."

"All I'm saying is when it comes down to it, don't be surprised if he sticks up for Damian. He may hate him, but he won't let his father die."

"I trust him to do the right thing."

He leaned forward, his elbows propped up on both arms of the chair. "I love my brother; he's the only family I have. I won't get in your way with Damian, but if Elijah tries to stop you, all I ask is you don't hurt him."

"I wouldn't hurt Elijah."

His eyebrows flicked upward. "Alex said you don't care about him."

"I don't."

"Hmm." He looked me up and down. "I'm going to check on her. Thanks for letting me stay, and for the talk. I figured you should know, as I'm in your house and I saw her throat. I could only feign ignorance for so long before it became obvious."

I nodded. The kid was smarter than I had given him credit for. "I still don't trust you."

He smiled. "Yet." He walked out and upstairs. I made a mental note to tell Cas as soon as he returned—and for him to keep a very close eye on Corbin—although in my heart, I felt he was telling the truth. Luckily, I didn't follow my heart.

Twenty-Six

Victoria

The hunter was pristine in his robes of white, with a garland made from red and white flowers atop his shoulders. The banisters of the grand staircase were spiraled with garlands similar to the one around the hunter's neck. Mistletoe hung from the doorways, and a fir tree stood at the side of the stairs, around nine feet tall and decorated with fancy ornaments and silver beads. He didn't see me at first, as he directed someone carrying a handful of tinsel, and he slicked back the few hairs at his receding hairline, as if it would help.

"Mr. Shaw," I said, clearing my throat.

He turned on his heel, anger flashing in his violent stare. "Victoria Amberwood."

My eyebrows knitted together. "It's Weathermore. Victoria Weathermore."

He scoffed. "Hmph."

I glanced down, then back at him, confusion flitting in my features. "May I talk with you about Elijah?"

He hesitated, his fingers flexing. The corner of his eye twitched, creasing the new scar that trailed down to his mouth. He wasn't sure, couldn't trust himself entirely. He would want to make certain I was truly a witch. "We can talk in the living room." He gestured, and I followed, holding my breath for a moment.

The potion Cas had created helped immensely. He said it was only temporary, that the madness would return and I would need to control it. As long as I performed no more dark magic, I might have been okay, but we were so close, I could taste it.

We reached the living area, which was decorated in the same reds and whites as the rest of the mansion. He clicked the door shut, then checked the other one was locked. With his back toward me, he let out a low growl. "Why are you here? Where is my son?"

Good. Elijah hadn't come back here after all. I had been banking on that. He must have gone to stay with a friend. "Safe," I said and stepped up behind am armchair, placing my painted nails against the cushioned back. "No thanks to you."

He laughed, turning to look at me. "You have no idea what you're talking about."

I dragged a fingernail across the fibers, smiling to myself. "You were right, you know, about my name."

He stepped forward, and I placed a hand in the air, stealing the air from his lungs. He gasped, dropping to his knees and clutching at his throat. I released the magic, and he drew in several deep breaths.

"I wouldn't do that if I were you," I warned. "I'm not like many of the innocent witches you've slaughtered. No, I'm one of the ones who most likely gave you those scars." I smirked. "Well, not all those scars, as we know. Your son is responsible for one. I'm pretty proud of him for it."

"Filthy demon," he said, lunging for me.

I rolled my eyes, lifting my fingers and stealing his air again. He fought against the magic rather valiantly, not begging even once. I released him from the spell, clicking my tongue as I did. "Damian, Damian, Damian." I loosed a sigh. "I won't give you a third warning. If you want to live to punish me, you're going to have to behave." I closed the distance between us, feeling the dark magic thrum in my veins. "Sit down," I ordered, forcing him onto the sofa, and sat across from him. "You're lucky I'm not finished with you yet."

"What does that mean?" He shook his leg against the sofa, his expression filled with more venom than my snakes.

"It means you may just keep your life for today if you listen."

He leaned forward, challenge glittering in those glacier-blue eyes. "I'm not afraid of you, witch. I've killed more of your kind than years you've been alive."

"I don't doubt it. You killed over half that in one night."

"Ah." He leaned back, amusement taking over his anger, though it still creased his lips. "You're here to avenge your sister. Emberly, wasn't it?"

"Good. You remember."

"Of course I do. She was very helpful."

"You despicable fuck."

"I still remember how her heart felt when it thrummed its last beat between my fingers." He looked up, enjoying himself far too much.

I reached out, closing my eyes until his blood began to boil. Every drop of rage and hatred crawled toward him through my magic, and I delighted in hearing him groan. I released the spell before it could do any real damage and opened my eyes. Sweat beaded his forehead. He clutched his chest, gasping, his venomous glare finding me once more.

I angled my head. "You're a glutton for punishment."

He released his hold on his chest, settling his breathing. "No, witch, I am the punisher."

"Then punish me."

A flash of anger crossed his expression, his lip curling ever so slightly. "Oh, I plan to."

"I'm sure you do. Now, when I leave here, you're going to want to hurt me, to follow me; however, I must remind you, I have your sons."

He gripped the sofa cushion. "If you hurt them…"

"No, no. I'm not you. I don't cause pain for pleasure."

He winced.

"I won't kill them if you don't try to execute me. I'm not the only witch here, you see."

"If you think I will let you leave this town alive, then you're delusional."

I pursed my lips. "Who will inherit the Shaw estate if you have no sons?"

His nostrils flared, but he didn't speak. He stared ahead at paintings on the wall for a good minute before he scowled. "Why come here and tell me you're a witch?"

"You already knew," I said. "I came here to make a deal."

"I don't negotiate with demons."

"Both your sons are at our house. If you try to hurt me now or come after me, I will kill them," I stated, shooting him an extra-hateful look to make sure he understood the seriousness of my statement. "It's your call." I stood and was walking to the door when he shouted after me.

"You think you're clever, don't you? Well, I promise you this: you will regret hurting my family."

I nodded, glancing over my shoulder. "As will you for hurting mine." I walked out, letting out a shaky exhale, and grabbed my jewelry from the table. He hadn't checked me to see if I was a witch. Why would he? I'd shown him my magic, and he'd *felt* it. It was all the confirmation he needed, so we'd wait. There was no way he would do nothing. He'd play the long game, I was sure, especially with the high priest's arrival the next day.

Within a few days, he would go mad from not being able to come after us. He would make plans to get his sons back, which was fine. I wanted him to try to hurt me in front of Elijah. I wanted him to warn people of witches and not be able to prove it, as my magic would be hidden using the ritual jewelry. To have Elijah vouch for me too would help my case. I wanted to drive him crazy, to loosen the screws of his mind until he lost the respect of his peers, his own family pitying and hating him. Then, I would kill him.

The next part was ensuring he lost his mind. Elijah had told me of something that scared the hunter, of his sexual repression and how he'd hurt himself when he felt anything of that kind. I knew what I needed to put the final nail in his coffin.

I walked out of the Shaw mansion and waited a few minutes to be sure. He didn't come after me, which was a good sign—and proof I was right. He wasn't going to run, torches blazing, when his sons could be in danger.

I made my way through the snow, to the edge of the woods and down through the narrowing trees and bare branches until I saw it: the haunted house. It really was the perfect place to perform dark magic, and it would be one of my last rituals. I hoped Cas's potions could hold me together until this was done.

***

The succubus demon appeared within my summoning circle. Her seductive stare landed on mine, her painted lips hooked into a smile. "Did you want to play?"

"No." I placed a hand on my hip, matching her smile. "I've summoned you to play with someone else."

"It doesn't work that way, witch." She stepped forward, her smoky-gray eyes widening. "Unless you want to divulge in our joint pleasure, then you may send me back."

"I know what you want." I looked her up and down. Her curvaceous figure was bronzed under the candlelight. She flicked her blonde hair over her shoulder. They appeared to each person based on what attracted them. I wondered how she would look to Damian, and what his desire was. "You want freedom, and I can help with that."

A flicker of hesitance crossed her expression. "If I did want that, how would you do it?"

"I'm going to give you the body of another."

"Ohh." She grinned, her fangs barely showing between her lips. "You're a dark magic witch."

"I am, and I'm willing to do anything to get what I want."

The glint in my eyes must have told her I was serious, because she nodded. "Who am I seducing?"

"His name is Damian Shaw."

She scoffed. "Even among us lesser demons, his name is whispered in the underworld. Many of my brothers and sisters haven't returned because of him."

"Then see this as the perfect revenge."

She shook her head. "He will trap my soul like he's done to my siblings. I can't help you."

I bit the inside of my bottom lip and glanced at the ceiling. "What if I could promise you even if he did trap you, I would get you out? What if I swear it?"

"A blood bond?" Her gaze snapped to my fingers. "You must be desperate."

My expression hardened. "As I said, I'll do anything to get what I want."

She arched a blonde eyebrow. "Which is?"

I paused for a moment. "Revenge."

"Ah, the second-best motivator."

"Second?"

"To love."

"Then I suppose I'm doing it for both those reasons."

She moved to the edge of the circle, mere inches from me. I could still smell the sulfur lingering on her clothes. "I'll assume he killed your lover."

Chills ran goose bumps along my arms. "Worse. He killed my sister."

"Now that is a motivator."

"Then he tore apart my family, chased us from our home, and he also murdered my cousin."

"I am presuming you don't want me to fuck him then?"

A slow smile spread across my face. "Oh, I want you to do much more than that."

She leaned in. "In my new body?"

"No, that will come later."

"And how do you plan on finding a willing participant?"

I held my breath. "Because the body you will be taking at the end of this all is mine."

Her arms dropped to her sides. "You're willing to give up your soul for your revenge?"

Tears glossed my vision. "What's the point in fighting for a cause if you're not willing to die for it?"

She paused for a good minute before she extended her hand. "You have yourself a deal, witch."

They were such dark, delicately tricky creatures to make deals with. If I did indeed lose my mind, she wouldn't be able to take over anyway; full permission was needed, and for that, the mind had to be whole. If that failed and I didn't lose my mind, then I'd have to trap her, becoming just like the hunter myself. Elijah told me how Damian captured demons, with dark objects, and being witches, we had one in our house: my brother's pocket watch. It was the only way to get out of a blood bond. I wouldn't be killing her or sending her back to the underworld.

As I walked away from the house, feeling the eyes of the dead upon me, a realization snaked up my spine. In all this revenge, I'd become a monster too. I was willing to hurt anyone in my way to get to him, to trap a demon and go back on my deals… to fuck with my own head. Alex could have died, and Cas had become a murderer by killing Richard Blackwood. At the end of all this, I wasn't sure if all of this had in fact been worth it.

Twenty-Seven

Elijah

I cracked the back of my neck, massaging out a knot in my shoulder, and stepped into the club. "Thanks again for letting me stay," I told Charles, who'd allowed me to sleep in his house for the past four days. I'd gone to check on Corbin, and he was making a miraculous recovery, so much I was beginning to think Victoria's brother was a miracle worker.

Victoria had seemed distant when I'd gone to visit her, like she was preoccupied with something else. She'd smiled and said the right thing, but there was a disconnect. She zoned out at the oddest of times, got headaches from nowhere, and slept and cried a lot. Every part of me felt helpless, but she'd asked me to come stay back at the house tonight, and I said I would. She needed help taking care of Eva, whose throat had been cut by some intruder. I should have been there, but Ambrose had told me to leave that night, so I had. I was never going to push my welcome. "I won't be staying tonight though."

"You going back with your father?"

I shoved my hands in my pockets. "No. I'm going to stay with a friend."

He arched an eyebrow. "I'm your only friend."

"I have other friends."

He chuckled, slapping me on the shoulder. "You have people who are afraid of you and those who work for you. There's a difference."

"Maybe it's a female friend."

He licked his lips. "That pretty girl from your ball?"

I couldn't help but smile. "Perhaps."

"Man, you're so secretive nowadays. We used to share everything."

"It's not like that. You'll always be my closest friend, but we don't have to tell each other everything."

"Fine, but I'm always here if you need to talk." He pulled up a stool beside me and tapped his glass against mine. "To friends."

"Friends." I clinked the glass back and downed my drink. "I should go and visit my father though, soon," I said, my thoughts turning back to matters of home.

"Be careful, with him going mad and all." He twirled his finger around, up by his temple.

"My father? Insane?" I shook my head, laughing. "I mean, I joke about it, but he's not actually mad."

"I thought you'd heard." He shrugged. "Sorry, Eli. There's been talking among the priest's wives. My mother has them over for lunch a lot."

I drank back the whiskey and slid my glass for another. I'd spent more time here in the past few days than ever before. "I'll go see him."

"Why did you fall out anyway?"

"Same old," I said, half explaining. "I know you'll do a good job with the club, but I don't want to sell it."

He squeezed my arm. "I know."

I downed the second whiskey before I stood. "Anything you want is on the house," I said at some attempt of control, but we both knew it was futile at this point. The club would soon be his. "I'll come by and grab my things later."

***

Noelle had taken over the mansion. Red flowers lined the paths, white and green garland hung from every surface, fir trees decorated each room, and fake snow had been placed inside to match the outdoors. The smell of cinnamon and chocolate filled the halls.

I bowed when I saw him, then rose slowly. "Your holiness," I said, addressing the high priest when I saw him walking in my direction. He wore robes of satin white and had flowing hair of gray. The wrinkles around his eyes crinkled when he smiled. He sandwiched my hand between his. "Elijah, it is good to see you, my boy."

He always had been kind, kinder than my father, by far. "How has your visit been?"

"Most humbling," he said vaguely. "Your father has been asking after you." He hesitated. "I believe him to be unwell."

"I heard." I nodded. "I'm going to look for him now."

"I will see you in a couple of days, for my final sermon."

"You're leaving so soon?" I asked, and he released my hand.

"I'm afraid so."

I didn't want to ask why. "I will be there."

He smiled again, and I bowed as he walked in the opposite direction, toward the kitchen with his three priests. I hurried up the staircase and to my father's room, where I found him digging his nails into his thigh.

His hair was thinning more than usual. His bony fingers were clasped around each other, his robes looser than the last time I'd seen him. He looked through me and then at me as if he'd seen a ghost. "Son?"

"It's me," I said, my mouth turning dry. I eyed his scar and looked down at my own healed knuckles.

He rushed to me with tears in his eyes, placing his hands on my shoulders. "You're home, away from those wretched things. I've been so worried. I was trying to find a way to get you and Corbin out of there. Where is he?"

"What are you—oh, you think they're witches. That's right." I rolled my eyes. "I see not much has changed."

"They've sent demons into my home." His lip trembled, his eyes unseeing as they moved to the staircase. "A woman comes in the night to..."

"What woman?"

He shuddered. "I don't know, but I think she's a demon. She made me... She tricked me..." He struggled, tears pushing from the corners of his eyes. "I am a good man."

My forehead wrinkled. "There's been talk, that you're losing your mind."

He took my hands in his. "No, I'm not. Who said that? No." He shook his head, hardly proving his point. He glanced at the staircase again and pointed. "There she is."

I looked at the empty space. "There's no one there."

"There was. She was right there." His expression crumpled. "Believe me, son."

I looked from him to the staircase, an unnerving feeling coming over me. He really was losing his mind. "I saw the high priest."

"Yes, he's going this evening to the church. He asked me to stay here today. He said I wasn't in the right state to perform a sermon, but it's only because I'm tired. She doesn't let me get any sleep. She comes in my dreams and—"

I grabbed his arms, my eyes focused on his. "I think you need some help. An herb to make you sleep? I have someone who can get it for you.

"No!" He jolted back. "It's them, isn't it? The Amberwoods. They're witches, Elijah. They're going to kill you, and Corbin. You must get him here."

"They're not witches, and their last name is Weathermore."

He groaned loudly. "No. She came here. Victoria. She hurt me with her magic. I know you hate me after everything that happened, but I'm telling you the truth. Who are you going to believe? Me or these people you barely know?"

I steadied my breathing, my heart racing as I looked around at the pitying eyes of servants. If anyone knew what was really going on, it was the staff. I needed to find Adeline. "Let's get you to bed." I took his weight on me and half carried him up the stairs. "I'll have the doctor bring you something to help you sleep." He calmed at that, and I rolled my eyes. I shouldn't be here at all helping him, but he was clearly sick.

"Come home," he croaked as I settled him onto his bed.

"Try to relax," I said, ignoring his question because there was no way in the heavens I was living back here after what he did. I looked at his legs, noticing fresh bruises. Was he hurting himself? I walked to the door, watching him mutter something at the wall, and sighed. I couldn't believe the rumors were true. He'd gone mad.

I spotted Adeline in the kitchens and pulled her into the gardens. "I'm glad I found you."

She offered me a kind smile. "I was hoping you'd come home."

"I'm not," I admitted. "Just visiting."

She looked at her feet. "I understand."

I clasped my hands behind my back. "How long has my father been this way? Please, speak plainly."

She bit her lip, curling it back behind her teeth. "A couple of days. It started suddenly, and he's declined quickly. The high priest has noticed." Her eyes filled with tears. "The priests traveling with him were talking in their rooms, and Amanda overheard them talking," she explained, referring to one of the scullery maids. "They may take away his priesthood if it continues—or even worse, have him taken into an... asylum."

I closed my eyes. "How did this happen so fast?"

"I'm not sure, but my uncle was the same. His mind declined quickly, and it never returned."

"Thanks, Adeline."

"Elijah." Her tone softened, not calling me Mr. Shaw for once. "Father Shaw has been talking to someone who isn't there. A woman, he says, and he keeps saying there are witches in the house and in the town."

I grabbed her hand. "There are no witches here. Trust me."

She nodded. "I'm worried what he'll do. He already shouts at the servants, and one found him screaming in his room that he wouldn't give in to destruction, but no one was in there with him. He's paranoid and calling everyone a witch. He thinks everyone is trying to hide Victoria. Isn't that the woman you, uh, spend time with?"

"It is." I loosed a sigh. "I will fix this, okay? You don't need to worry."

"Please," she said one last time. "He's been hitting himself too, you know. They will lock him up if you don't do something soon."

I inhaled sharply, watching her leave. I needed to go back to Victoria's before I could do anything else. Corbin was there, and I had to protect him and Victoria's family. They were all in danger, especially with my father in this state. Once there, I'd figure out what my next move would be.

Twenty-Eight

Victoria

The succubus smiled far too sweetly for my liking when she slipped between the shadows of my room. "I'm rather enjoying the hunter. You were right; I didn't need to fuck him to drive him crazy. He hurts himself when I turn him on. He's terrified of sinning. It's most delightful."

"Good, but please, keep those details to yourself." I placed my hot tea on my dresser and looked at the mirror where my reflection showed. "Has anyone suspected anything?"

"No." She giggled, running her hand along her thigh. "He's terrified of a beautiful woman, you know. I reach into his mind..." She popped a finger in the air, laughing. "Pull out a fear and use it. He hasn't slept much, and when he does, I create more nightmares."

"Well done."

She angled her head, her blonde waves falling around her shoulders and cleavage. "Remember our deal, little witch. I'm only doing this so you will give me your body to use."

"I know." I scowled and picked up my hairbrush, then pulled it through my strands haphazardly. "You can return now. Make sure to report to me tomorrow evening, only when no one is around."

She nodded and left through the window. As soon as she was gone, my mind swarmed. I barely made it to the kitchen when the splitting started. I grabbed a jar of the amber liquid, noting it was the last one, and drank the cloying, thick mixture. I coughed once it went down and followed it with water.

I heard footsteps and saw Alex walk inside, the cut on her neck now scabbing. She brushed her fingertips against it, her watery gaze on the tea kettle. "Peppermint?"

She shook her head.

"Orange? Raspberry?"

She nodded.

"Raspberry it is."

She screeched out a chair and took a seat at the table.

Corbin walked in not long after. "Hi."

I tensed. "Hello." I handed Alex her tea. "I'm glad you're staying," I told her. Cas had decided not to flee town in his panic after everything, although persuading him to stay hadn't just been me, but Corbin and Alex too—her plea through a letter. "I would miss you."

She gave me a look and I laughed.

"Even without words, you know how to get me."

She rolled her eyes, turning back toward Corbin, but I saw the way her face crumpled when I'd said it. I despised the sadness etched between the worry lines that shouldn't be on a seventeen-year-old's forehead. I had failed her, and she knew I felt that way because she kept coming to me in the evenings and playing with Ebony and Buttercup on my bed, trying to make me feel better in her own way.

I didn't deserve any of them.

The door opened and shut. I went to greet Cas but saw Elijah. He dropped his bag by the foot of the stairs and pulled me into an unexpected embrace. "We need to talk," he whispered in my ear, and my stomach dipped. "Alone."

Once we were in my room, he buried his head in his hands, sitting at the edge of my bed. "My father's gone mad."

I almost grinned but suppressed it. "Oh, really?"

He couldn't even look at me. "This is all my fault."

Any bit of satisfaction I had disappeared. "No, it's not."

"I shouldn't have hit him back. Maybe I did something to his brain."

I balled my fist but quickly uncurled my fingers before he could see. "He almost killed your brother. You did the right thing, and besides, I've never heard of a fall turning someone mad."

"It was so sudden."

I sat at his side, placing my hand on his. "I think he's been going that way for a while. I noticed things when I met him but didn't dare want to say."

"Like what?"

"The one time I met him, he seemed a bit strange was all. I couldn't put my finger on it," I lied.

He ate it up, thankfully. "I can't leave him there alone. The staff are concerned, and I'm worried he will hurt one of them."

It had all gone far better than I'd planned. "Should we take him to an asylum?" I asked tentatively.

"Not yet." He gritted his teeth, forcing back the tears I could see were threatening to break from the corners. "I can't condemn him there if he's not actually mad. Maybe he's taking something and it's making him like that. I need to make sure."

I repressed the urge to roll my eyes. "Then what do we do?"

He pulled me on top of him in a surprise move, so quick I couldn't catch my breath. I curled around his lap, his eyes searching mine with an intensity that made me nervous. "I love it when you say we."

Before I could speak, his lips were on mine, and for once, I wasn't thinking about Damian or my inevitable insanity. Even the darkness in my mind seemed to retreat a little. I closed my eyes, deepening the kiss. His fingers danced along my skin and stopped at my neck. Every touch was deliberate, gentle, kind.

He brushed a thumb on my neck and pulled away. "I'll figure things out tomorrow, but for now, I need to not think about him—or anything. I just need you."

He moved his thumb to my lips and pulled down the bottom one, his pupils dilating. He kissed me again, this time softer. His pain matched mine; I heard it in the confliction in his tone when he spoke about his dad, in every touch when he trailed lines so gently along my skin, giving me exactly what I needed without him knowing it.

I let the moment swallow me whole, entangling my limbs with his as I dove deep into every touch, moaning at every kiss and nip. Soon I wouldn't have him or anyone anymore. I always knew I wasn't going to get out of this alive. The deal with the succubus, continuing to use dark magic, was proof of what I knew but didn't want to admit. My revenge was going to destroy me too, and at the very least, I should allow myself some enjoyment, some feeling of pleasure before it happened.

Because when we stopped for air and I looked into his face, I didn't see the younger version of the hunter. I saw a man who'd do anything for the people he loves, someone just as tortured as me in their own way, trying to find their way in the world.

I saw the face of someone I would miss.

We lay on the bed, a sheet sticking to our sweaty bodies. I looked up at the ceiling, and he kissed my temple.

"You could always take over the household now," I said, realizing that if I couldn't get a life after this, at least he could. "If he's branded insane, then you can take over the estate. It would be as if he died." I softened my tone. "Sorry."

"Don't be." He inhaled sharply. "I'd already thought of it, and you're right. I can keep my club, take care of Corbin, and not have to become a hunter."

I moved gently. "You should."

"Victoria."

"It would be easy."

He sat upright, running his hand through his hair. "I know, okay?" He clenched his jaw. "It's just—"

"He's your father," I said, finishing for him. It was like Corbin had said.

"I need to let him go. He's not the man I thought he was. Even with his darkness, I truly believed one day he would see the light, but I was wrong. I should take over the house. I saw the high priest. He's leaving in two days, which is unusual. He normally stays for much longer. They're going to take away Father's priesthood. I just know it."

I hadn't ever heard such good news. "Maybe if you take over the estate, if they find him insane, then you can keep in the house, under a doctor's care of course," I said because I didn't want them to send him away. I still needed to kill him.

"I will. This will be good for me and for Corbin."

I kissed his cheek. "It's okay still to be sad."

"Does that make me crazy?"

I shook my head. "No, it just makes you human."

He paused, running his fingers through mine. "If I didn't have you these past few weeks, I don't know what I'd have done. You're an angel who's come into my life."

I held my breath. I was far from an angel. For the first time since starting our plan, I felt a twinge of guilt, but I quickly pushed the feeling aside. "You're too kind."

"No, you are." He looked into my eyes with an intensity I couldn't match. "When I inherit the estate, I'm going to do something for you."

"There's no need, truly."

He kissed my hand softly. "I want to. Come with me tomorrow. I'll have two of the doctors come to the house to check him, and I'll need to discuss everything with my lawyers, but first, I should tell him in person."

"Is that such a good idea with him being… unhinged?"

"It's the right thing to do."

He lay next to me, and I pushed my hand through his hair until he fell asleep. I turned my mind back to the plan. Damian would most likely attack me in front of Elijah, which had been the plan all along, and the revenge was almost done. Cas had already started spreading rumors through the church, not about him beating them as I'd asked him not to, but about his insanity.

Everything would be coming to an end soon, and I would have to leave. I looked at Elijah sleeping, so peaceful under my covers, and my heart sank a little.

Twenty-Nine

Elijah

The visit to the house couldn't have gone worse. As soon as we were alone with my father, he'd grabbed her in a chokehold.

"Touch her again, and I'll run this across your throat." I pulled out my pocketknife. She had been right; I shouldn't have come and told him first.

His eyes widened, rage glittering in them. "You would choose this witch over your own blood?"

I balled my fists. "She's not a witch."

He grabbed Victoria's arm, forcing her wrist around. Anyone else would have yelped when his nails dug in, but she didn't show an ounce of fear. I stepped forward, gritting my teeth. "See her wrist? This crystal is a dark object. It will show if she has magic." He pulled it from his pocket, placing it against her skin. "See?"

I looked at the crystal. "Nothing is happening."

The corner of his lips tugged upward. "Back at your old tricks?" he asked her.

Victoria struggled against him, her nostrils flaring. "I don't know what you're talking about."

"Where is it? The thing hiding your powers?" Madness danced in his stare. "Where is it?" A trail of saliva trickled over his bottom lip.

She looked at me, her wide gaze focused, sad. "Elijah, please. He's fucking insane."

My stomach fluttered. Turning my attention back to Father, I tensed my shoulders. "Let. Her. Go."

He pulled her tighter against him. "You wouldn't dare."

I shook my head. "For years I've protected you. I've made excuses for your behavior, and I shouldn't have." I paused, my eyes never leaving his.

He shook her. "You're blinded by lust, you fool. She's a witch. She's trying to turn you against me. Don't you see?"

"This isn't just about Victoria. For years you hurt us. Corbin. You were so afraid of him going down the wrong path, but you're the one who pushed him down it."

"That's not true."

Victoria struggled against his grip once more. "It is. I've seen their scars. I'm not the monster here."

He dug his nails in again. "Shut up, witch."

"Do that again!" I warned, stepping forward. "Do it."

He hesitated. There was a first for everything, I supposed. "Your brother carved his own path."

"It was your bullying, your words, your scars that led him that way. You blame him for something he had no control over. Mother didn't die because of him, and I doubt she died because of any witch."

He loosened his hold on her. "How can you say that?"

"You said she only took a potion to help with conceiving Corbin. I don't see how it could kill her all those months later. I don't know a lot about it all, but I'm assuming there aren't such long delays."

He hesitated. "He was born of witchcraft. It's in your brother's blood."

"Have you checked him for magic? Because I've never seen him show a shred of it."

His lips parted, but he fell silent.

I took the opportunity. "He's terrified, every day, of you. You speak about being a good man, one worthy of anointment from Zerheus, and you can't even see past your own ignorance."

His expression hardened. I glanced from him to Victoria, inhaling sharply.

"No!" he shouted. "She left the hexed bag and brought demons into my house. She cursed Lady Abor. She died in that tuberculosis hospital, didn't you know? She has been playing us all since she came into your life. Please see sense."

Confusion flitted her features. "Wait, what? I haven't been doing anything."

"She doesn't know who you're talking about." I scowled. "She's innocent. Let her go. Whoever left that hexed bag, we will find, and Lady Abor had tuberculosis. Many are dying from it."

"Don't be naïve, son. I brought you up better than this. Bleeding from the eyes and nose are not symptoms of tuberculosis."

"The doctor said some experience strange symptoms. He's seen them," I replied.

"Nothing I say will help you see the truth." He sighed, drooping his head, and dropped the crystal. "You leave me no choice. You may not always understand the choices I make, but I'm doing this for your own good." He reached into his pocket with his free hand and slowly pulled out a small knife.

I ran cold.

Her eyes glossed. "Elijah."

My heart skipped a beat. He pressed the sharp side against her throat. A trickle of blood appeared in a curve, and I moved faster than I knew I could.

I still had my own knife in my hand, but I never thought I'd have to use it, especially against my own father.

I slammed my hand into his arm, knocking my fist between the inside of his elbow. The knife slipped from his fingers, dropping between Victoria and me. His startled gaze climbed up to mine. Breathless, I pushed him back into the wall behind him, knocking the air from his lungs.

"Run."

"I'm not leaving you," she replied, standing at my side. She picked up Father's knife from the ground and took a step forward.

I placed my arm out to stop her. "Don't."

Her lips parted. A tear struggled from her eye and down her cheek. "He was going to kill me!"

"I know. The lawyers already agreed for the estate to be handed to me."

She arched a dark eyebrow. "So he is no longer head of this household?"

"You've done what? I am not insane!" he shouted.

"You are. We can all attest to it. Even the high priest has seen it." My heart felt ten times heavier in my chest, and my stomach felt as if it had turned to lead.

Father angled his head. "The high priest thinks I am insane?"

"Yes."

He looked at Victoria. "This was all you. I'm going to kill you."

I pushed him against the wall before he could hurt her. "Don't touch her. I mean it. I will choose her over you if I have to."

He shook his head. "You fool."

I let him go, and he rubbed his arm. I looked toward the door, hearing voices approach from down the hall.

"Good, the doctors are here."

"I'm not mad," he said, his eyes wide. "I captured the demon in that crystal. I trapped her this morning. My mind is fine now. Son, please."

I escorted him out into the hallway, spotting the straitjacket and chair. "Take him to the east wing. There's a room secure there."

Chapter Thirty

Victoria

I waited until Elijah escorted him into the hallway before I picked up the crystal from the ground and pocketed it. I could feel the succubus's presence inside of it, dark and thrumming with power. I had to give it to Damian. He was a damn good hunter, but not quite good enough.

"Saves me one job," I said under my breath, and I felt the succubus's anger pulse through the dark object. "I'll be putting you somewhere safe."

I walked out into the hallway, watching Damian get wrapped in a straitjacket. I let myself smile behind Elijah's back when no one was looking but the hunter. He wrestled harder, screaming "witch" and "demon" as he was carried upstairs. I followed Elijah and noticed a man in white robes, surrounded by others with blue robes, watching. He must have been the high priest. They all placed their hands over their hearts.

Elijah slumped. "That was harder than I thought." He turned, brushing his hand along my cheek. "Are you okay? Did he hurt you?"

I shook my head. "You saved me."

He rested his head against my forehead. "I couldn't have done this without you." He closed his eyes, and the joy I'd felt moments ago slipped away. I wanted to hold him back, to tell him I wasn't going anywhere, but it would have been a lie, because there was only one final step left in our plan.

To kill Damian Shaw.

"I'm going to hold a ball," he said, interrupting my thoughts. "It's customary when becoming the head of a household, but in reality, I'm going to do it for you. My life has been filled with so much unhappiness, as has yours. We deserve some joy." He looked up the stairs. "I just need a day first."

"Take all the time you need, and also, a ball isn't necessary."

"Please, I want to do this. Will you stay here with me until then?"

I pressed my lips together. It would allow me to be close to Damian, and a ball was a good cover for murder, with loud music to cover the screams and a ton of suspects in attendance. "I'll stay here. Besides, Eva loves a ball."

***

Alex may have been without a voice, but it didn't stop her from still somehow being the loudest in the room. Her very presence demanded attention.

My navy-blue, floor-length dress trailed out behind me, glittering as if it were made of a thousand stars. It clung tight to my curves. Alex's deep-purple dress flowered at her knees, with roses wrapped delicately around her waist like a belt. Her hair was tied up into a high ponytail, falling down one shoulder as if her hair were wound of silk. Cas removed his top hat, disheveling his dark hair. He picked a piece of lint from his tailcoat and smirked when he looked around the room.

Everyone was looking at us, and for once, we didn't shy away. We were out for blood, and we didn't care who knew.

"Ambrose." Lady Montague didn't try to hide her delight at seeing my brother. Her cheeks pinkened when she stepped away from her husband. "I owe you a dance. You're on my card."

Ambrose took her arm, his chin lifted as he led her onto the dance floor.

Her husband extended his hand toward us, but Alex recoiled away, and I pressed my lips together. "No."

His eyebrows flicked upward. "What a rude young lady."

Alex bared her teeth, and he backed away.

I couldn't help but chuckle. "Fuck, Alex, you could try some subtlety."

She gave me a look.

"I know, that's like asking a fish not to swim."

She smiled and I spotted Corbin enter the room. He was handsome in his dress suit. He'd even slicked his hair back.

"I'm glad you met him. He cares about you."

She nodded and brushed her hand against mine. Corbin found her from across the room and looked at her as if she were the only person who existed among the sea of people. She steadied herself, holding my hand, and I saw her swallow hard before she stepped away from me.

When she reached him, he cupped both sides of her face, resting his forehead against hers. In a gentle motion, he lightly touched her throat, his eye twitching when his finger grazed the still-healing scab. His eyes glossed, or maybe it was the low light, but I wished I could somehow capture the moment for her. I'd never seen a person look at another like that. He might have been human, and she a witch, but I was certain they'd do anything for each other.

A hand reached around my waist from behind and pulled me into a hard body. "That dress should be illegal."

Elijah. My heart settled, if only a little. I turned in his grip, and his pupils dilated as he looked down at me. "I wore it for you. It was hard sneaking in the order for fabric under your nose."

He leaned down, whispering a kiss against my lips. "It was worth it. My beautiful woman," he said against my mouth.

"Oh. So no 'fuck' or 'I drive you crazy' then?"

His expression softened. "Not tonight."

My heart skipped a beat. He led me into the steps of the next dance, but I couldn't pull myself away. If it weren't for the layers of clothing between us, we'd be melded together with how close his body was against mine. I could feel every muscle, every want of his. "You look handsome in your suit," I said, brushing my lips upward until we were kissing mid-song. I deepened the kiss until I couldn't tell where he began and I ended.

He pulled back an inch. "I wore it for you."

I grinned. "I see you've pulled out all the stops tonight."

"I was inspired, and I told you I would. It's my entry into society as head of the Shaw household." He ran his hand into my hair. "I needed the perfect evening. For everyone." He looked at his brother. "Zerheus knows we all needed some fun after everything that's happened. I also may have another reason too."

"What's that?"

He tightened his embrace. "You'll see at the end of the night."

He twirled me outward, loosing my curls around my shoulders, then we knotted back together in the center.

"If your father gets out of his room, he will try to kill me," I said. "Where is it again, so I can make sure to avoid the entire area."

"East wing. It's the largest corner room, but don't worry. He can't get out. I have men stationed outside." His expression dropped. "I may have him transferred into an asylum soon. It might be the best thing for him."

"I think you're right."

"Anyway, enough of this talk." He twirled me around again, and I clasped his hand when we met back together. I caught my breath, and he kissed me.

I splayed my hand against his chest, feeling his heartbeat. I closed my eyes, engulfing myself in the moment. If he weren't human, I weren't a witch, and his father weren't my sworn enemy, we could have been everything together. I almost caught myself wishing things were different, but after this dance, everything would be different. I would kill the hunter and flee. Elijah and Corbin would be free. Cas could stay here as Ambrose, along with Alex, undetected, and they could live out the lives they'd built here.

I never could fit in like the rest of my family. I couldn't be with a human, especially knowing that if Elijah ever found out the truth about me, lover or not, I would end up at the end of a rope. I couldn't watch him hate me like that. My leaving was best for everyone. I would go to my mother, try to fix our relationship, and try to build some life for myself up in Blackburn.

If I didn't lose my mind first. The madness continued to creep in every day, and after tonight, it would be even worse. I didn't know how sane I'd be afterward.

I placed my fingers against his lips when he leaned in for another kiss. "I have something I need to take care of."

"Anything I can help with?" he asked against my finger.

I pulled away, my lips parting. A shallow breath passed between them as I took in every feature of his. "Elijah." I closed my eyes for a moment, finding some resolve in the darkness. "You should network. Go find Charles. I need to see my brother and discuss a few things."

He kissed my forehead. "Come find me."

"I will."

I watched him walk away for the last time. I could still feel his kiss lingering on my lips and feel the plea in his voice rock through my heart. Tears tried to breach the corner of my eyes as I searched for Cas.

I found him with Lady Montague, by the drinks table. "Brother."

He lifted his glass, excusing himself, then walked with me to a secluded corner.

"I'm going to the hunter's room. Keep the music loud," I said.

"You're not doing this alone." He grabbed my hand. "He will kill you."

"I have friends," I explained. "Trust me. This way, Alex won't be involved either. She's happy, with Corbin." I spotted them a little ways away, dancing. "The party is in full swing. It's a good time."

"Then I'm coming with you."

"No." I searched for the high priest in the crowd. "I need you to stay here, where people can see you. You can cover for me if needed. I'm counting on you." I walked away, and he called after me, but I didn't look back. I heard him swear loudly when I reached the middle of the room, fighting my way through the dancing couples and talking groups of people. I left out the hall and navigated my way to the east wing, stopping in the study to grab the whip.

It was how I had always planned it. I would do this part myself. It wasn't fair for me to put it on Alex or Cas. I pursed my crimson-painted lips and adjusted my bracelet. Three men were standing outside the door. With a sweep of my hand, I allowed the dark magic to run through me and reach them, knocking them unconscious.

The door to his room was locked when I reached it. Placing my hand on the handle, I felt power thrum through my hands and arms, like flames licking through my veins. The lock turned and clicked. I pushed the handle down and whispered Ember's name on my lips. This was all to avenge her, but in its way, it had become more than that. It was for every witch who had suffered at his hand and for his sons, especially Corbin, who'd almost died at his hand. It was ironic Damian hated witches when it was us who'd saved his son from becoming a person of the past.

The door creaked open, and I stepped inside, closing it behind me. The music loudened in the ballroom, building until the voices of chatter were drowned out completely. Cas had pulled it off.

"Good evening." I placed my hands in front of my stomach. "I've been waiting to see you."

He didn't turn around. He leaned over his desk, his voice gruff when he spoke. "As I have you. I've been waiting for my chance to kill you, to get you away from my son."

"You think you can overpower me?" I laughed, feeling raw magic seep through every ounce of my being.

Elijah stepped in front of me with his fists clenched, his stance poised to fight. "Victoria?" he asked. "Why are you here?"

"You followed me."

"I saw you leave," he stated. "How did you knock out my security?"

I swallowed thickly. "You need to leave."

"No, let him stay," Damian said, wiping his forehead as he stood. "You came to kill me. Let him see."

"Love?"

"He's right," I admitted. "I wanted to keep you out of this." Regret pulsed into my mind. Feeling power thrum through me, I curled my fingers. I'd come this far, and I couldn't give up now, not when the opportunity was so perfect. It didn't matter anyway. I'd be gone soon.

Damian's eyes widened when I looked at him, his pupils thinning under the yellow light. His blood began to boil but stopped after a few seconds. Beads of sweat had formed over his brows and on his neck.

"What are you doing?" Elijah pulled me back, close to him.

"Don't," I warned and pressed my hand against his chest. I couldn't do this without putting him in danger. "Try not to move." I let my magic seep into my fingertips, then leave my body, twisting and shaping around Elijah's heart, weakening him until he dropped to his knees. The color drained from his face. It was a simple yet effective incapacitation spell.

He'd hate me for it, but I couldn't have him get in the way of my revenge finale. He slumped against the back wall, helpless only to watch.

Damian closed his eyes, praying under his breath.

I stepped forward. "Your god won't save you now."

His eyelids flicked open, his cheeks whitening. "What did you do to my son?"

"Saved him from himself." I didn't look back. "This is between me and you."

"What now?" he spat. "Do you think you've won? You will never beat me." He tugged at his collar.

"I've already ruined you." I took another step forward, relishing in the flinch I caught in his right hand. "You keep preaching how we witches are demonic. I made sure not to disappoint. I became evil, for you. Because you were wrong about us, about my Ember. See, my sister was light, with a good heart and a human soul. Ironically, if she were here, she would be the one who'd show you mercy. Looks like you killed the wrong one." I paused. "When you took her heart, you killed an innocent person and gods know how many more. You thought you were doing good when really, you were committing murder."

He scoffed a laugh. "You believe you can trick me into believing you're good? That you're not darkness?"

The corners of my lips lifted into a sadistic smile, baring my teeth. "Oh, no. There are good and bad witches, just like there are good and bad humans. I'm not good. I'm not my sister, and thank the gods for it." I closed the distance between us, placed my hand on his chest before he could fight me off, and sent a shockwave through his body, forcing him to his knees. "If I were, I wouldn't do this." I placed my fingers against his temples, feeling his blood pump under my fingertips. Closing my eyes, it bent to the magic in my veins. The demons around me charged the energy, so every spell was as easy as taking my next breath.

His blue eyes rolled back, his lips curling as a scream erupted from his mouth. He crouched forward, gripping his nails into the floorboards, blood seeping from his fingers. "This is merely a taste of what I have in store for you." I released my spell with force, stepping back and kicking him back with the heel of my boot. "Get up, you fucking coward. I want you aware enough for what's coming next."

On shaking arms, he pulled himself up slowly. My patience was wearing thin. I grabbed a handful of his blond hair and pulled him up. He stumbled backward but steadied himself against a turned-over chair.

"Evil," he managed to spit out.

"Darkness recognizes darkness." I glanced over my shoulder at Elijah. He was struggling to open his mouth, still trying to fight against my spell. He didn't need words to show his disappointment in me. It was written all over his face. I looked back at Damian. "You will never become high priest. Everyone thinks you're mad."

He wiped the blood from his mouth, remnants of my spell on his brain. "They'll see through you soon enough," he replied. "My son has finally seen you for the evil creature you are."

My stomach knotted. Elijah was never supposed to be here, not for this part, but it mattered not. I clenched my fist, strengthening my resolve. "I won't let anything get in the way of your demise, not even Elijah."

He peered around me. "See, I told you. She never cared about you. They don't have hearts. They don't know love."

I reached for his throat, my magic weakening his resolve to fight back. Digging my nails into his windpipe was far too satisfying. If I didn't want his suffering to be prolonged, I'd have happily kept squeezing. "You know nothing about me."

He grappled at my fingers on his throat, and it was only when I saw the first vessels burst in the whites of his eyes did I release my grip.

"My sister is dead because of you. My cousin is also dead because of you. I lost my home, my shop. When you tore out her heart, you took mine too. She was my favorite person, and I loved her with every ounce of my soul. I was meant to protect her." A tear escaped and trickled down my cheek. "I can never get her back." My voice croaked, my tone waning. "She deserved a life, a future. She wanted to make fucking perfumes and open her own shop. She dreams, more than you and I." I swallowed hard, trying to remove the lump in my throat. Goose bumps spread along my arms. "You took everything from me, and now I'm going to take it from you. I've been working against you this whole time. You were right about everything: the hexed bag, the succubus, about who me and my family truly are, and your precious town will never know. Don't worry, we'll take care of them when you're locked up—and Corbin. Gods know he needs it after the way you've treated him, which is why I brought this."

I squeezed the leather of the whip in my palm, a smile on my face. Elijah watched from where he sat against the wall, his bloodshot eyes never moving from me.

"Now it's time to see how good you really are." The leather creaked when I twirled it in my hand. "If you really care about your son, you'll allow me to whip you the number of times you whipped Corbin. If you don't, then I will kill Elijah." I lied, but I didn't dare look at him. I had to look convincing so Elijah would believe me. I couldn't come back from this, but he had to see what his father really was, even at the hand of a witch. "Well, remove your shirt and bend over the chair."

He swallowed thickly, fear finally clouding his sharp features. To my dismay, he pulled off his shirt. His fingers trembled as he leaned over the splintering wood. His back convulsed before I even landed the first hit. Pulling the whip back, I let it whoosh through the air, not holding anything back. The strings and leather cut into his back, drawing blood on first contact.

I'd never heard a man scream like that. His legs buckled, and he fell to the floor. I lifted the whip again, and he cried out when it slapped against his back, this time harder. Tears fell thick and fast down his cheeks. I moved back for a third, but he pleaded between sobs, sniffing back snot. More dripped down his face.

"Please, no."

"Twenty more, or Elijah dies."

"No," he cried, his voice barely a whisper.

I whipped him again, and his back arched. He stretched out on the ground, a cold sweat breaking out across his body.

"Take him," he said finally, the words I wanted to hear.

"Louder," I ordered, but he didn't budge. I pulled back the whip in warning, and he cowered into a ball.

"Please, no more."

"Then I'll kill your son."

His teeth clenched; he couldn't even look in Elijah's direction. "What else do you want?"

"It's your son or you. A Shaw will pay with their life today. If you want to live, if you want the pain to stop, then you know what to do."

His shaking, trembling arms failed to lift him from the ground.

"Say it."

His lips parted, but the words wouldn't come out.

I brought the whip down on his back again, and he vomited, choking when it came up. "Corbin took far more than this. Now you know how it feels." I brought the whip back and picked a piece of hanging flesh from the end. "Eighteen more."

"No." His dried voice screeched. "Take Elijah."

"What was that?"

"He's yours, please."

I looked at the dark stain on his pants. He'd wet himself. So much for me not being able to beat him. "You willingly exchange your son's life for your sins?"

"I have no sins," he said.

Ah, finally, some resolve. I bent down, hissing in his ear. "Lies." I stood back up. "Do you offer his life as punishment for your sins?"

After a minute, he cried against the vomit, sticky between the floorboard and his cheek. "Yes. Please, make it stop."

I stepped back and dropped the whip. He cried with relief when I walked toward Elijah. He didn't cower, like his father, his stare fixated on mine, his jaw hardened. He wasn't going to make it easy. Elijah would make it so I had to look into his eyes when I took his life. I crouched to place my hand on his chest and released the spell on him. "I won't kill you."

I stood. He got to his feet too and looked from me to his beaten father. I held my breath with anxious anticipation. He hated me—that much was obvious—and he knew I was a witch. He reached out, and I didn't move or fight back. His hand touched my hair, beyond my ear. My eyes trailed his fingers, my heart racing.

"You betrayed me." The words barely hit me before he turned, leaving me and Damian alone in the room. He didn't even attempt to beg for his father's life or try to protect him. At least he didn't lash out at me, which I had expected, but his words punched like he may as well have.

Damian bawled in the corner, crying, unable to move from his injuries. I wanted to kill him, but I had to stop Elijah first. I'd put Cas and Alex in danger.

***

He wasn't in the ballroom, or in any of the corridors, or the garden. I headed back upstairs and found him standing in his room, looking out his window, his hands clasped behind his back. "Have you come to keep me quiet?"

Chapter Thirty-One

Elijah

"No," she answered, hovering in the doorway. "Well, a little, honestly, but it's not the only reason I'm here."

I looked over the sprawling gardens, coated in a blanket of white. Noelle was coming soon, but it didn't feel like it. The decorations did nothing but add a splash of color to the awful season. "You could have told me you were a witch."

"So you could string me up at the gallows?"

The muscle in my jaw ticked. I turned slowly. "Do you think so low of me?"

She didn't look at me. I couldn't help but stare at the spatters of blood on her cheek. At least the black of her dress hid most of the truth of what had happened in his room. I still couldn't believe she was a witch, but the evidence was overwhelming. I couldn't deny what had happened right in front of my eyes. Words of warning flickered into my mind, ones I'd heard all my life of their trickery and lack of emotions, but it didn't feel true—not when she'd spoken so painfully of her heartbreak over her sister.

"Don't pretend you would have understood. I was protecting my family. I couldn't risk them by telling you."

"You lied so much to me. To us. Was any of it real?" I held my breath, but I wasn't sure why. Did it really matter? Yet I needed to hear her response before I decided what to do next.

"At first you were a means to an end, the perfect person to get closer to Damian."

Pain jilted in my chest, but I didn't let it show. "Good to know."

She took a step into the room. "It all changed. I'm not sure when, but I felt things." She shuffled on the spot. "I feel things, for you."

I raised my eyebrows. That looked way more painful than it should have been. "So you're a witch," I said, as if somehow it still may not be true.

"Yes."

"Your parents never really died, did they?"

She shook her head. "My dad did years ago. My mother's alive."

"My father killed your sister."

She nodded, her eyes glossing. "He ripped out her heart."

I winced. "You said she was light."

She looked off into the distance. "She was a better person than I."

"You hurt him in there, with your magic."

"Yes, but most witches don't use magic sourced from the underworld," she explained. "I have dark magic inside of me, but it's still of this world. Some call it blood magic, but it's not strong enough to take down my enemies. Magic taken from demons, from the underworld, has no boundaries like normal magic. I can use it to harm others."

"Witches can't harm others normally then?"

"No."

I hadn't expected that. "But you wanted to harm my father."

"He also killed my cousin," she said. "We had to flee our family home and everything we had built. My mother is far from us, suffering. I couldn't let him continue to get away with murder."

My head swarmed with questions and flashbacks of my father lying on the floor, beaten and bleeding and offering my life for his. I shook my head as if to scatter my thoughts. "Why doesn't everyone use the underworld magic then?"

"It does come at a price." She pressed a finger against her bottom lip. "It takes a toll on the mind. I've started falling apart since I've been using it, but I had no choice. It's also how I kept my and my family's magic from being detected."

"Do they use it too?"

"No, they haven't."

She took all the responsibility and the burden. Half of me wanted to hold her, to keep her together because I could see her breaking, but the other half said she couldn't be trusted, that she was one of the monsters I'd spent my life fearing, who'd lied and used me. "Is my father dead?"

"Not yet."

"Why?"

"Because I wanted him to suffer, to see everything he cares about collapse around him." Vengeance filled her expression. "I plan on killing him tonight."

"What will you do if I try to intervene?" I asked, baiting her. Was her revenge more important than any connection she had with me? If it was all pretend, her answer would prove it.

She hesitated and sat on the end of my bed. "Elijah..."

"Tell me."

"I'm asking you not to."

"But what if I do?" I asked.

"Then I'll stop you," she admitted, her eyes glossing with tears. "I won't hurt you, but I won't let you stand in my way."

My heart softened an inch, but I didn't move from where I stood. She appeared so human, but I still didn't understand. "You are no murderer, Victoria. Murder darkens the soul."

She laughed. "Didn't you hear? I'm a witch. My soul is already dark."

I couldn't see it, even after everything she'd shown me with the demons and magic. "You said some time ago you believed witches were created from humans and old gods?"

She nodded. "It's true. We are people, just like you. Mostly human, but we have magic."

"Why should I believe you?"

She huffed out a breath, puffing out her cheeks. "Because, Elijah, if I were lying, I wouldn't bother coming up here. I would simply kill you if I were some emotionless being."

She had a good point. "You used me back there to show me my father's true side."

"Yes."

"It hurt," I admitted, and the words felt as childish coming out of my mouth as they sounded in my head.

"I know," she said and inched in my direction, but she thought better of it.

"My brother—"

"He knows. Alex told him everything." She rolled her eyes—at her sister, I imagined.

"He wasn't upset?"

"No. He listened and understood. He's more open-minded than I realized."

"I'm not surprised."

"We did save him," she said. "When you brought us to him that night your dad had whipped him, he was going to die. I'll tell you the truth. If we hadn't performed a spell on him, he wouldn't have made it."

A lump formed in my throat. "Anything else I should know?"

She sighed. "When the snake bit you, I performed a spell to take half the venom into myself. My sister wasn't going to make it back on time, and you were dying. We both took the potion."

I recalled her murmuring some incantation, but I thought it had been hallucinations brought on by the venom. "You cared even then?"

"Sort of," she said, biting her bottom lip. "I couldn't have you die, because our plan against your father had just begun."

"Well, at least you're honest."

"It's why I was leaving. My mind is broken, Elijah. All these spells have taken a toll on me. I can't think properly half the time. My nightmares are becoming hard to distinguish against reality, and I can't burden anyone with that. I wanted my sister and brother to stay here, to build their lives, but I guess now they can't."

My chest tightened. "I'm not going to tell anyone."

She dared a glance. "Why not?"

"Because I believe what you're saying," I said, and my mouth went dry. "But I won't have my father killed."

"Then what? Have him roam free to hunt me? To continue to kill?"

"No." Nausea crept through me as an idea formulated. "We send him to an asylum still. He's murdered people, but we can't argue a witch's innocence against an entire kingdom, so this is the only way. I also don't want him out. He's hurt my brother—and me—for the last time, but I won't see him dead. I can't have that.

He's still a person, and I don't condone murder. Under any circumstance."

She tucked a lock of hair behind her ear. "I can't... He needs to die."

"Why?"

"Because it's why I came here. It has to end with me holding his heart in my hand."

I touched her arm, but she flinched. I looked at her, and she was still as captivating as the first day we met. Every snarky comment, laugh, smile, and talk surfaced, softening me to her. She could have killed me, but she didn't, and she was dark. She did summon demons and use magic, but I think she thought of herself as evil, and being dark and evil were two very different things. "You're not a bad person. You don't need to do this."

Her eyes lit up. "How can you say that after everything you've seen?"

"You loved your sister, you love your family, you saved my brother twice, and you came up here and were honest with me. I'm not happy about any of this or how it happened, but I don't hate you, and I don't think you're a bad person—which is why I know you can walk away from this, to lock him away. You can't play the role of a god. We don't get to decide who lives or dies."

She looked down at her feet. "I'm sorry, Elijah. I want to do this for you, but I can't walk away from this now. Not after what he's done. His life will end."

I shook my head. "I can't stop you. Like you proved downstairs, you can put your hand on my chest and stop me from moving, but know this: if you murder him, you are becoming just like him. He will have *won*."

Something changed in her eyes.

"I'll be ending the ball now."

She stood and looked at me for half a second before she left the room. I watched her leave, my stomach sinking. I hoped she'd do the right thing, by some miracle.

I touched the box in my pocket, with the engagement ring inside it. The evening had ended far differently than I'd expected. I turned back toward the window, listening to the music from downstairs.

Chapter Thirty-Two

Victoria

I looked at Damian Shaw as he lay crumpled on his bed, whimpering in the dimply lit room. "This is where I kill you."

His bloodshot eyes found me. "My son hates me."

"Sons, plural," I said to correct him. "Yes, they do, although don't give me all the credit for it. It was mostly you."

He pushed himself up from the bed. "You're evil."

"Your son doesn't think so. I told him everything, about my being a witch."

"Then he's a fool."

I paused, my heart skipping a beat. I took a step forward. "You know what? He's not a fool at all. He's an amazing man with a good heart, despite growing up in this head-fuck of a household. Now, I admit I've done things I'm not proud of, but I don't go around murdering people like you, so don't you lie there and call me evil."

He laughed, coughing as he did. "You say this with a dagger between your fingers, ready to take my life. You will rot in the underworld for this."

The dagger trembled in my hands. "No." I wanted to scream at him, to make him see beyond his own ignorance. I needed him to know why he was dying and why these bad things had happened to him. "My sister was a good person."

"She was a witch."

"We were born from gods and humans. We are not demons."

"Yet you brought demons into my house."

I stammered, squeezing the handle of the dagger until my nails hurt. "Why can't you see what you've done?"

He shook his head. "I've protected this town and my family."

"No, you haven't. You're blind and using your church and your beliefs to justify both your sadistic desire for killing and your blind hatred for witches."

"My wife trusted a witch," he said slowly. "She died for it."

"That's why you hate us so much?"

"She gave her a potion to help us conceive a second child."

Everything clicked into place. "It's why you hate Corbin."

"She died during childbirth."

"As do so many people. It has nothing to do with a potion. Potions don't work like that."

"More trickery."

"If she took it to conceive, there's no way any potion or spell or even curse can wait that long before enacting. Killing spells are extremely difficult and immediate."

"You're lying."

I stepped forward. "I'm not." I looked directly into his eyes, realizing how different he looked from Elijah. There was no softness to this man, no love or compassion. "You think whatever you want, but I'm telling you the truth. You've killed hundreds of people—yes, people, not witches or demons, but souls—all over a misunderstanding. I'm not going to be the one going to the underworld." I held the dagger over his chest. This was it, everything I'd worked up to. Cas, Alex, and I had given up everything so we could enact our revenge, and it had worked perfectly. Yet as I readied myself to plunge the blade into his chest, I found myself unable to catch my breath.

There was fear lacing his eyes, as Ember had had in hers. He'd killed her and every witch out of revenge for his wife. He could pretend otherwise, but it was obvious now. It was no "message from Zerheus" or "his calling." He'd acted out of vengeance and anger, like me.

"Victoria." Elijah hesitated, holding his hands up when I looked over my shoulder. "Don't do this. This isn't you."

"Leave now." Tears fell down my cheeks, thick and fast. I loosed a sob, catching a glimpse of my reflection in the windowpane. I was breaking apart. I'd felt it for so long, and the truth hit colder than stone: killing him wouldn't bring Ember back. It wouldn't truly free my family because we'd always be on the run from some hunter in some town. We were bound to a life of secrecy because we weren't accepted, and it hurt so much, I could hardly breathe.

Elijah had reached me sometime in my panic. His hands were around my waist, turning me slowly, softly. He placed his hand on the handle of the dagger, lowering it. "You're not a murderer."

"I'm already broken," I said, my voice cracking. "My mind is fractured, my sister is dead, and no matter what I do, my family and I will never be accepted in Salvius. What do I have to live for? Revenge is all I have."

He brushed his thumb against mine. "That's not true, love. You have me."

I looked away. "Don't do that."

"It's true."

"I've done bad things."

"So have I. I can be an asshole when I want to be. I've treated people badly. We've all made mistakes, but that's the great thing. We can always change ourselves for the better. You're better than this. You're a good sister. You care about me, even Corbin. I've seen it." He touched my tears, wiping them downward under my eyes. "If you were a demon, you wouldn't be capable of any of that, so I believe you. I trust you, Victoria, to make the right choice here. It doesn't have to end like this."

"How do I know you won't hand me over if I don't kill him?"

"You don't," he admitted, "but you can take a leap of faith."

I couldn't focus. "I don't know."

"I know this is difficult for you, but you also have your sister and brother. Please, give me the dagger. You can still walk away from this."

I wanted to trust him, but trusting humans had only ever brought me heartache. I still had the dagger. I could push Elijah away and end the hunter now. At least then I could die knowing I finished what I had started. Alex and Cas could stay here. They seemed happy here. "My family needs him dead. He'll always hunt them."

"He won't. They'll lock him up. I promise I'll keep you all safe."

"I want to believe you..."

He rested his forehead against mine. He could turn me over to the church as soon as I handed it to him. He could have those shackles with him now. "I'm not going to hurt you," he said, as if he could read my thoughts. "Don't you know? I'm in love with you."

His words sliced through me. "No, you're not."

He pulled out an engagement ring from his pocket. "I do. I was going to give you this tonight."

I averted my gaze. "I don't deserve that."

"I say you do."

Damian ran up behind us and wrapped his hands around Elijah's neck. Whatever strength he had in him, he used in that final moment. I spun around, watching as Elijah pushed him back into the wall.

"I won't let you. She's a witch!" he shouted, tears falling down his cheeks. It was then I realized the most hurtful thing for the hunter was seeing Elijah love me. My heart pounded. I pushed out my arm, using dark magic for what I hoped was the last time. Power crept toward him like smoke, wrapping around his senses until he dropped to the floor.

Elijah turned around, pale-faced, the ring still in his hand. "Did you kill him?"

"No." My chest heaved. "I knocked him out. Have him sent away."

"You're going to let him go?"

I'd never felt so vulnerable. Honestly, I wanted to squirm on the spot. "I want to be the good you see in me, the good Ember saw in me too." I looked down. For the first time in my life, I wanted to be worthy of those around me. I looked at Damian, unconscious, and sighed. It wasn't the revenge I'd planned, but in so many ways, he'd done it to himself.

Elijah wrapped his arms around me, pulling me tight against his chest and holding the back of my head. "I'm right here, love. I won't hurt you."

I closed my eyes, holding him back. "How can you love me knowing I'm a witch?"

"Because I trust you. I trust everything you've told me, and honestly, witch, human, or something else, nothing can stop how I feel for you."

I almost collapsed against him as the weight of everything came loose—all the dark magic, grief, heartache, plotting, and pain. He held me up as my tears fell thick and fast. For the first time in what felt like ever, I was myself, and someone loved me for it. He loved me for it, and I didn't have to pretend anymore. It was over. It was all finally over.

Epilogue

Victoria

Elijah was right. It really was all about networking. I couldn't go on a stampede through the kingdom, explaining how witches weren't evil, but I could change the mind of one person at a time. It was how the world could change. That one person could change the mind of another, and it would spread.

He leaned down and kissed my cheek. "You've made a lot of new friends."

"I'm shocked too, but not all humans are terrible."

He lifted an eyebrow, playfulness glittering in his eyes. "Oh, really?"

I shrugged, grinning. "Some are okay."

"I'd say the same about witches."

Cas rolled his eyes from the back of the shop. "Get a room."

"We have one," Elijah called. "You're in it. Aren't you supposed to be closed?"

"I have to count inventory still," he called back. "Mother is coming by tonight to see everything."

I turned toward Elijah. "Ignore him."

"I do," he said with a smirk. "I'm glad your mother's back with you all. She seems happy."

"It's still hard to look at her," I admitted. "But things are a little easier now."

"Now that you've opened up a little?"

"I guess."

"You are most welcome."

"Ugh." I nudged him in his side. "Your ego needs to come down a few notches. I'm just saying."

He kissed me again, softer this time. "I can't help it. You make me feel so high."

Alex walked in with Corbin. "Brother," he said to Elijah, then looked at me. "My new sister."

"We're not married yet." I looked at the rock on my finger and let out a small smile. Alex caught it and made a face—unspoken, but I understood every word. I'd never believed I would be excited about getting married, or ever settling down. When we'd told Cas, he'd almost fainted in shock, then muttered something about me "actually having a heart after all." It had all gone perfectly, except that Elijah insisted Ebony and Buttercup could not be bridesmaids as it would frighten our guests, but I was still going to marry him.

He turned, chatting to Corbin about their next business venture, which had been booming since Elijah had taken over the estate, and I turned my attention to a newsletter. I walked to the cashier stand and leaned over the countertop to read the articles when I found one about Damian.

"It looks like he's stuck in there. They took away his priesthood."

"No surprise there," Cas replied. "They can't have a madman giving sermons."

"Except he's not actually mad."

He placed a jar into a drawer, and it rattled when it closed. "You did the right thing, letting him live. Richard Blackwood may have been a murderer and a prick, but a day doesn't go by when I don't think about what I did." He shuddered, despite the warm air. "It hurts the soul, taking a life."

"I thought I had killed someone once, remember? The woman in the church. It didn't haunt me."

He shrugged. "You didn't actually kill her though, and if you had, it was an accident. It's different."

I grabbed his hand before he could pull away. "Brother, you saved Alex's life."

"I know. I tell myself that every day." He inhaled sharply and pulled out the jar of amber liquid. "Here's your daily medicine."

My nose wrinkled. "When can I stop taking it?"

"Once I'm certain your mind is healed, as long as you don't perform any more dark magic."

"I'm not sure it'll ever fully heal."

"Maybe not entirely, but enough so you can live normally. How're the nightmares?"

"Less with your medicines. You're so talented, you know. You should do what Elijah said and become a doctor."

"No, I like doing this." He mixed two herbs into a grinding dish. "I get to meet lots of women too."

I rolled my eyes. "There it is, my cue to end this conversation."

"Drink it all," he said, passing the jar to me. "At least you don't have to explain to everyone why your name has changed. I had to tell them Ambrose was my middle name."

"Life is so complicated," I said, feigning sympathy, and drank my medicine. Within a few seconds, the grogginess in my mind relinquished a little. "Thanks."

"I know it's not easy starting over," he said, picking up the empty jar, "but I really do believe we can make a home here."

"Ironic how our new home is in the top witch-fearing town in Salvius."

"It's not as bad with Damian gone and with our whispers changing a few hearts here and there."

"You're right. I miss our old house though."

"Elijah said everything's gone..." He looked down at his hands. "We still have the memories, Victoria. Up here." He pointed at his temple, and I gave him a watery smile. "It's not all perfect, but we're together as a family, and we're building a home. I'm proud of us."

"You know, Cas, for the first time ever, I think you might be making sense."

He rolled his eyes, nudging my arm. "We should go. We promised Alex and Corbin dinner for their graduation."

"She wants you to cook because gods know I can't."

He nodded. "I'll cook, you clean."

Alex skipped up beside me and rested her head against my shoulder. We'd grown closer since I decided to say.

I looked outside and smiled as the sky darkened. Ember's death had brought us all closer together. She'd have been happy with that. There wasn't a day that went by when I didn't think about her, and I didn't want the day to come when I wouldn't. Grief never went away, not really. It just felt less and less suffocating with each passing week. I learned to shape my life around it, to do things that would make her proud, and mostly, I learned to be kind to myself. I found happiness in the little things, and I let myself feel sad when I needed to. I'd learned so much, through every person in my life: Alex, Cas, Ember, Elijah, Corbin, and my mother. They had each taught me something important, but in the end, it was my choices that had changed me the most. I had decided not to kill him. I'd heard reports that he was treated well, but they'd never let him out after the testimonies, especially considering the high priest had confirmed his madness. He wasn't dead, but he didn't need to be. I'd gotten him out of our lives, laid the path for him to show his true colors. His family and the town were safer for it.

"Let's go home," I said to Alex, patting her head. "I'm proud of you for finishing at the academy. You have so many talents. I can't wait to see what you do."

She flicked both eyebrows upward, smirking. I followed her out, and Elijah caught my waist. "I hope you're not leaving without me."

I planted a kiss on his lips. "I wouldn't dream of it."

Alex pretended to gag, and I laughed. I looked around as Cas closed. Corbin joined Elijah's side, and I smiled. We walked outside and I looked up at the night sky, imagining Ember was with us, and a star winked against the deep blue.

Free eBook

Get your free eBook now of *Ruin*, a fantasy romance novella, when you sign up for Rebecca's monthly newsletter. It will be packed with updates, information on upcoming releases, book trailers, cover reveals, quizzes, giveaways, and other book-related content!

Ruin is a spin-off novella of The Fate of Crowns Trilogy and can be read as a standalone.
Get your free copy here: http://bit.ly/RebeccaNewsletterRuin

Acknowledgments

A huge thank-you, as always, to my incredible beta readers: Kelly Kortright, Rebecca Waggner, Linda Hamonou, Belle Manuel, and Lauren Churchwell. Your comments are invaluable, and your enthusiasm and notes help me perfect the first drafts.

Thank-you to my editor, Angie Wade, who is the coolest, funniest editor I've met, a grammar nerd—well, all-around nerd, but I love you for it—and an incredible editor. You help me polish my book babies and I trust you inexplicably. Also, a big thank-you Janna for your perfect proofreading skills. You guys are the dream team.

To my friend Sarah Cradit, for co-releasing *The Raven and the Rush* with *Heart of a Witch.* I had so much fun doing this together!

Finally, *Heart of a Witch* wouldn't be anywhere without marketing, so thank you to Kiki and the whole team at The Next Step PR and Amanda at BOMM Tours.

Glossary

Celeste: The goddess many in Salvius worship

Dawnridge: The main city in Salvius

Dramair: Currency in Salvius

Istinia: Territory of witches and magic

Noelle: Christmas

Salvius: Kingdom of humans

Redforest: The town *Heart of a Witch* is set in

Underworld: Ruled by Thalia

Zerheus: The god many in Salvius worship

Also by Rebecca L. Garcia

THE FATE OF CROWNS SERIES

The Fate of Crowns

The Princess of Nothing

The Court of Secrets

Ruin

EMBRACING DARKNESS COLLECTION

Spellbound

Heart of a Witch

Rebecca lives in San Antonio, Texas, with her husband and son. Originally from England, you can find her drinking tea, writing new worlds, and designing covers. She writes fantasy romance. She devoured every book she was given and fell in love with magical worlds, and when she got older, her imagination grew with her.

When she's not writing or spending time with her family, you can find her traveling and hosting book signings with Spellbinding Events.

You can find more information, updates, social media, and more on her website: www.rebeccalgarciabooks.com

Printed in the USA
CPSIA information can be obtained
at www.ICGtesting.com
LVHW091718131223
766098LV00123BA/386/J

9 781912 405947